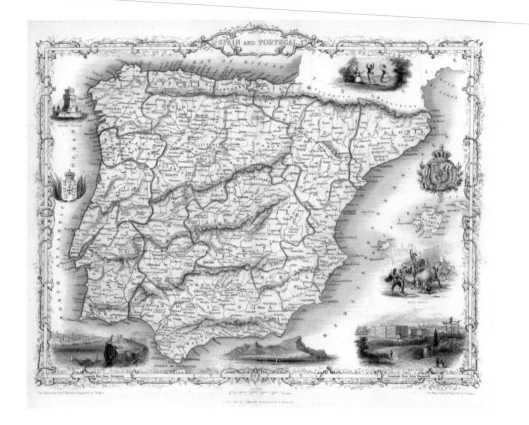

Spain and Portugal 1851

Steve Bartrick Antique Prints and Maps

Foreword

A glossary of foreign words is provided on page 287.

A reading group guide begins on page 291.

Niña, Pinta and Santa María

Engraving 1882

Los Feliz
April 6, 2011

Mrs. Elena Catalina Dougherty tried to ignore the yearning in her heart. For over seventy-seven years she skimmed the surface, nibbled at the edges, looked and listened only selectively. She led an unexamined and perfectly dreamy life inside a gossamer bubble of luxury and privilege. Until one night when she screamed in her sleep.

"*Lagundu! Lagundu!*" moaned Mrs. Elena Catalina Dougherty as she tossed and turned her aged and veiny body in her teak bed encrusted with mother-of-pearl. She mumbled unintelligibly under her goose down comforter while the baby monitor on the ivory granite-top nightstand flashed a faint green light. Four LED night lights illuminated the corners of the room, and the monitor's green light reflected off the headboard onto the Venetian plastered walls. The entire room was an iridescent grotto engulfing tiny Mrs. Dougherty.

She opened her eyes a crack in the fog of sleep, and her nearsightedness made her think she dwelled in a snow-speckled woodland. Awake or asleep she considered herself a forest dweller. As a child she pretended to be Gretel or Little Red Riding Hood strolling innocently among the tall oaks of her family's estate in Pasadena. Now, in her seventy-eighth year, Mrs. Dougherty felt like a withering forest nymph, a haggard hamadryad of Greek mythology. With her pint-sized body, long hair still dyed black, and her olive skin showing the signs of the elements, she indeed looked a little like a woodland creature. Elena had lived a long and luxurious life, most of it tied to her late husband and to this wooded villa in the affluent Los Feliz neighborhood of Los Angeles. Lately, she had to remind her successful and domineering daughters that just as the Greek hamadryads died when their trees were cut down, she too would die if they removed her from her forest home to the wasteland of an assisted living residence. She was not being dramatic. Lately she had tapped into something off the beaten path, and it was here in this place or in her or both. Maybe it was just the familiarity of her home, or her attachment to the people she had loved under its roof who were all gone now. She didn't know, and she didn't care. If Elena Dougherty were to leave this house it would literally be, as she told her daughters and her doctors and anyone else who asked, "over my dead body."

Mrs. Dougherty had no complaints about her solitary life on her property overlooking Los Angeles. On balmy summer evenings she loved to sit under the oak trees and listen to the strains of music floating from the Greek Theatre a few blocks away. In her garden she cultivated fragrant flowers and healthy herbs. And she wasn't completely alone. Her youthful gardener Octavio pruned the tougher branches she could no longer cut. Her daughters would not have called Octavio youthful. They would say something insulting but well-intentioned like, "he's aging well." But don't all men do that at least longer than women do? Octavio still had dark hair and a face weathered enough to be masculine. His body was trim and solid from a lifetime of working outdoors. People used to say her husband Randall was aging well, until he stopped aging at all.

After graduating college in 1953, she had spent all her married life in this Spanish Revival house, where every arch entrance and hand-forged iron gate reminded her of her daughters Cynthia and Catlin sliding on the parquet floors. Randall had carried her across its threshold singing:

Que Será, Será,

Whatever will be, will be,

The future's not ours, to see,

Que Será, Será

The song was her husband's attempt to acknowledge Elena's Spanish heritage on her mother's side of the family. Her ancestors had been early settlers in Los Angeles, but after four generations, Elena's sense of her Iberian heritage had dissipated. Randall seemed to enjoy her heritage more than she did. He would often brag to friends at the California Club that Elena's ancestors had established Los Angeles. They were not impressed. Randall's peers grouped all Spanish-speaking people into one ordinary brown bag. But Randall loved the radiance of her oblong face as it contrasted against her shiny dark hair that made her resemble a spry Audrey Hepburn.

Cynthia was now an entrepreneur in Silicon Valley, and Catlin, an attorney in the Bay area. Randall had passed on six years ago, and Elena learned to keep on living because by then *que será, será* had become her motto.

There were others in the house besides Elena and Octavio out on the grounds. Her daughters did not trust in her solitude or in her gardener as Elena did. It was Catlin, recovering from her own divorce and an empty nest since her own son went off to college, who had hired Yolanda as Mrs. Dougherty's live-in caregiver. Catlin would not listen to her mother's reluctance at having a caregiver despite acknowledging that Mrs. Dougherty was in stout health and with an agile mind. Catlin and Cynthia needed to reassure themselves that they were not neglecting their mother.

Her acquiescence gave her girls the peace of mind to concentrate on their own lives. It was what she wanted for them, and so she let them believe it was for her benefit that Yolanda moved in. The house was big enough, and Elena knew that whatever would be would be. She seemed to be fighting things less and less these days, pushing away the things that came to her unbidden less and less. Something was opening in her, something unfamiliar and yet part of her, something in her bones. She hoped it wasn't death coming for her a little at a time. Maybe this was how it started. But it didn't feel like death. It felt like life, and so she stayed in her house and watched and listened and waited for it to come.

❖ ❖ ❖

Tonight's spring rain had become a downpour complete with thunder and lightning. It was April of 2011 and the chaotic weather magnified the intensity of Mrs. Dougherty's dreams by keeping her somehow closer to waking than a true dreamer should be. At least that was her sensation; a creeping confusion about whether or not she was actually dreaming. A change in her state of being almost more like a trance than a dream. She was moaning in her sleep, next panting, now groaning. Part of her wondered if someone might hear, but the other part, the larger part wailed with abandon, "*Lagundu! Lagundu!*"

And in the stupor and frenzy of the dream and the storm, she wrapped her withered legs tight around a king-size pillow raising her hips as high as she could and thrashing them back down again.

⊞ ⊞ ⊞

Elena preferred the term "companion" to describe Yolanda rather than "caregiver," as the latter made her seem bedridden, which was far from true. But "companion" bothered everyone else. Cynthia and Catlin wanted Yolanda to realize she was an employee. They needn't have bothered with the reminder. Yolanda had left her family behind in Mexico to earn money in the states. She had sacrificed everything to care for them, and here were these two spoiled brats calling her an employee and looking at her always as if she might have the good silverware hidden in her pockets.

Yolanda didn't like the word "companion" either, because she had looked it up and knew it meant "friend." She was not a woman to accept money for friendship. It struck her as an odd sort of prostitution, and she didn't want to do anything that would make the daughters suspicious of her. She had identified them early as the kind that think all poor people steal. Actually, Yolanda thought, they were the type that made poor people *want* to steal. It was because they held themselves entitled to what they had only inherited and not earned. And they held tightly to what they did earn, thinking that because they worked hard, they should keep every penny, as if no one worked harder than they did. Yolanda kept almost nothing she earned and was grateful to send money to her aunt and her children in Mexico, and to share the rest with her sister and infant niece who lived in a decayed apartment nearby in downtown. Yolanda did not much like the daughters, but she prayed for them, and she reported to them, followed their orders, and took their money.

Yolanda slept in the bedroom across from Mrs. Dougherty's master suite. She did not trust the baby monitor. She had never used such a device, not even for her own children. So she slept very lightly so as to not miss any calls from Mrs. Dougherty. Unlike her previous elderly employers and their demanding adult children, Yolanda appreciated Mrs. Dougherty's respectful and gentle nature.

In Yolanda's sleep, she heard Mrs. Dougherty call out "Lolanda! Lolanda!" and she was touched by the mispronunciation of her own name. She was accustomed to her elderly employers calling her by the wrong name or simply addressing her as "girl," despite being thirty-five years old with three young children back in Mexico. She did look slightly younger than she was just because she was shorter than even her shrinking clients and wore her long black hair nearly to her waist. One particularly difficult insomniac patient, now deceased, had insisted on spouting commands to her. He addressed her as "you, the Mexican maid," and demanded that she bring him this or that all day and night long.

❖ ❖ ❖

Yolanda jumped out of her bed and went directly to Mrs. Dougherty's bedside. Yolanda had learned long ago in this job to sleep in a t-shirt and sweatpants and to keep a pair of shoes by the bed. If an employer's health was going to take a turn for the worse, it was usually in the small hours of the dark morning and there wasn't always time to dress before paramedics arrived. In the enormous master bedroom, Yolanda leaned close to her employer's face and whispered, "I am here now Mrs. Dougherty, do not worry."

Yolanda stroked Mrs. Dougherty's forehead gently, and in return, a sleepy but agitated Mrs. Dougherty tried to kiss Yolanda's lips. Yolanda was startled and repulsed at the same time and she stepped back. It had not been a small peck that her employer attempted. Mrs. Dougherty turned on the antique porcelain lamp on the nightstand, almost knocking it over in the process, but was clearly still asleep. She raised her bony thighs and squeezed the pillow she had wedged between them tightly. Her delirious moan of release was indescribable and Yolanda reflexively closed her eyes and covered her ears with her hands in order to muffle Mrs. Dougherty's cry of: "Ahhhhh!"

Yolanda squealed, "Ay, please, Mrs. Dougherty, wake up, please! You are having a nightmare." Yolanda opened her eyes and quickly yanked the pillow from the grip of Mrs. Dougherty's clamped legs, and finally her employer woke up. Yolanda tried to hide the pillow behind her back but then couldn't think of why. "You drop this," she said, "From your nightmare." And she replaced the pillow under Mrs. Dougherty's head.

"My goodness, what an intense dream I was having," Elena said and sat up to let Yolanda adjust her pillows. "I'm terribly sorry for waking you up, dear Yolanda."

"Do not worry, Mrs. Dougherty. I sleep very little. I always be ready any time you need me. I tell Miss Cynthia, no to worry, I take special care of her *mamacita,*" rambled Yolanda. It seemed very important for the moment that she continue talking. She fluffed and smoothed the pillows and blankets so she wouldn't have to look Mrs. Dougherty in the eye.

Mrs. Dougherty cleared her throat and said, "Thank you, dear. Please go back to bed. I'll just go downstairs and make some coffee. It's practically sunrise, anyway."

Yolanda shook her sleepy head and replied instantly, "No, Mrs. Dougherty. You wait right here, and I make your coffee and bring up to you." Yolanda wanted very badly to leave the room if only long enough to make coffee. "Lawyer Catlin say to me to never ever leave her *mamacita* alone. Your eyes not too perfect no more, she say."

Mrs. Dougherty smiled at the thought of Catlin making those demands. She was certain Catlin must have been much more dictatorial and threatening to patient Yolanda. Mrs. Dougherty answered, "O.K. dear, but it's not necessary to call Catlin *lawyer* Catlin. In the United States, we don't usually refer to a person's profession along with her name."

Yolanda always appreciated Mrs. Dougherty's explanations but she was still a bit confused. She asked, "But Mrs. Dougherty, how can other people know how educated and cultured someone is if they do not use their professional title? My nephew in Mexico is engineer, and we always call him *Ingeniero* Rodolfo. Is nice to have title, do you not think so, Mrs. Dougherty?"

"I'm glad to hear he has a good profession, Yolanda," replied Mrs. Dougherty, as she rose dreamily from bed.

Yolanda had expected a longer explanation. Mrs. Dougherty loved to explain the differences between Americans and other cultures when it came to things like class and race. Americans liked to pretend the world was as they would have it, not as it was. This fascinated Yolanda, and Mrs. Dougherty enjoyed being her guide. She thought she was helping Yolanda to become more of an American because isn't that what everyone wants? She had missed the point of Yolanda's employment here in this country. It was a necessity and she would give anything to be back with her children instead of making small talk with this woman who was refined and kind to her but whose orgasm she had been forced to witness. While caring for her clients Yolanda had witnessed many things the human body could do, and she tried always to allow for as much dignity and privacy as possible. But this was a first, and this was different.

Yolanda stiffly assisted Mrs. Dougherty with her mono-grammed slippers and matching peach-colored robe. Mrs. Dougherty thanked her for her kindness. They were both trying too hard to play their roles but something had changed between them, something powerful. Both women felt a profound and tec-tonic movement in Mrs. Dougherty's soul. Yolanda likened it to a 4.3 Southern California tremor. After her first experience with an earthquake, everything had seemed cast in a different light. The suddenness, the unpredictability—the illusion that every-thing could be controlled and planned for shattered. It was obvious that Yolanda had just witnessed a private erotic moment, yet her senior employer preferred to disregard it as a nightmare. This was intimacy and denial and a shared adrena-line rush that had no place in their previous relationship. Yolanda knew her daily pattern with Mrs. Dougherty would no longer be symmetrical or simple.

As for Mrs. Dougherty, the hanging objects in her heart and mind swung back and forth releasing not just pleasure, but memories as well. It was a little bit exciting like finding a box you had hidden away and forgotten, but mostly it frightened her, and she could see in Yolanda's dark eyes that it frightened her too. Neither woman got any more sleep that night.

◈ ◈ ◈

The heavy rain continued all that night and into the next day. By afternoon, both women were relieved at the arrival of Mrs. Dougherty's personal massage therapist. Claire knew her way around the large property, and she came in through the solarium door wiping her wet shoes on a mat Yolanda had placed there for her. "Phew, it's raining cats and dogs out there," she said as she dragged in her equipment that included a portable massage bed. "This isn't our usual sunny California day, is it, Mrs. Dougherty?" Claire shook her shoulder-length dark hair as she released it from under a baseball cap and then tied it back into a loose ponytail. She went about unfolding and setting up her table.

"Oh, it certainly is not. I slept terribly and woke up poor Yolanda with my frightful screams," replied Mrs. Dougherty. Elena was embarrassed at her own attempt to cover what had been a very erotic dream. She had no idea what Yolanda had seen, only what she had experienced. But she knew she had made enough noise to wake her, and she knew how the dream had ended.

Claire saw Mrs. Dougherty's face flush and worried that she might have a fever. She asked, "Yoli, did you take her temperature? Perhaps we should postpone the massage?"

"Her temperature is normal," replied Yolanda.

Mrs. Dougherty blushed again and said, "I feel fine. I think that I just had a sharp leg cramp last night, that's all. I could use a nice Swedish massage."

Claire continued setting up the massage bed near the oversize fireplace. "Whatever you want, Mrs. Dougherty. Although I was prepared to give you craniosacral therapy."

"Well, I guess we could try a new type of therapy. I, I, uh, I am feeling a little out of s-s-sorts after my incredible dream, uh, I mean to say, my nightmare, last night," stuttered Mrs. Dougherty. "And the leg cramp, of course. I wonder, can dreams cause leg cramps?"

Claire had never heard the quietly poised elderly woman stammer, or seen her blush, for that matter. She resolved to pay close attention to these subtle changes in Mrs. Dougherty during her massage. Claire knew from living with her own eighty-three-year-old grandmother in nearby Echo Park that even the subtlest of changes in the elderly could forecast a turn for the worse.

"Yoli, can you please help me get our little Mrs. D onto the massage table. I placed it a bit closer to the fireplace so she'll be nice and toasty," Claire said with a chipper smile.

"My Randall used to say he could roast a bison on a spit in there," said Elena. "Of course, he never tried. It's a Batchelder fireplace, don't you know. Design 578A, I think." The addition of "I think" was just coyness on Elena's part. She loved to explain the architectural and design features of her home and she knew them by heart. "Randall used to say that old man Batchelder made the tiles especially for him since he loved to hunt. Can you see the two hunters with the spears? How about the Pegasus horse near the hearth? Yolanda, that tile is still legible, isn't it?"

"Mrs. Dougherty, you have too good memory. I do not know about the Pegasus, but I think this one is a horse," said Yolanda.

"Precisely, dear. Well, Randall used to tease me since I've always been petite that I could fit in the fireplace like a little troll in its warm cave."

Claire laughed at the thought of pretty and dainty Mrs. D being compared to a troll. Yolanda on the other hand did not find any mention of trolls amusing. "We never mention trolls in Mexico. My great-grandmother told me the *duende* live in dark caves, now they live in the walls of our homes, and they hurt children." Her voice cracked with emotion. "I wish to be at home taking care of my children next year."

It was hard for Elena when Yolanda spoke of missing her children. She felt selfish for keeping her from them, but knew employment was what Yolanda needed most to care for them. It could get complicated when you were paying the people who lived in your house. But Elena was used to it; there had been nannies and housekeepers throughout their years here. Elena couldn't help but think of these people as family, and it wounded her in a way when they spoke openly of wanting to be somewhere else.

"I would never let the *duende* get my babies," Yolanda said. "I would have to chop him with a machete, I think."

Both Claire and Mrs. Dougherty looked perplexed at the depth of emotion Yolanda showed about some silly troll. Claire, always the diplomat, said, "I think all the trolls or *duende* as you say, are all extinct from the world. Don't worry, Yolanda."

"No, Claire. My third cousin's fifth baby lost his toes to a *duende* that crept out of the wall in the bedroom. This is what the *duende* do. He take the dirty toenails of the children and sometimes he take the whole toe. Ay, I hope my aunt is washing my children's toes."

Claire knew all about missing your loved one so much that it actually made your muscles cramp up with pain. Instead of allowing melancholy to grasp her again, she rearranged the massage table and knelt down to admire the Pegasus tile. She said, "What an incredible range of earth tones on all the tiles! Did you say this house dates from the 1920's?"

"Yes, 1929 to be precise," Mrs. Dougherty said. "Batchelder's studio, which was nearby in Pasadena, was known for its production of relief tiles. Ernest Batchelder loved to design leaping deer and other animals and he let the tiles sun-dry in a yard, although he later glazed and fired them in the kiln. Do you notice the tiles with the tree designs? Why those are California live oak trees, just like the ones in my yard! I do believe that I was meant to live around oak trees all my life. Strange that I've always felt that way isn't it?"

"Your property does have gorgeous oaks, Mrs. D., and these tiles are still in pristine condition, although the wings on the Pegasus are all gone. He's just an ordinary horse in your cavernous fireplace." Claire said this so sadly, as if all the magic of a happier time had gone out of the world as the Pegasus wings faded to white.

A worried Yolanda grasped the silver locket around her neck that contained her children's photo. Maybe the *duende* in California homes eats part of the tiles, maybe he wants part of the soil people have taken from his caves, maybe the *duende* takes little by little, then he attacks the innocents, she thought. Something was clearly wrong in this house. Maybe in America the *duende* brought bad weather as a trick so the family would track dirt into the house. She must be careful to keep the floors mopped and to protect Mrs. Daugherty's claw-like feet. She still had her toenails painted once a week with bright colors. This could be dangerous. Yolanda felt as if she was in a strange place where she no longer understood the rules. She held her locket tighter and whispered a prayer of protection.

Mrs. Dougherty smiled gently at the sweetness of these two young and sad women who took such good care of her. But she did not like it that they seemed to be blaming so much on her house. Why had they suffered so much in their young years? Good fortune had always smiled upon her here, even now in her old age; these two young women seemed to genuinely care about her well-being. She wanted them to draw solace from this place the way that she did. There was memory stored down every hallway, behind every cupboard, secrets under every rug, arguments resolved or forgotten hanging from the eves. She wondered if there was more than just the projection of memory to what she felt here. Could there be something measurable in a place that had contained a life even when the people had gone? Where did memory reside? Elena was more certain than ever that she would die if she left this place. She was this container and its grounds, and all of it was her. Randall was right, this was her warm cave.

Some might criticize her daughters for letting paid strangers do what some would consider their responsibilities, but Elena knew Cynthia and Catlin's careers were top priority in their lives. She had passed up on a professional life to create a beautiful home for Randall and her girls. Some might have wanted more passion and lust from their husbands, but she settled for a steady and prosperous provider. After last night's erotic experience—it was hard to think of it as only a dream—Elena wondered if she could have been more seductive with Randall, more assertive, but those were different days. It all seemed very old-fashioned now, but she had known contentment, unlike the sadness that Yolanda and Claire tracked into her house like mud from the garden.

🔲 🔲 🔲

Two months ago on Valentine's Day, while she trimmed some verbena shrubs, Mrs. Dougherty had overheard Claire and Yolanda talking about their broken hearts. She sat immobile on her gardening stool eavesdropping and staring at some unwanted mushrooms that had sprouted in a dank corner of her garden. Under a live oak tree and amidst the large boulders that created a landscaped cavern effect, the mushrooms made themselves at home. This annoyed her, as she considered them both invaders and pests. She thought they might be the terribly poisonous Death Cap mushrooms. She leaned a bit closer and noticed that the mushrooms did not have the white cup around the base of the stalk nor did they have the partial veil of the Death Cap. She wanted to ask Octavio about them, but it was his day off.

🔲 🔲 🔲

Last November, Octavio had warned her about poisonous mushrooms. Octavio was punctilious about exterminating any unwanted weeds or mushrooms. He was almost territorial about the most distant and heavy foliaged sections of her three-acre estate. Whenever he saw her approaching the farthest sections, he called out to Yolanda to take better care of Mrs. Dougherty. Yolanda did not appreciate the implication that she wasn't doing her job. Yolanda did not trust Octavio. "Our little boss will fall," he yelled. "We will get blamed for not taking care of her. You know Miss Catlin is a clever attorney and she will sue me for not keeping the grounds nice and even for her mother."

Yolanda glared at Octavio that day. She shook her head in frustration and disgust at his false interest, and she said, "I know how to take care of Mrs. Dougherty. You better take care of the weeds and the other filth that grows in that dark corner, or I think Lawyer Catlin might hear about it." Octavio stared daggers at her when Yolanda threatened his part of the garden. For now it was a stalemate of mutually assured destruction. But Yolanda swore to herself if she found out Octavio was doing anything to harm Mrs. Dougherty in the back garden she would turn the daughters on him even if it cost her this job. And Octavio knew it.

Mrs. Dougherty didn't like to witness any friction between her helpers. She said, "Don't worry, Octavio, I prefer to stay close to my herb garden and my lemon trees. I'll stay away from your mossy corner. I was just wondering about these mushrooms, that's all."

Octavio told her, "Do not even touch the mushrooms, Mrs. Dougherty. I do not want you to get poisoned. Do not believe people who say that no poisonous mushrooms grow on wood. Sure, many mushrooms grow near the roots of oak or cork trees because they provide phosphorus, magnesium, and other nutrients to the tree in exchange for carbohydrates, but many are still poisonous."

Mrs. Dougherty had asked him, "But don't you think that in your country certain types of mushrooms might have different characteristics from those in California?"

"Of course, Missus. We have many, many types of mush-rooms in Ecuador. Some are tasty with a meal, but some can only be used by a shaman because only they know how to help you interpret the dreams. The chemical structure of psilocybin resembles that of *ayahua*...."

Mrs. Dougherty leaned forward to hear Octavio's professo-rial lecture on mushrooms, only to hear him change his tone and clarity by saying, "I talk crazy nonsense. I no know nothing. Excuse me, Missus." She knew he spoke better English than he let on. She had noticed it just as he had noticed his half-hearted excuses about un-even ground keeping her and everyone else out of the back garden. She had assumed he was over qualified to be a groundskeeper, but couldn't find other work so he pre-tended to be a simple laborer. Elena thought it polite to let him keep his secrets. She liked Octavio, and she liked having him in her garden and in her small but growing family of strangers.

"On the contrary, Octavio," Elena insisted. "Please contin-ue. I have heard about psychedelic mushrooms, isn't that what you're referring to?" She was trying to sound both non-judg-mental and hip, but Octavio had already walked to the front of the yard and turned on the leaf blower at full blast. They never spoke of the poisonous mushroom again nor did she approach the farthest dank corner of her yard. She did not want to risk driving him away.

◼ ◼ ◼

But on that Valentine's Day that was Octavio's day off, Mrs. Dougherty inhaled the bouquet of her verbena shrubs and the nearby herb garden overflowing with rosemary and thyme, and wondered why she just couldn't yank those putrid mushrooms from the ground. They offended her vision of her garden. They shouldn't have come here. Let them try someone else's yard. Whether or not they were poisonous didn't matter, they contaminated the beauty of her herbs, lemon trees, and the intoxicating spice of verbena and moist soil. They were ruining something that had been just right without them. It agitated her to no end, though she wasn't sure why she reacted so strongly to them. Maybe she was miffed that the only man currently in her life had taken Valentine's Day off. She was ready to yank out the garden intruders, when she heard Claire and Yolanda.

Claire's soft sobs made Mrs. Dougherty's ears stand at attention, like the rabbits that often trotted along her garden. She heard Claire say to Yolanda, "I am a massage therapist, dear God, and I could not massage any life back to his withering muscles."

Yolanda wrapped her arms around Claire and cried along with her. "Ay, *que tristeza*, Claire. I so sad for you. I so sorry about your fiancé."

"I know all there is to know about muscles, and I couldn't help Phil at all. He lost control of all his muscles. His head drooped, he couldn't swallow, and finally, he couldn't even breathe," Claire sobbed. "I shouldn't even be a massage therapist; I'm a fraud. All my elderly patients wait anxiously for me to arrive, and I really can't help them at all."

Yolanda grasped Claire's hands tightly and said, "Clarita, you have kind hands. You help many of the elderly people here in Los Feliz. I hear from the other caregivers in the neighborhood that all your clients look forward to their massages. You have healing hands, yes, I think so."

Claire stopped crying, but only briefly. "I love massaging my seniors. I know that on some days I am the only one who can bring a bit of relief to their aching bodies."

Elena was beginning to regret her eavesdropping. She resented being referred to as a "senior." It was only her body that was aging. Inside she still felt seventeen just like everyone else does. Elena knew instinctively that parts of her were untouched by her age or even by herself. Elena had always believed her soul was older than she was and hers for only a while. There was something bigger, and Elena liked to think she was right in the middle of it, not at the end, not a "senior."

"It is more than that, Clarita," said Yolanda. "You bring human touch to their empty lives, *pobrecitos*. It's not like in our countries, we don't abandon our *abuelitos*, no never."

Empty lives? Elena sat still and silent as a statue focusing all her resentment at those damn mushrooms.

"Thank you, Yolanda," said Claire. "But this is my country, it's my grandmother who is from Ecuador, and I live with her now. She's the one who took care of me when Phil died. Now it's my turn to take care of her. But don't be so harsh on others who can't take care of their old folks. I think people always want to take care of their elderly relatives, but life gets very complicated. Sometimes we just can't help those we love the most. I couldn't help Phil. I miss Phil so very much." Claire wept.

Yolanda cried along with Claire. "Yes, that is true. I miss my three children too much, Clarita, it hurts me deep inside; past my skin, past my muscles, past everything. *Me duele hasta la médula.*"

Claire had never heard this expression: that something hurts so badly that it hurts right through to the spinal marrow. This expression struck a raw nerve in Claire. It defined the last year of her life; the year since Phil died. *Me duele hasta la médula.* Yes, indeed, this expression put her sorrow into words. Her pain had traveled to the core of all her organs; to her spinal cord, to the central axis of her nervous system; to the myelin covering of her nerves. To the same myelin that in Phil's athletic body had remained intact while all his nerve cells under the myelin sheath had died. Phil could only communicate his complex thoughts and his deep love for her with a debilitated blink from his teary and bloodshot right eye.

"Yes, Yolanda, I understand your pain. *Me duele hasta la médula,*" Claire sighed.

◼ ◼ ◼

Claire and Yolanda helped Mrs. Dougherty onto the massage table. The rain drops on the solarium glass ceiling galloped a measured pace like the hoofs of Peruvian Pasos on a cobblestone street in a village in Peru. The fireplace flames flickered with a warm and welcoming energy. The lights in the room were turned down low and the sound system played a simple flute composition.

"Would you like me to remove your socks, Mrs. Dougherty?" asked Yolanda.

"It won't be necessary. Claire said she will be doing a different type of massage today,one where I don't remove my clothing, right Claire?" asked Mrs. Dougherty.

"That's right, you just keep your comfy p.j., and I'll be right back. I have a little surprise for you, but I left it in the car. Be right back." Yolanda hurried to grab an umbrella for Claire as she braved the storm outside once more.

"Shall I go and get you a glass of water?" asked Yolanda.

"No, please stay here. It will be nice to have you listen to Claire tell us about this new massage."

Claire returned from her car with a bottle of massage oil. She placed a few drops on her palms and rubbed them together while Yolanda used a small towel to wipe up any hint of Claire's wet footprints on the floor. Claire's eyes twinkled as she said, "Okey dokey, Mrs. D., take a nice deep breath of this."

Mrs. Dougherty did as told and cooed at the scent. The sound she made was involuntary and came from deep in her lungs. Claire smiled, delighted. It was in her nature to make people happy and she had found something just right for her Mrs. D. "My goodness, that's my favorite verbena, isn't it? But there's something very different, very tangy, what is it?"

"My grandmother and Octavio made this oil of lemon verbena using your very own verbena, but grandma added lemon, clary sage, clove, basil, aniseed, thyme, and pimento, as they do in Ecuador. They say that lemon verbena oil can boost liver functions and help with insomnia. Since you said you didn't sleep well, I thought I could just apply a bit to your neck. Although the protocol for craniosacral therapy does not call for the application of any massage oil since the client is fully clothed, I thought you would enjoy its calming effects. Are you ready?"

"Yes, dear, and please tell your grandmother how much I appreciate it. What else is this essential oil good for?"

"It's also an antispasmodic since you said you had a leg cramp last night, right Yoli?"

Yolanda just nodded yes, but Claire didn't notice it, so Claire rephrased it: "How strong was that leg cramp or did both legs cramp?"

Yolanda and Mrs. Dougherty remained silent, wishing Clare would drop the subject of her fake cramp. Mrs. Dougherty's cheeks flushed a vibrant crimson, and Yolanda looked down at the Persian carpet on the parquet floor. Claire continued delineating the benefits of the lemon verbena oil. "It's a sedative, an emollient for your skin, and an aphrodi..." Claire stopped short; it seemed rude and inappropriate to talk about aphrodisiacs with the proper and elderly Mrs. D. Not appropriate for a senior.

Mrs. Dougherty couldn't hear the rest of Claire's sentence. "What was the last benefit of the oil, Claire?"

"Let's get started, shall we?"

Mrs. Dougherty appreciated the pampering. She usually felt better after her massage, and she was certain her daughters would give a sigh of relief. Mrs. Dougherty assumed that Catlin would grill poor Yolanda about her mother's reaction to the new therapy, and Cynthia would make sure that Claire was paid promptly and received a hefty tip for her services. Elena knew Yolanda reported back to Catlin. She had overheard Catlin's commands to Yolanda: "At the end of each day, I want you to text or email me a recap of my mother's well-being. Is that understood?"

Yolanda had responded sweetly, "I would like to do as you wish, Lawyer Catlin, but I do not know about this text or email or recap, but I learn. Can you please teach me?"

"Oh, never mind. You do know how to make a phone call, don't you?"

Catlin's sharp rebuke made Yolanda nervous. She said, "Of course, Lawyer Catlin. I will make a telephone to you every-thing, I mean, every day to her and then to you, yes?"

Catlin's frustration showed in the abrupt manner she grabbed her own cell phone. She said, "For pity's sake. Dial my number and leave me a message. Got it? Do it now so I know that you understand what I'm saying. I gotta catch a plane back to San Francisco. Do it now."

Yolanda fumbled at first, but she soon became so adept at reporting to Catlin that for the last three months, Catlin had instructed her to call in only every other week. Before hanging up with Yolanda, Catlin had said, "I'm totally stressed and I don't want to hear about my mother's bowel movements. I'm in deep shit already. Got it. In fact, keep taking your notes but only call me once a month, for pity's sake."

Yolanda still needed reassurance. "Should I call Miss Cynthia?"

"Are you kidding me? She only pays for Mother's care, but I'm killing myself with worry. Besides, Cynthia will be in Europe for the next three months."

※ ※ ※

Yolanda heard Claire's calm voice as she explained this new type of therapy, and she tried to take notes to report to Catlin. It was a gentle therapy never using more than five grams of pressure which was the weight of a nickel. Yolanda tried to remember, five grams, nickel. But the music and the fireplace and Claire's soothing voice put her to sleep on the wingback leather chair. She heard something about craniosacral therapy taking the whole-person approach to healing. Something about it connecting the mind, body and spirit, and that it was suitable for all ages. She glanced at Mrs. Dougherty who seemed to be inhaling deeply and snoring. Claire's other comments about the tide and the cranial rhythmic impulse made no sense to Yolanda other than to put her to sleep. She awoke to the now familiar sound of Mrs. Dougherty screaming.

"*Lagundu!* Pablo! *Lagundu!*" screamed Mrs. Dougherty. She continued to speak in a language Yolanda had never heard. Claire stopped her treatment and tried to wake Mrs. Dougherty, but she kept shouting in what seemed like gibberish.

"*Lamia!* Mari! *Lagundu!*" shouted Mrs. Dougherty.

Claire finally succeeded in waking Mrs. Dougherty. "Are you ok, Mrs. D? Were you having a nightmare?"

"No, I don't think so. It was actually a wonderful dream about, uh, about, that is to say, uh, it was not a nightmare. Please continue."

"O.K. but shall we talk a bit while I massage you? I would not want you to sleep now and be up all night, right Yoli?"

Yolanda was embarrassed for Mrs. Dougherty. She recognized the same glazed eyes and hot desire on the face of her employer. She decided to remain silent, so she sunk back into her wingback chair and pretended that she had not felt the shock wave going on in Mrs. Dougherty's *médula*. Something was changing her employer, something deep in her bones. Yolanda made a quick sign of the cross and pretended to go back to sleep.

CHAPTER TWO

Berástegui,
Guipúzcoa
Spain 1610

Cruelties of the Inquisition
Engraving circa 1882
iStockphoto.com

Berástegui, Guipúzcoa
Spain
1610

It was on a foggy day in April when Juan de Valle Alvarado and his agents made their way to Catalina's quiet hamlet nestled in the ancient valley of Araiz in northwest Iberia. Catalina could still hear twelve-year-old Mari crying for help, "*Lagundu! Lagundu!*"— as they dragged her limp body a fortnight ago to the Inquisitor's secret prison cells. No one had helped her.

Everyone in Berástegui and the nearby valley of Bertizaun knew Mari could not hold up to torture. Mari was only a child. It may be why they had chosen her. Mari's confession would be extracted. She would admit to being part of a witch's *aquellarre*. She would name others as members of her coven, and sixteen-year-old Catalina knew it was only a matter of time. The Inquisitor would come for her. This was a certainty.

Juan de Valle had cast a pall of terror in the ancient Basque homeland of Guipúzcoa and neighboring Navarra. The villagers, still recovering from a recent pestilence, had become malleable to the draconian justice of the *Malleus Maleficarum,* or the

Witches' Hammer, the manual of the professional witch hunters. Since 1609, Juan de Valle traversed from placid Basque village to bucolic Basque hamlet inciting terror, confession through torture, and death on the pyres of the *auto de fe.*

Old Diego had tried to warn the girls. "Girls, beware that you are not out at night alone, look what happened to the five girls of Zugarramurdi."

Mari's timid twelve-year-old voice wavered when she asked, "How old were they, Diego?"

Diego raised his bushy white eyebrows and stared at the girls. "The youngest one, María de Lecumberri, was barely twelve-years-old, but had been influenced by her sixteen-year-old cousin."

Catalina's practical mind would not accept that youngsters in Guipúzcoa and Navarra would conjure up such fantasies. "But Diego, you know we have to labor night and day to maintain our farms and herds while our fathers and brothers are away," she said. "We take turns helping one another on the farms, and we have to go out at night. How else can we finish all our work?"

"But sometimes," Mari added with a mischievous grin, "if we are in need of coins and we see a drunk out at night, we hit him on the head and take his coins, don't we Catalina?" Mari giggled and swung an invisible bottle as if hitting her drunk on the head.

"You are a dreadful liar, Mari," said Catalina. And she shivered at the possibility that she would not be able to impress on Mari the importance of not telling stories to strangers, or even to neighbors these days. "Let Diego finish."

Diego pretended not to have heard Mari's tall tales. "These are evil times, girls," Diego continued. "Remember that once the inquisitor clutches a suspected witch, she will be tortured until she confesses. Although it is a foregone conclusion that she is guilty of witchcraft." Diego's shriveled eyes managed to look up at Catalina with both fear and dread. "They ask them if they know how to make salve," he said. "You should not doubt the power of the inquisitors, Cati."

"But of course any Basque woman knows how to make all sorts of salve," said Cati. "Are they asking us in our language? Maybe the women don't understand what the inquisitors are asking."

"They bring Basque interpreters. Unless your blood is Basque, our language is impossible to learn. It is said that we have spoken it since we lived in caves," Diego said, "and the rest of the word was full of ice."

⌘ ⌘ ⌘

Talk of caves always reminded Catalina of two summers ago with Pablo. Just as their ancestors had done since primeval times, the young lovers had fearlessly explored the hidden cave near Pablo's family home and, within its sanctuary, the contours of each other's bodies. Many of the animals their ancestors had painted and carved into the limestone were no longer in existence, but the mushrooms with bell-shaped caps remained a treasure trove for the wise women of Guipúzcoa. As the proliferation of paintings on the walls attested, the women knew the enchanted mushrooms were an oracle from their ancestors.

After running his fingers along Catalina's legs, Pablo ran his strong hands along the curvature of the auroch painted on the cave walls. "My great-grandfather told me these beasts grazed all the way to the Bay of Biscay," he said. "I want to see more incredible creatures. They say there are lizards as big as goats in the New World." Catalina feigned disinterest—she did not want to think of Pablo leaving this place. "Father and I will be heading south to Seville, and then boarding the caravel owned by Martín de Aramburu," Pablo continued. "He is a fellow Basque from Guipúzcoa."

"Our men are seafarers," she whispered. "Their boats chase the baleen all across the western ocean. I know it is your destiny. In the past we could count on our whalers to always return, but the New World and its dusky sirens entice our men for eternity." Catalina wondered which type of sailor her love would be.

❖ ❖ ❖

Old Diego interrupted Catalina's memory. "Cati, I am sorry I must ask—do you have a salve for my aching joints? I could also use some herbs to help me fall asleep." He seemed ashamed to ask after his warnings, and Catalina knew he must be in a great pain. He was 95 years old, and in desperate need of salve since his wife died. "Can you help me?" he asked.

Catalina had known Diego all her life. He was as old as the deep-rooted oaks dotting the hills that protected their valley. She didn't hesitate. "I will send Mari tonight." She looked at Mari still so young and changed her mind. "No, not tonight, tomorrow morning."

That night the icy winds that ruin crops and kill livestock hit the valley again with a vengeance. Prompted by the arrival of the inquisitors, the villagers blamed this new disaster on witchcraft. They could not accept the randomness and cruelty of a universe in which their village could suffer the fevers and the loss of its crops so close together. There must be a reason for their misfortune. Someone had to be blamed. They were harboring witches, and by burning they would atone. Catalina knew Diego would be in even greater pain in the severe weather, so she and Mari risked walking to his hovel that night to help him. The girls were spotted trotting like the Spanish lynx to get the *belar osasungarriak*, the medicinal herbs, to creaky Diego. Some neighbor turned them all in to the Inquisition.

Diego was the first to disappear, then Mari and her grandmother. Their trio of distinctly painful laments escaped the torturous dungeons of the Inquisition, and Catalina despaired. Old Diego wouldn't last five minutes if they put him on the rack and pulled apart his already screaming joints. At night she saw little Mari in her dreams hanging from the ceiling by her small wrists bound behind her back, her own body weight slowly dislocating both shoulders. Once the inquisitors paid a visit to a village, they only left after the burnings. It was a matter of pride.

Before the dust from Juan de Valle's caravan had time to settle on her lands, Catalina fled her empty stone house and hiked in the dark to her and Pablo's summer cave. It was the only place she thought she might be safe, the only place he might think to look for her. She prayed he would return in time.

◈ ◈ ◈

When Pablo came back, he found Catalina's house empty and his village gone insane with fear. Yet he sensed that no harm had yet come to Catalina, and there was only one place she could be. He found her in their cave, enveloped by the limestone walls with pre-historic carvings and paintings of bison and the disappeared auroch. From their hiding place, Pablo could hear the raging crowd in the village. "Catalina, my *burualdi*, my stubborn one," he said, "this time I promise you that I will not leave

Guipúzcoa until I take you with me to Seville. Your father gave me his blessing to come and retrieve you, your mother and your little sisters..."

Catalina wept at the mention of her mother and sisters. She sighed, "My poor sisters and mother were no match for the scourge; they couldn't even hold out eight days. We were all so very weakened by working day and night on our farm while our men navigate the seas. I am so sorry for the passing of your mother, Pablo."

By the time he returned to Berástegui, Pablo's mother had already been buried along with all his sisters after the scourge razed the village. He was too late to save them, but he vowed that he would save Catalina from the evil that had overtaken their village. He whispered Catalina's name and dug into the metal chest that his mother had left behind. She had kept a cornucopia of *belarberza*, healing herbs, and Pablo grabbed an assortment of enchanted herbs, mushroom powder, and pulverized green toad skin. He needed them now to keep Catalina entertained with a kaleidoscope mind as her body and mind began to heal inside the cave while he left to investigate the brewing furor. In the cave Pablo swallowed his sorrows for now, because that is what he had to do in order to rescue Catalina and flee this superstitious backwater. He took another pinch of the *belarberza* from his leather pouch and placed it under Catalina's tongue. He waited until her wide awake dreaming was in full bloom, and then he mounted his horse making sure no one had seen him leave Catalina's hiding place. He headed for the *txoko* tavern.

▣ ▣ ▣

Catalina rode the kaleidoscope and heard Pablo's voice and the sound of his horse outside, and suddenly she was not in the cave exhausted and dehydrated but on a hillside riding her own horse after Pablo's at a hard gallop. She smelled not the smoke of the bonfires but the earthy sweet smells of the wind and the hills around her and the horse beneath her. Young Pablo and Catalina raced their horses up the steep hills surrounding Berástegui. They stopped at the hermitage of San Lorenzo one day and the convent of San Sebastian the next. They reenacted ancient medieval battles between the Oñacinos and the Gambinos. Catalina would be the first to charge Pablo and shout, "I will slice your head off, you worthless Gambino!"

Pablo would laugh and periodically let her win since she was three years younger. But he knew her joy for life had its mischievous streak. She would sneak up behind the pilgrims and startle them into dropping the handfuls of nails they'd brought as a devotional gesture to their patron saint San Lorenzo. Pablo found the pilgrims tragically pathetic. "Look at those dumb oxen, they're rubbing their boils with nails and then leaving them at the feet of San Lorenzo. They should all go see my mother, who will create a poultice for their boils. Cati, you should learn how to be a healer." Pablo had never been one to put his faith in superstition.

Catalina swatted him hard on the head for his suggestion. He fell to the ground, and feigned unconsciousness. Catalina jumped off her horse and rubbed his head. "Your head is a wild field of verbena," she said. She kept inhaling the verbena, and then she stared at him with eyes as dreamy as if she had just opened up a chest full of gold.

⬛ ⬛ ⬛

Shouts of "*epa!*" rang throughout the tavern and pats on the back welcomed Pablo. The men left in the village wanted to know which of their kinsmen had become wealthy on the Spanish Indies trade.

"Why did you return to our valley?" asked Iñigo. "Aren't the streets of Seville full of gold from Peru and silver from Nueva España?" Pablo was glad to see his childhood friend. Iñigo had a malformed foot that prevented him from sailing abroad with all the other men, and Pablo had missed him. Between the two, Iñigo's countenance was praised by all the girls, but his misshapen leg and limp made him undesirable. Whenever possible, Iñigo preferred to remain on horseback where his deficient leg remained hidden.

Pablo answered, "Seville is teeming with men seeking their fortu—"

An older man demanded, "My son Mikel was supposed to send for us as soon as he established himself in Seville. Have you heard from him?" Pablo ducked into the crowd. He didn't have the heart to tell the man his overly ambitious son had deserted as soon as the caravel docked in Callao, Peru, and no one heard from him again. More often than not, gold-hungry deserters met their demise through New World diseases or to the penetrating dagger of an equally invidious fellow deserter.

"How easy is it for a man to sign up with a ship on the Indies trade?" asked Iñigo.

Pablo knew Iñigo and his damaged leg would get booted out of town since the shipping dock area of the Arenal in Seville was teeming with able men desperate to strike it rich on a voyage to the Indies. "Iñigo, you know you always get *almadiamiento* any time you're on ship," he said. "Stay away from seasickness and from the harsh Andalusian sun. You should stay here working your land."

"Why should I be left behind?" asked Iñigo. "I want to accrue riches, like you."

"Times are changing. The creation of the University of Seafarers in Seville is making it more difficult for a simple sailor to join the fleet."

This last unconvincing comment encouraged the rude drunks in their favorite game: shouting insults at Iñigo. One man screamed, "He's not a full man, just a three-legged stool. Crawl over here and let me rest my feet on your back!"

Iñigo laughed good-naturedly, but his clutched fists disheartened Pablo. Pablo didn't have the time to feel compassion for his friend. He wanted to speed up the conversation since he didn't know how much time he had before Catalina was found or the herbs wore off, and she came looking for him. The welcome-home banter was turning uglier with each drink, but he entertained more questions and finally tried to sound uninterested as he asked about Mari. "Where have they taken the women accused of belonging to the *aquellarre*? Are they still nearby or are they already in Logroño?" When no one volunteered any information, he added, "They tell me that Mari and her grandmother are in front of the tribunal in Logroño. Do you think Don Alonso de Salazar Frías will be able to convince the other judges that our local women are not involved in any Witches' Sabbat, but simply working day and night while we men are away at sea?"

He hoped this would cause the men to rally around their women, to blame what was happening on outsiders and not on themselves. Pablo was not prepared for their rude reaction. The men belched, passed thunderous wind, and threw bits of crusty old bread at Pablo. How could things have changed so much while he was gone? How could the men be reacting like this in the face of so much death? Pablo was tempted to pull out his dagger, but remembered Catalina's trusting eyes in the cave. He let go of his last hope that sanity could be restored to his people and focused his interrogation of the assembled drunks in order to determine how to best haul Catalina out of this frigid valley burning with the fever of mob rage.

Suddenly a man named Juanes singled him out. "Did you expect us to work your lands while you were away hoarding riches from Peru? We know you and your clansmen are outfitting your own vessels in Seville so you can sail with agility to the Canaries and the Azores. You and your limber bodies and sticky fingers transport a little registered cargo here along with a larger amount of contraband there. You and the Oñates are nothing but a pack of cunning corsairs, ain't that so, boys?"

Pablo made sure he could reach his dagger and glanced towards Iñigo, but instead of support he thought he saw a sardonic expression on Iñigo's handsome face. It was the wave of fear that washed over him then that almost convinced Pablo he could do nothing for Mari or her grandmother. He began to doubt he would even get Catalina out in time. He shouldn't have come here. He should have taken Catalina from their cave right away and never looked back.

Both the inebriated and the sober men howled their approval of Juanes's accusation.

Juanes jumped on top of the tavern's oak table, pounded his chest, and grabbed his genitals, and bellowed. "We men who stayed behind know how to take care of our families and our ancestral lands. 'Gora Euskadi!' Long live our Basque homeland. There's more treasure in tilling our lands, hunting our wild boar in our forests, and planting Basque seeds into our own women instead of impregnating some bronze wenches in the Indies."

The tavern shook as the men shouted their ancient chants, "Gora Euskadi! We bow down to no one, we are all nobles, and this is our land since time immemorial."

Another thin man who looked typically Basque with his fair skin and long narrow face rose to say something. Some other fellow, who had a virtually identical face, pulled him down. Pablo now understood why the Basque sailors were easily recognized by their similar facial characteristics, whether in New Spain,

Peru, the Philippines, Goa, or the Moluccas. The thin man persevered and shouted. "What lands are you talking about, jackass? We continue to till the lands belonging to the lords of Berástegui, and those highwaymen cloaked as counts still rob us blind."

Juanes flung himself at the man, but his punches were intercepted by the burly blacksmith Javi. Javi's iron hands stabilized Juanes as he sat him down on a bench. He addressed the shabby group. "Juanes makes sense even when he's four sheets to the wind. Those greedy counts of Berástegui are not any nobler than the rest of us. Our ancestors were all recognized as nobles at the assembly to recognize the *fueros,* our laws, at the giant oak tree in Guernica ages ago. It just so happens that the counts of Berástegui's lands border the royal highway from Pamplona to San Sebastian. They charge road tolls to protect the caravans from their own bandits."

Cries of "Thieves! Bandits!" bombarded the fetid air, and added a noxious layer of envy, fear, and disappointment to the already dank *txoko.*

Pablo found himself disgusted by these men and desperately tried to maneuver the conversation back to the whereabouts of Judge Salazar, the only juror of the Inquisition known for attempting to use a certain amount of genuine jurisprudence in the witch trials, but the men ignored him. Instead, they wanted to vent about their lack of status and their hurt pride in their small hidden valley.

Javi commanded respect. He told all assembled, "The Berástegui clan took the proceeds of their tolls and the tithes our elders had to pay them, and they built mansions in Tolosa. They even sent their youngest son Ojer on the first voyage of Columbus. This nearsighted scribe didn't man the sails or pilot the caravel like the rest of our great-grandfathers. He couldn't see beyond his quill, but he sure knew how to keep records of riches accumulated by the Admiral of the Ocean Sea. Ojer de Berástegui ended his career with enough wealth to settle branches of his own family in Seville and in Cádiz. They are clever foxes."

An elderly man interrupted with a fist crashing on the oak table as he managed to raise his feeble voice in admiration of the counts of Berástegui. "Don't you wish you were as clever? The Berástegui's continued to send their men to settle in Quito and Nueva España for generations. They knew how to extend their fishing-for-treasures nets all over the Indies—"

Another old-timer applauded this fellow's approbation. He hoarsely added, "Ojer de Berástegui was nearsighted but he sure knew how to maintain a ship's ledger of accounts. He bobbed and swayed in the boat all the way to the Indies and back, yet he managed to keep the records to the liking of Admiral Columbus. I say that we *all* should have been so farsighted."

All the men paused to hear Javi's retort, but he seemed temporarily dumfounded by such clarity coming from a decayed cerebrum. He managed a weak and crass statement. "Who gives a seagull's turd about the counts of Berástegui? I'm fed up with having to look up to their coat of arms all over our village. Their manor and tower stay empty while they fill their coffers with our tithes and the bounty from the Indies. We should burn their manor down."

Cries of "Burn the manor, burn the tower" quickly turned into "Burn the witches, burn the demons!" Pablo watched in horror as these men transformed in front of him. Their eyes were fixed and red, filled with something between hatred and glee. These men were the demons filled with the courage of the mob. Juanes downed a tankard of *aguardiente* moonshine and dropped his head like a lumberjack's ax on a wood stump, and passed out. All the men clapped, and they downed more of their own *aguardiente*.

Pablo recognized that he had but minutes to extract the information as to the whereabouts of Mari, as he had promised Catalina. More importantly, he wanted to determine how many of the Inquisition's henchmen roamed their hamlet so that he could plan an escape route. Pablo attempted to sound *blasé*. "So, where are the inquisitors and their hangers-on hiding out? Do you all see them wandering in the village, or are they riding the hills near the hermitages as well?"

Pablo thought his voice sounded serene, but Javi caught on. He shouted loud enough for the entire *txoko* to hear, "What you're really asking is this: Where's that witch Catalina, isn't it? Don't you worry; you're just in time to smell your sweetheart's skin sizzling. Valle's men will flush her out from whichever hole she's hiding in. None of the women are leaving this village alive. Not my dead wife, not your dead mother, and not Catalina." He took a swig of his strong *aguardiente*, and concluded: "Our ancestors may have lived in this region forever, but when the men started to desert their homes and their women, chasing gold instead of tending their farms and hunting whales, they invited the horned goat to enter their homes and ravish their women. Those witches deserve what they have coming to them."

One of the village's buffoons jumped around the floor stamping out non-existing flames with his filthy feet and shouting in a child's high-pitched voice, *"Lagundu! Lagundu!"* just as Mari had done. The rest of the men broke out in hysterical howls and obscene gestures as if preparing for a nighttime wild boar hunt. The buffoon's cries turned into hysterical yelps. "Let's burn the witches, let's burn the witches!"

Another village simpleton, his mouth lathered with thick saliva, jumped on top of the serving table and removed the stuffed ibex head from the tavern's wall. He ran around trying to penetrate the other buffoon's bottom with the ibex's curved ringed horns. With a powerful but hoarse voice he cheered the men into savagery. His flying saliva splattered on the drunken men as he screamed. "Let's show those witches what real horns feel like before they burn!"

The men howled in the night. They growled at their broken and old bodies that had obstructed them from manning the sails on merchant ships or from spearing whales in the icy western seas. They struck one another with canes, clubs, and tankards as punishment for their weakness in their bodies, minds, and souls. Iñigo limped out of the fray and gestured to Pablo to follow him. Pablo allowed himself a glimmer of hope. Perhaps an ally at last, and one who had kept his wits.

After escaping the ruckus at the *txoko*, Iñigo said, "You must stop asking about the witches and their inquisitors. We're all in a state of fear. Once the women confess to their wickedness, their men folk get thrown into the bonfires, too. In Zugarramurdi, they not only burned María de Arburu and María Bastán de la Borda, but also Domingo de Subildegui. So unless you want to leave your charred remains in this forsaken land, leave now. I'll even give you my horse; just leave."

Pablo was touched by Iñigo's concern and by his generosity in warning him to leave when he had thrown his crippled friend no such lifeline in return. Iñigo was still a good man and a good friend.

"I hear that Judge Salazar is in Tolosa, just a few leagues away," said Iñigo. "Shall we ride there now and stay at my uncle's house for a couple of days?"

Pablo's already pale face blanched further. He had no intention of putting any more distance between himself and Catalina. He stammered, "Uh, no, I, I'd better stay here until I find out about Mari."

"Mari and the four other accused left on a coach this afternoon. We really should head west to Tolosa now. Unless, of course, you want me to help you hide Catalina in a mule cart and take you both to San Sebastian. From there you can take a ship to Seville."

Pablo was grateful for Iñigo's help, but he still didn't dare tell him that he knew Catalina's hiding place. He would never put her life in another man's hands. Never. He tried one last time to get information about Mari's location, and if the Inquisition was ready to move on to the next village. He said, "From what I've heard, the tribunal can't decide how to pass down their verdict on the witches. They say that Dr. San Vicente wants to sentence them quickly and decree a forfeiture of their property. But Valle wants to impose reconciliation and life imprisonment, plus the confiscation of all their properties. Have you heard if Judge Salazar is nearby or in Logroño?"

"What difference would one judge's decision make against Valle? He's the final say in these proceedings, isn't he?" asked Iñigo.

"I hear that Salazar uses a more rational approach in these trials. He tries to determine if the supporting evidence is independent and factual. They say he is out to prove that the current method accepts accusations that are based on fantasy and dreams, and not on reality. If he is truly a reasonable man, perhaps we can somehow influence him to release Mari; she's just 12 years old. And then they will leave other local suspects alone, don't you think? We know that this village has never had any covens or any other evil mumbo jumbo, right Iñigo?"

"Absolutely! Our women are strong and dedicated to their families. Who has time for such nonsense? But I don't think that you should get too optimistic about Judge Salazar. He recommends torture as a first step in the proceedings. Look at what he did to María de Zozaya; he had her tortured mercilessly for being accused as a proselytizing witch. Salazar just wants to make his mark as a different kind of jurist, but he's as cruel as they come. And don't forget, all the judges, regardless of their stripes, always confiscate the property of the accused. You don't want Catalina to lose all her lands, do you?"

Pablo looked down and did not answer. Iñigo continued, "On the other hand, if Salazar is truly after the facts, perhaps Mari will be released. That is, if she hasn't succumbed to the torture. Let's ride to Tolosa, shall we?"

Pablo muttered an unconvincing excuse about repairing some farm tools. He said a brief goodnight to his friend and headed towards his family's lonely house. Once he neared his property he looked to all four corners to make sure no one noticed him, and then circled around the tenebrous streets of the desolate village, and headed toward the cave.

▣ ▣ ▣

As they waited for the darkness to become complete before leaving, Catalina whispered to Pablo, "I think some animal entered the cave. Can you see anything?"

Their small fire lit up her face, and Pablo could see fear in her eyes.

"No, it isn't anything to worry about," Pablo assured her, but he grasped the handle of his dagger.

A flock of birds flew from a branch *en masse*, producing a loud fluttering. Catalina relaxed and laughed. "You're right; it's just the birds flying from tree to tree." Catalina pulled Pablo closer to her and sighed. "I can tell when you're near by the trail of verbena oil. Do you think it's true that verbena has supernatural forces?"

"My mother massaged it on us boys because of its calming effects. Now I apply it because it reminds me of her, and I like the way your eyes gleam when you smell it on my neck!"

In the end, it was the smell of verbena that made Iñigo do it. Flat on the ground like a frozen salamander at the entrance of the cave, Iñigo trembled with rage and envy. The redolence of verbena and sweat from Pablo and Catalina's lovemaking formed steam in the small chamber, and the unique incense of love, lust, and promise overcame Iñigo. Instead of crawling slowly like a venomous serpent, Iñigo gagged and growled as a rabid beast. He gave himself away, and Pablo was ready for him.

Pablo leapt up from his place by the fire and thrust his dagger at the assailant. With one deep stab, he ended Iñigo. Pablo had struck blindly in the dark at an unknown attacker. He was stunned that his lifelong friend would have slithered up on them as a snake in the grass. The Iñigo of old would have never acted this way. There was no time to stop and think about what he had done to his friend or what his old friend had meant for him and Catalina. He had killed Iñigo while hiding an accused witch, and if Iñigo could find their cave then more might be coming. Instantly, he picked up Catalina, whose mind remained distorted from the *belarberza*. She asked in a panic, "What is that beast on the ground?"

"Close your eyes. It was a dreaded *lamia*, the evil troll that lives in caves, that's all."

"Oh, no, they do exist! Please, get me out of here," she said.

◈ ◈ ◈

Catalina rested her head on Pablo's shoulder and smelled the tang of verbena and musk. Pablo's bouquet calmed and excited her. As they rode down the slopes of their ancient village on

Iñigo's horse heading toward San Sebastian, Pablo covered himself with Iñigo's hat and his heavy woolen cape. He rode with his right leg drooping at an abnormal angle, just as Iñigo had ridden. They passed a neighbor who greeted him jovially, "*Epa!* Iñigo!" Catalina, who was wearing Pablo's cape and hat, pulled on Pablo's leather amulet that she was wearing around her neck. Pablo was known in town for always tossing and pulling on his mother's amulet. As the neighbor walked away from them, he pretended to limp along the road mocking the rider who he assumed was Iñigo. Pablo let a few tears roll down his cheek at the memory of the taunting Iñigo had experienced since childhood.

Pablo and Catalina kept a good pace and stopped only once to glance back at the distant stone tower of the counts of Berástegui. Since antediluvian times, their ancestors claimed these grassy hills, full of wildlife and rich soil, as their own land. Hence their name: Berástegui, a place of high grass. Pablo and Catalina promised to tell their descendants about the cave, the carved auroch they would never see, and they would sing to them in their enigma of a language. Catalina would grow tangy lemons and verbena plants so she could massage her energetic sons and grandsons with verbena oil. Their sons would be as passionate as her Pablo, and she would grow old with dozens of grandchildren.

Catalina asked, "Will Iñigo join us at the port?"

Pablo choked up for a second time at the mention of his lifelong friend. Finally, he answered, "No, Iñigo belongs to the soil of *Euskal Herria*. He is part of the barbarous herds of bison carved on the limestone caves of our Basque homeland. *Gora Euskadi!*"

CHAPTER THREE

Los Feliz

April 8, 2011

...and the Amazon 1969-1999

Native of Peru

Illustration created by Riou

Published Le Tour du Monde, Paris 1864

Bigstockphoto.com

Los Feliz
April 8, 2011

Octavio's panel van curved along the hilly streets of Los Feliz bearing the faded graffiti of decades of failed businesses: a section of the word "plumbing" in orange letters near the driver's door, a few scraped letters of the word "carpet" somewhat visible towards the rear. This collage of faded letters and lost dreams meant nothing to Octavio. His calling was a higher one than plumbing repair or carpet cleaning. Octavio worked with the earth and its plants, learned from them, harnessed their power.

Octavio's ladders, long fruit hooks, and ropes were attached and ordered on the side of his van with military precision. He would not risk being stopped by a bored cop due to a loose ladder. They might want to search the miniature rainforest he carried in the back of his van where he kept shrubs in buckets and shelves growing with exotic cuttings in large coffee cans. There were seeds and roots he had carefully smuggled into the country from the Amazon. There were plants the authorities in this country would not recognize as dangerous and some that they knew all too well.

Octavio was a child of the Amazon, and his morality was based on the jungle. The ways of the anaconda and the jaguar were not complex. Eat or be eaten was not a form of evil—it was the jungle when it was most alive. Octavio knew the rules were different here, and that to obey the rule of law rather than the rule of the warrior meant he would go unnoticed and not be interfered with. It meant he would continue his work to its ultimate conclusion.

But some things about himself he could not change. The axes and the picks and the serrated spades hung within reach. There were things in his van and in the greenhouses he had so generously built on the extensive lands of the clients he chose to cultivate, and there were things hidden deeper in the dark corners of their estates these elderly people could never suspect. It was always the paid women who were called "caregivers" who were suspicious. They watched him and shook their fingers at him and pretended they knew what he was up to. They couldn't begin to guess, but they all seemed to notice the axes and the picks and the serrated spades as more than simple garden implements. He could see it in their eyes. They were wary of large men who could wield such things. But none of them had been brave enough yet to seek him out in the greenhouses and the secret corners of the yards. Something in their pasts had taught them when it was safer to keep their mouths shut. And besides, he knew these women would never push things far enough to risk losing their jobs, and none of them were born here in this country. If they meddled too deeply, the authorities might dismiss their complaints against Octavio. They might demand to see their green cards; they might deport them.

To the home owners and the retired residents of Los Feliz, an immigrant gardener in a used van loaded down with equipment was ubiquitous. These were people who had always had the details of daily living taken care of by others. Most of them didn't own a single gardening tool of their own unless it was an expensive pair of leather gloves and a delicate set of shears for cutting flowers to put in the crystal and porcelain vases on tables. This they considered gardening. Octavio would show them how to trim their roses in the right place when they took blooms for the table, and they instantly listed gardening as one of their hobbies. They would tell their friends how it sustained them to care for the roses or the orchids they were becoming such experts in. They looked up botanical names in books just in case someone questioned their new found expertise.

Octavio knew much more than where to trim a rose bush so it continued to produce blooms. There were more varieties of poison in nature than there were varieties of roses. There were far more deadly defenses employed by plants than the thorns on a rose bush, and no pair of expensive leather gardening gloves would be protection enough.

◈ ◈ ◈

Mrs. Dougherty tried to compliment Octavio once.

"Octavio, do you know that you and your van remind me of the bakery man who used to drive in a panel van tooting the distinct whistles that announced his coconut frosted cakes and loaves of bread when my girls were just little girls?" She seemed so pleased with herself and seemed to think Octavio should be pleased as well, but Octavio was no bakery man. He did not toot. She had tried to diminish him by transforming him into a player in one of her own memories and wearing him around her neck. Octavio knew all about transformation. There were powerful transformations for warriors and diminishing ones for enemies. He had once been expert at them both.

"That is a nice memory for you, yes?" asked Octavio. He cast her off making sure she knew this was her own vision she was enjoying, not his.

Mrs. Dougherty wanted to chastise him for his abrupt dismissal, especially since she had been on the verge of paying him a compliment. Why, just seeing Octavio drive up in his woodland wagon, with its promise of resurgent plant life, filled her heart with wonderful memories. But instead of waiting for her comments, Octavio was soon planting and pruning and adjusting his prized plants inside the greenhouse he had constructed in her yard three years ago. Mrs. Dougherty accepted his difficult nature, satisfied that his orchids would soon be the envy of all her friends; that is, her very few remaining friends.

⊞ ⊞ ⊞

Mrs. Dougherty's ornery neighbor a few doors down the street, Dr. Zeke Nunez, liked to think he didn't put up with any of Octavio's "impertinent" behavior, but he did just like all the others. He told Octavio, "I know you built a bootleg greenhouse in Elena's huge yard. Don't think that just because my vision is no longer acute, I don't know the illegal shenanigans you illegals are up to. I ran my own medical practice for 48 years, so don't think you can pull the wool over my eyes, got it?"

"Yes, sir, Doctor Nuñez, I do—"

"Damn it, how many times do I have to tell you people that I am not Hispanic. The proper pronunciation of my last names is NUNS, not the Hispanic version, got it?" shouted Dr. Nunez.

Octavio powered up the lawn mower and saw Dr. Nunez's mouth moving like a jabbering old woman. He moved quickly down the long narrow lawn and left Dr. Nunez throwing a fit; small and alone in his yard.

Dr. Nunez's Filipina caregiver Soledad watched all of this from the kitchen window while making lunch for the old man. She was preparing his favorite beet salad, but she wasn't doing it to please him. Octavio was here and it frustrated old Dr. Nunez that Octavio had coaxed two varieties of beets from the ground on the Nunez estate. After his retirement, part of Dr. Nunez's plan was to spend his days tending his vegetable garden and preparing impressive meals with homegrown beets, heirloom tomatoes, and Japanese eggplants, all of his favorites. Soledad got a perverse pleasure from the fact that Dr. Nunez's old age had not gone according to his script. The ground had not presented him with fresh salads worthy of vegetarian magazine covers the way he imagined it would, and his eyesight dimmed so quickly it was either give up gardening altogether or risk losing toes to his hoe and fingertips to the pruning shears. Kneeling in the garden became difficult too, and getting up again without help, impossible. The whole thing had been humiliating for a man who was accustomed to getting what he wanted. Dr. Nunez did not like old age, and Soledad did not like Dr. Nunez. So she made him a beautiful beet salad with Octavio's beets and relished watching the old man fuming in the yard. Soledad also liked the way Octavio moved. He strutted away like a peacock, and his back muscles protruded through the damp t-shirt.

"I suppose I should talk the old fart into calming down before he has a heart attack," she said to herself. No old man meant no job, and Soledad needed her job. Her life had not gone quite according to script either. She saw the old man remove his thick glasses and rub his eyes with a violent windshield wiper motion. "Your eyesight is gone with the wind," she said to him from the confines of the kitchen window. She laughed at her own cinematic reference, even though she was sick and tired of watching old movies with the old codger. She waited until she saw Dr. Nunez's bulging veins at his temples before going outside. Soledad was not an overly kind woman, but for the most part she did her job.

"Dr. Nunez, calm down. Please tell me what is bothering you?" asked Soledad in her well-honed, phony, caregiver voice.

"What do you think? It's that wise ass illegal gardener, who else?" he shouted. Dr. Nunez had a little bit of a hunch to his back, but he could still flail his arms around when angry. He must have made his share of nurses and interns jump in his day before he was small, gray, and half-blind.

"That Octavio has the worst manners," said Soledad. "In the Philippines he would be fired for his rudeness. I will be glad to tell him that you do not want him working here."

"I don't need you to do my hiring or firing." He flailed his arms some more only this time in her direction instead of Octavio's as if he were attempting to scratch at the air in front of him. He probably couldn't tell how far away she was with those eyes. Soledad had to wonder if he would even have recognized her if she hadn't spoken to him first. She made a mental note to test this sometime soon. "And I don't care what they do in your country; this is America, damn it. Don't think that I'm weak of character just because my health is declining. I can still fire him and you, for that matter!" Soledad took one experimental step backwards and noticed that her boss squinted harder and stuck his head out on his neck like a turtle trying to telescope his eyes out closer to her.

"Of course, sir. You are the big boss, yes sir." She walked towards him and took his arm. "May I help you walk back to the kitchen; I made your favorite beet salad."

"Yeah, let me lean on you a bit." He grabbed her arm like a small child lost in the woods. "I forgot my walker. Are those the beets that Octavio planted?" he asked.

"Yes, sir, big boss. Two types of beets: Golden beet and Chioggia."

"Damn that Octavio! I tried for years to grow beets without any success. I thought I needed sandier soil with a pH of 8, then he comes along and now we have two types of beets. Do you think that we should ask him to build us a greenhouse, too?" he asked softly as he leaned very heavily onto Soledad's small frame. She practically towed him back into the house and noticed that he stubbed his toe when he forgot about the flagstone step at the back door.

Soledad had been doing this caregiving gig too long with too many old people, and now they were breaking her back slowly but surely. She had come to California to be in the movies twenty years ago, but all she ever got in her earlier years were offers to perform lewd acts in trashy movies. Had they offered her bigger money, she might have accepted their sleazy offers, but now her looks had faded and her prodigious natural breasts were easily replicated by any flimflam doctor on any flat-chested wannabe actress.

Soledad's days were now spent watching tedious black and white movies with a cantankerous old doctor and listening to him complain about two kinds of beets. When she first arrived at his home, she thought that maybe if she let him cop a feel of her breasts, he would give her a bonus. Instead, he lectured her incessantly about behaving honorably. How else could she increase her nest egg? She wanted to return to the Philippines and invest in a neighborhood bar and still have a little left over to pay for handsome young escorts who would satisfy *her* needs for once. Instead, she waited hand and foot on Dr. Nunez, and yet he complained that she'd better call Claire for another massage since his body ached terribly. Didn't she also deserve a massage once in a while? What had she done in a past life to have the bad luck to waste her years with whining and decrepit old farts?

Without ever turning around to see what Dr. Nunez and Soledad were doing, Octavio knew they both wanted something from him. He felt their dark and needy energy from a distance. Their need was a fact running through his veins just as the secondary veins of the *caimito* tree leaves cling to the mid-vein. He heard Doctor Nunez's body creak as he leaned into his caregiver with the despair of a man at the gallows, and he felt Soledad's desire for him. It had been swirling around him since he started the lawn mower. Octavio knew that Dr. Nunez's constant haranguing about the poor condition of the vegetable garden echoed a cry of futility at having missed a fruitful season when he was in his youth. Octavio realized that all the luscious vegetables in the world wouldn't bring back the robust life that Dr. Nunez had wasted. These were the everlasting truths the mighty Amazon taught Octavio to see.

▣ ▣ ▣

When the other pubescent boys from Octavio's settlement were still learning how to paint the tips of their blowgun darts with poisonous *curare*, he was using the same leaves from the canopy of trees as a treatment for fever. While the other boys monkeyed around throwing rotting *camu camu* fruit at one another, their faces and chests drenched in the red purple juice of the fruit, Octavio snuck off deeper into the forest to enjoy the juicy pleasures of the girls. He was more serious than the others, maturing at a faster rate, and intelligent enough to begin discovering the secrets of plants and trees without being taught. It seemed Octavio had never had time to waste with a childhood. He behaved like someone with a destiny. The elders had seen it before and they watched him. They made their plans to test him and when the time was right they moved against him to see if what they suspected about him was true. Before pouncing on Octavio while he frolicked with the girls, the elders stalked him with the same silent paws and sharp fangs the jaguar kept for a plump tapir.

Octavio heard the faint rustle of the leaves meters away in the forest. He closed his eyes and sifted the information, looking for evidence of his enemies on the wind. It was easy to do, and no one had taught it to him. He knew the forest. Octavio knew every sound, color, texture. He knew what belonged and what didn't. He could discern stillness from movement. His quick mind eliminated all the probable animal sounds, and then he knew what was left and that they had come for him. He jumped off the smiling girl, and quickly ran up the trunk of a *capinurí* tree.

The elders had sent the most able of the young warriors to attack Octavio, but they had lost the element of surprise and the high ground before they even saw him. Their numbers and their skill now gave them no advantage. One by one he foresaw their amateur moves and knocked them down or knocked them out. Octavio ridiculed the last opponent. "You limp monkeys think you can attack me when I am near my tree? Look around imbeciles, what do you see? That's right, can't you see that the branches from my tree are in the powerful shape of a rock-hard penis?" He grabbed a branch of the *capinurí* and crushed the head of the last man-boy standing. With all the adrenaline rushing through him, Octavio even had time to finish off what he had started with the girl.

Octavio's prowess as a warrior and as a lover brought him to the attention of the *uwishin,* the elder shaman. He asked Octavio, "How did you learn to make dragon's blood to stop the bleeding of the men you attacked?"

Octavio responded in a matter of fact way. "I've been watching you since I was an infant. I used the sap of the *Sangre del Grado's* tree and applied it to their wounds. Most of them were surface wounds anyway."

"What would you have done if this did not stop the bleeding?" probed the *uwishin*.

Octavio quickly answered, "I would have used the yellow resin of the *renaquilla* tree to heal their internal fractures."

Octavio never saw it coming. The *uwishin* wacked him with a stick to the side of his head. Octavio fell to the ground and heard loud ringing in his right ear. He felt blood trickle from the ear, and he lost his balance.

The *uwishin* said, "I didn't ask you about internal injuries, did I?"

Octavio shook his head, no. He just stared at the drops of blood now running down his neck to his chest. Octavio said, "I have much to learn from my elders."

The *uwishin* struck him again, and then he said, "No, you have much to learn from ME. You have the force, the *arutam,* which makes for a great warrior and a future shaman. Your *arutam* can be the greatest we have seen in many generations. Do you want to learn from me?"

Octavio suspected it was the *uwishin* who could learn from him, but he bit his tongue and instead answered, "I have much to learn from you."

Then both men bored into each other's eyes and they exchanged looks of fear and power. The *uwishin's* pride did not allow him to acknowledge that perhaps he was peering into the spirit of a true *kakáram*, a warrior whose *arutam* exceeds all others. The old *uwishin* said, "Soon we will dream together with the soul vine, and I will tell YOU what I see for your future. I will look deep into your soul and I will decide when and what you do next." The old man was too late to introduce Octavio to the *natem* teacher plant. Octavio had already consumed it, and he had journeyed to hell and back. He did not need a lowly shaman to tell him what was in store for him: he was the greatest *kakáram* the Shuar had ever seen.

⊠ ⊠ ⊠

The Shuar territory extended from the steep eastern slopes of the Andes to the unnavigable rapids of the Pastaza and Upano Rivers, near the mighty Amazon's headwaters. This rugged and forbidding terrain kept nosy strangers away, but it didn't stop them from fighting over Shuar lands on maps. From century to century, Ecuador lost this portion of land and Peru gained that parcel. All of this meant less than nothing to the Shuar. Octavio's people didn't care what the foreign maps said or who supposedly owned their lands. They had been semi-nomadic people who lived in autonomous settlements the others called *centros*. This had been their land and as long as they kept the foreigners far away, their way of life continued as it had always been.

Nineteen-sixty-nine was the year of Octavio's birth and the year the federation of indigenous people, including the Shuar, signed an accord with the Ecuadorian government. Soon the area was bustling with foreign oil interests. The few truly wise *uwishin* sensed the danger and ordered the various family units to go deeper into the rainforest. That is where Octavio learned to remain true to his Shuar ways. He learned all the ancient adult rituals and became a healer without peers. He used *Amor Seco* or Spanish needles to treat dysentery and worms. He applied a poultice of the *Piñon Blanco* shrub to treat infection, and the latex from the same shrub to reduce a toothache. He was satisfied in helping the elderly and children with their aches and pains, but deep inside him lived a jaguar who wanted to hunt and attack. He was not just a healer. The warrior was still part of him, too.

Octavio roamed far away from the settlement and disappeared for days. Everyone assumed he was up to his woman-hunting again, and they waited for him to return satiated. The Shuar women were known for being aggressive warriors themselves. In fact, the colonials feared them almost as much as they feared the Shuar warrior males. What the other Shuar did not realize was that Octavio was in fact a jaguar. He not only wanted numerous mates; he wanted blood. Under the influence of the *natem* he prepared, and after the initial bout of vomiting and diarrhea, Octavio cleansed his human interior and reached a higher level of awareness as a fearless jaguar.

When he shifted into his jaguar-self he prowled dauntlessly. His eyes could see clearly even in the starless nights in the rainforest. He could smell a pack of stinky foreigners trying to tap another oil well nearer and nearer to his territory. Helicopters circled overhead trying to determine which section of his forest to clear. All his senses were on ready alert. He wanted to taste his enemies' blood and touch their skulls as he removed them in preparation for shrinking. His jaguar-self waited impatiently above his trees for the moment to leap from the canopy.

◈ ◈ ◈

Previous generations of *kakáram* had killed dozens of enemies and performed the head-shrinking ceremonies. They had been true warriors who protected their women and their hunting territories. The famed warrior Tukupi had accumulated the heads of thirty-three dead enemies. The whereabouts of Tukupi's treasure of shrunken heads remains a mystery. Many warriors had been offered guns, rifles, and bullets in exchange for a handful of dangling heads. Tukupi must have made a similar exchange. It annoyed Octavio to think of the shrunken heads that had once contained the spirits of his enemies now roamed somewhere in a foreign museum collection or a collector's cabinet of curiosities. Octavio would never release the shrunken heads of his enemies; he would guard their spirits so that they would never escape and shoot invisible poisonous darts into his neck. But first he craved the hand-to-hand combat. He wanted to hear their bones break and smell their hot blood oozing from their sliced necks. Only then would he shrink their heads and keep their angry spirits sealed forever.

The Shuar's aggressive nature had instilled fear in others for ages, and with good reason. Whenever a foreigner encroached on their territory looking for balsa wood or women, he would never be seen again in full size. Only a mini version of his head was a reminder that he had ever existed. With this type of retaliation on the part of the Shuar, the others called the Shuar by the pejorative name: *Jívaros,* meaning savages. Unlike the Shuar who had agreed to remain in the settlements and who had become domesticated, or as they preferred to say, civilized, Octavio remained feral and had an immense disdain for both the weak Shuar and their colonizers.

Since 1969 the Shuar who had settled in the *centros* no longer had a reputation as indomitable combatants. They were now perceived as placid men waiting for a handout from the government or as lowly laborers for the oil industry. Octavio dreamed of one day leading a pack of warrior jaguars into the watering hole of the oil workers as they drank the local *chicha*. Once the workers were totally drunk they would fondle the Shuar women. That's where Octavio would end their days with fangs so sharp that he would decapitate them as easily as removing the cap from a mushroom.

Days later, after the oil company would notice that some of their men were missing, Octavio and his jaguars would return stealthily in the middle of the night to dangle their prey's now miniaturized heads from the oil drill. He could already envision their heads bobbing up and down on the oil drills like red *granadilla venenosa* flowers. The government would realize that the old Shuar ways didn't die when documents were signed or lines were drawn on maps or oily dollars changed hands. Most importantly, by recognizing the features of their missing acquaintances on the tiny bobbing heads, everyone would understand that the Shuar had not forgotten how to dispense fates worse than death.

▣ ▣ ▣

The Shuar who had agreed to become "civilized" would still have evidence that the old ways were truly moral and reasonable. They would come back to the traditions of the Amazon and allow themselves to be led by Octavio. The rainforest and its twisting lianas and ravenous caymans would devour the intruders and their oil-sucking machines. The anacondas would be rotund with the anguished bodies of the invaders. Octavio would make the whole region scream with fear at the word "*Jívaro.*" *Jívaro* indeed. This *Jívaro*, this head-shrinking beast the others created, would make them all heave with fear.

Octavio prepared himself for the day his jaguar-self would taste revenge. He would hear the wind telling him when to venture out into the forest. With the help of the transforming *natem* teaching plant, he set off at dusk to search the advice of the spirit world. He would attempt to suck the power force, the *arutam,* from the spirits of the departed *kakáram* who still inhabited the jungle. He struggled with the spirits until they finally relented and taught him how to turn his enemies' heads into *tsantsa.*

"Sever your enemy's head quickly and preferably when he is still alive," said the *kakáram* spirit.

"Make a slit in the neck and up the back of the head, and peel the skin and hair carefully," said another *kakáram*.

"Don't forget to take the skull and put it in the river as a gift for the anaconda," added Octavio's third spirit guide.

"Yes, I will do as you instruct me, elders. I must go and find my enemy now," answered Octavio.

But the first *kakáram* paralyzed Octavio with the *tsentsak*, the invisible darts to force him to listen further. He hissed in Octavio's right ear, "Listen carefully, you are too brash and you will stay immobile until you understand the importance of our rites. This isn't a Hollywood movie brought by the enemy to make you weak. This is real life, and this is life and death."

The second spirit continued describing the steps of sewing shut the lips and eyes, and the process of boiling the head and filling it with hot sand. Finally, the eldest of the *kakáram* said, "It will take you one week to capture the vengeful spirit of your enemy. You must be careful to maintain the likeness of your enemy's head. You must treat him with respect. Don't make him look like all the cheap goat skin imitations they sell in Sucua, they're probably made in China."

All three *kakáram* spirits laughed, and before departing they shouted to Octavio, "Once you have contained your enemy's spirit tightly in his reduced head, wear the *tsantsa* around your neck to remind you daily of your own power."

◧ ◩ ◧

Octavio stalked his enemy in the nearest *centros* now inhabited by tame Shuar, *mestizos* from the highlands, and the mercenary corporate types and their local henchmen. Octavio despised them all equally. He observed them from afar during the day and at night. In his jaguar-self, he came close enough to smell their alcoholic breath. Octavio was only fifteen years old, but his soul was that of a *kakáram* twice his age. He was ready to attack and lacerate their necks and run off with their heads; all he needed were a couple of dexterous and bloodthirsty jaguars to assist him. His dream of restoring his people to the old ways was near. Young Octavio went to raise his jaguar army.

Octavio hunted deeper and deeper into the rainforest in search of his confederates. The strongest, the most dedicated to their true way of life would have fled farthest from the oil companies. He tried to convince the few remaining warriors he found that it was time to attack the intruders. Octavio believed they had only been waiting for a leader brave enough. But they dismissed him. They were too few, and unlike Octavio could see only blank futures in the ever increasing deforested areas of their primordial lands. They had no spirit guides to teach them, they heard nothing in the wind. All that these weak warriors still had was their rage, but they lacked the sense to turn it against their common enemy. They struck out against their own women and their children and one another instead. Octavio was disgusted by them. These men were not jaguars. They were not even men.

The oil company had done this. It was counting on the would-be warriors who knew the perils of the rainforest and who would work endlessly to make the profits. It tempted the workers with alcohol, petty cash, easy women, and round-the-clock soccer matches on the satellite televisions installed here and there. It made promises of health care and education. One by one the warriors and their families approached the *centros*, as so many of the Shuar had done since the day Octavio was born, and within a short period of time their *arutam*, their power force, had diminished until only a flash of their ancient power was left.

When Octavio met up with his *amikri*, his childhood blood brother, he found him unfocused and lethargic, leaning against the dense cone of the belly palm with blood and mucus running down his droopy face.

"Why aren't you up and fighting, you are not a small child or a woman with child, get up!" said Octavio. His friend looked up to Octavio in a stupor. "Are you sick or did you ingest *yagé?*"

His former fellow warrior just stared blankly at the forest and allowed giant ants to crawl up his nostrils. Octavio struck him with his ever present *capinurí* branch. He shouted, "Get up and fight me. You are a man. You are a Shuar warrior, honor your *arutam*!" But his friend fell asleep.

◈ ◈ ◈

Soon Octavio discovered he was affected too. He could no longer shift into his jaguar-self. He tweaked with the *natem* recipe, adding more *datura*, but all he saw were visions of himself as a tapir waiting to be eaten. Octavio found he could only travel a few kilometers without seeing a cluster of men clearing the forest. He had lost his camouflage abilities, and now the men looked up and noticed him with the same look of pity they gave the Hyacinth Macaw. Some of the workers even dared to wave to Octavio, as if he were a friendly child. He wanted to shoot poisonous arrows at them to remind them not to stare at a Shuar *kakáram*, but he had wasted his last batch of darts. He attempted to shoot the waving men with invisible darts to help him look into their hearts, but their souls were empty, so he paddled along past debris and foreign poisons on a fishless and rotting river.

Everything was gone. The life had been pulled out of the forest and its power slowly leached from his people. Its power was leaving him too, and Octavio stood on the bank of the river feeling that he was the last of his race on this earth. At night when he looked at the stars and the machines were quiet for a time he could imagine thousands of his people looking up at the same stars, every one of them knowing the same words to the same stories. They were all still here, the young and the old hidden from sight. This comforted him for a time until even the silence of the dark was broken by the despairing sound of drunken laughter and music that was ugly and foreign to the forest. He could no longer pretend there were legions of his people hidden behind the few remaining trees. Octavio knew in the way he knew all things that were not taught to him that he was the last of his kind. His spirit guides never came again.

※ ※ ※

When the Salesian priests found Octavio high up on the oil rig limp and seemingly lifeless, they took him into a makeshift clinic in the *centro*. Some of them had gray hair and seemed to be the elders of their tribe. They carried him gently and with reverence as if he was something precious they didn't want to break. They prayed for him in their own words and shot him with a thin metal dart that made him dream. Sometimes they even kept the dart in his vein with clear water dripping from a bag he could see through. It was the cleanest water he had ever seen, and he wondered where they got it. He thought that they must be draining him of his blood and filling him with clean water from another place, from a river near their home, because Octavio's river had been fouled and could never restore him now.

 These medicine men were filling him just as he would fill his enemies' heads with hot sand. He didn't care that they were preparing him for sacrifice since they seemed to be doing their enemy-shrinking ceremony with respect for the great *kakáram* he once had been. It was in the way they moved, the garments they wore on his behalf. There was a reverence to what they did, and he knew instinctively that these were people who had once apprenticed as he did. They possessed the knowledge of their culture's magic and they had found him worthy of its practice. He was glad to be dying this way. It was a fitting death for the last of his kind.

※ ※ ※

But Octavio the jaguar did not die. The Salesian priests' magic had healed him rather than delivered him to his death. The priests never asked him why he attempted to kill himself. Months later, when he was fully recovered, Octavio found some of his old friends in the *centro,* but he avoided them and began helping at the clinic. He had bonded with the men who had saved him and felt that he and his skills belonged to them now. Octavio had been only half jaguar. The other half was healer, and it was that half asserting itself now. The medical staff found his now calm nature and knowledge of the local healing plants helpful in their research on medicinal and psychotropic herbs and plants of the Amazon. He took them in his canoe through the small tributaries collecting specimens, and showed them how to prepare the leaves, the bark, the sap and flowers.

Sometimes he went by himself into the rainforest escaping into the ever shrinking territory of his ancestors, but he found no solace in being alone and could never reclaim his jaguar self. He returned only with plants and grew them in the clinic compound, trying to save what he could. He had been given the gift of healing others by the goddess Nunqui. She had enlightened him with an understanding of which plants should be given for one illness or another. Soon he was administering seeds of *mucuna* as an anti-hemorrhoidal when Western medicine was scarce. The Shuar workers came by to see him when they had a snake bite, diarrhea or a fever. Once all he had wanted was to see his enemies' heads bobbing like red *granadilla venenosa* on the oil rigs; now he used the same red passion vine to treat fevers.

❖ ❖ ❖

In 1990, when Octavio turned twenty-one years old, the *centro* turned into a pool of oily black sludge. The ancient lands were contaminated beyond redemption; dumping waste in unlined pits was standard practice for the oil company. They filled the ground and the streams and the jungle until their money was made and the forest was poison. One small tribe known as the Tetetes vanished and along with them all evidence of their language and their culture.

The Shamans lost their power to heal when cancer oozed from the tar pits and into the people. The shamans boiled *jengibre* roots as an anti-inflammatory for the soil, and the oil company brought in bulldozers and covered tar pits with dirt. The black sludge oozed easily from under the dirt and the sickness continued.

Something dark and evil stirred in Octavio's stomach, grunting when he couldn't help his patients, gnarling when he couldn't paddle the river, snarling when he couldn't hunt, and growling to find footprints, feces, or any evidence of his jaguar-self. Octavio knew his jaguar was still there. He sensed the jaguar, smelled his musky scent, and heard him purring in his ears. The healer alone was no longer enough. Octavio longed to be whole again. When he could no longer do anything useful for what was left of his people, when even the gift of Nunqui abandoned him, he took what he had saved in the form of seeds, roots and clippings and left the Amazon.

Even if he couldn't touch him or see him the jaguar was still on this earth, and Octavio would find him. He would prove to himself that he was still the greatest *kakáram* of the Shuar people and not just another Southern California gardener in a used van. He would sniff out his jaguar and feed his soul and become the jaguar hunting his enemies and wearing their captured shrunken heads around his jaguar chest no matter where in the world the scent would take him, and no matter how long it would take.

Los Feliz
April 11, 2011

usk approached brusquely for an early spring afternoon in Southern California. The dark clouds and light fog created a gauzy curtain on the street. Under this slate cloak the live-in caregivers of Los Feliz emerged from their respective homes and gathered in their favorite spot. Under the leafy canopy created by two pepper trees in Dr. Nunez's front yard they formed their secret society of caregivers. Others preferred to call them companions to the elderly, but these women were not given to euphemism of any kind. Life had dealt them too many lessons in reality to indulge in the delusion of being companions to these employers who paid them $9.00 an hour. Companionship is what they had with those they left behind and what they sought at night with one another under the pepper trees.

While their elderly charges sat calmly in their reclining chairs or hospital beds, their televisions or sound systems lulling them to sleep, the women knew they had a good hour to whine about their elderly employers. They knew all the nooks and crannies on their streets and they alternated the spot where they met. Tonight, under foggy camouflage, they were certain to go undetected from the prying eyes of younger neighbors, and so they finally rested their tired bodies on the well-kept lawn.

Soledad sat on the grass and waved the others over as she lit up a joint. She said, "That old doctor nearly broke my back today, so I guess I'm in need of some medical marijuana for pain, don't you think?"

Round chubby Margarita and slender Ofelia with her long hair in a ponytail joined her on the grass. Getting comfortable in their green orderly uniforms they looked like a bizarre collection of garden gnomes strewn at awkward angles, as if some wise pranksters had placed the women-gnomes there deliberately. Margarita and Ofelia laughed at Soledad's audacity, but declined to take a hit of her joint. After smelling the smoke, Margarita relented and took a delicate puff.

Soledad teased both of them. She said, "You two should have been nuns. You don't know how to hang loose."

They didn't hear the heavy footsteps then or the voice in the darkness. They didn't know they were not alone in their search for solace in the foggy night.

"What does 'hang loose' mean, Soledad?" asked Margarita.

"It means: have some fun, relax a little bit," answered Soledad as she exhaled slowly. "You Latinas need to improve your English real fast. We learn English in the Philippines, that's why I'm so good at it. You never know when our old employers are going to wake up ice cold, and then off we go and we hotfoot over to another house."

Margarita said, "Judge Carrera tries to improve my English, but I don't want to stay up all night writing down definitions to her long list of words. I'm exhausted, I'd rather watch TV."

Ofelia, who was angry at the world, shouted, "Easy for both of you to say have fun and learn English! Your old doctor growls but doesn't bite and the judge doesn't hit you. That mean La Linda strikes me with her tambourine if I don't move fast enough." Ofelia tended to hover at the edge of rage and sorrow.

"Don't call her La Linda in front of us," commanded Soledad. "She's not pretty in any way. She's just as gnarled and bumpy as the cork trees by her dance studio." Soledad raised herself up on her elbows, crossed her legs at the ankles and blew smoke at the sky.

Margarita, who parroted Soledad or any other strong female figure, added a jab of her own. "Yeah, her name should be La Ugly."

They all laughed, but Soledad laughed the longest and then couldn't stop laughing. The others waited while Soledad laughed herself out, and when she was quiet again, Margarita leaned close to her and whispered, "La Ugly." Soledad burst into another round of laughter so loud her friends covered her mouth with their hands. It was too much fun to play with Soledad when she was stoned. After a while, the women grew less playful and quiet settled on them again.

Ofelia yanked clumps of grass from the lawn and threw them as far as she could into the street. Finally she said, "La Linda used to be a beautiful woman; you should see all her black and white photos in every single wall in the house. In her prime, she was the greatest flamenco dancer in America, maybe even in Spain. All the famous men wanted her, well, that's what she tells me every day anyway."

"So what if men lusted after her 100 years ago, she doesn't have the right to hit you," Soledad said. "Next time, take the tambourine away and hit her on top of her puny head. She's not the only one who was once beautiful. We were all beautiful when we were young, too. Ofelia, you're still pretty and you're only thirty-five years old. You should sneak out and go dancing in Hollywood. I'll check in on La Ugly for you while you dance with some hot young man."

"When I first came to California from Ecuador, I did go to every Latino dance hall in the city, but I was looking for my daughter and not dance partners," whimpered Ofelia.

The other women looked away, at the ground, at the sky, anywhere but at Ofelia. Some things couldn't be accepted, because that would be the end of you. You hoped in spite of what you already knew because that was the only way to get up tomorrow. They didn't want Ofelia to break down hysterically again. It had been three years, but the tears were always close. Ofelia's daughter had vanished from Los Angeles and she would never be found, but they couldn't tell her this brutal truth. They all knew it, but not one of them would give it the power of saying it out loud. Young pretty girls on their own in Los Angeles who disappeared simply did not appear again. They were gone like smoke to the traffickers.

Neither Soledad nor Margarita had any children, and they couldn't comprehend a mother's anguish at not knowing the whereabouts of a child. But everyone they knew had a missing relative who just vanished into thin air once they arrived in America. This is the risk they all took in gambling that they would arrive and find good jobs in L.A. so they could send their families enough to live on. Those who lost the gamble ended up dead in the desert, missing in the chaos of the border, or swallowed up by human traffickers whose bottomless pit was deeper than the San Andreas Fault.

And of course Soledad and Ofelia had their own burdens and dreams that would go unfulfilled in this land of dreams and caregiving at $9.00 an hour.

Ofelia's tears streamed down her face. "My baby would have been nineteen years old this Christmas," she barely whispered.

"Maybe our Holy Mother will bring her back to me then. I just can't go out looking for her anymore. Those awful men see me coming into their disgusting strip joints and they throw me out. She loved to dance, that is why I think they trapped her there. Why did I let her come to his country alone when she was only sixteen years old? If I ever find the woman who brought her from Ecuador, I will kill her."

Each of them nodded silently in agreement. No one was shocked by this comment. They would all have liked to kill the women who helped to lure young girls away to slavery and ultimately death. Life was hard enough without traitors helping the devil. Ofelia's friends were good women, often kind women, but not women given to euphemism. Reality had seen to that.

Soledad took a big hit of her dwindling joint and held it in. Ofelia's tale of woe was a familiar one and after years of hearing it repeated, frankly, she didn't give a damn. Soledad liked that expression from one of the old movies Dr. Nunez forced her to watch. She had a mental list of her favorite sayings and was waiting for the day she could use them on Dr. Nunez: Frankly, you blind old fool, I don't give a damn and I'm outta here. In the meantime, she felt the effects of the joint so she lay spread-eagled on the grass and watched the smoke drift past the leaves of the pepper trees and into the night. Soledad smelled the moist grass. "I wish that Octavio would kick back with me on this grass," she said. "I bet we could be hot together."

Margarita asked, "Did you say that Octavio kicked you and now you have a fever?"

Soledad didn't answer Margarita. It wasn't worth wasting her high. Sometimes Margarita only pretended to misunderstand in order to change the subject or to make someone uncomfortable. Soledad was beginning to suspect Margarita had a crush on Octavio herself.

"Don't let him kick you," Margarita continued. "Take the scissors and cut his *chorizo* off." She made scissors with her fingers and snipped in the air. "That's what I should have done when Sergio hit me. Instead I escaped to this country and now I am rotting along with Judge Carrera. My sister says that I can go live with her and her babies in MacArthur Park, but she has a colicky newborn. I'd rather stay with the Judge and say, 'Yes, Your Honor, you're absolutely correct,' all day long!"

Soledad didn't feel like going down the feeling-sorry-for-myself path with Margarita. It was too easy, and there was nothing she could use at the end of it. Her thoughts meandered to her favorite place in her head, a place she hoped to make real someday. She planned to open a bar in the Philippines, and sexy young men would escort her around town. Normally, she dispensed tough-love advice like falling coconuts to Margarita and Ofelia. She could be brutally honest with them—they could take a hard brown nut on the crown, unlike the other two goody-goody caregivers, Yolanda and Fatima. Yolanda never left Mrs. Dougherty alone for one minute and Fatima cooked day and night with Mrs. Hamieh. Those two caregivers made Ofelia and Margarita look and sound like untamed women.

Soledad wished she could find someone, anyone, more interesting than her four fellow caregivers. All their depressing tales about their families and illnesses and death were choking the life right out of her. To make matters worse, Dr. Nunez's vision was getting worse by the day and this made him intolerable. Just as Soledad was ready to doze off, Margarita finally said something provocative. Margarita extended her plump body on the fresh cut grass, and complained. "At least Dr. Nunez doesn't go around rubbing himself all day."

Soledad cackled a tad too loud at the vision of serious Judge Carrera rubbing herself. She wanted to ask Margarita to describe all the details, but by now she was pretty high and kept on laughing loudly and uncontrollably. That was when they heard the footsteps and all three women froze.

The women were chronically afraid of getting nabbed by immigration officers or who knows who. Look what happened to Ofelia's daughter—one night she was conjugating the past tense of the verb "to think" in her ESL class, and the next day she disappeared. The women were foreigners without any legal documents, and they lived fearfully in the shadows. The heavy footsteps quieted down when they walked on the grass. Ofelia closed her eyes, and Margarita covered her face with her ample arms; both expected the worst.

Soledad was the one who spoke. "May I help you? You're trespassing on Dr. Nunez's property. What do you want?"

"It's me, Alma," said a female voice from under the hood of a jogging sweatshirt. "Don't you remember me? I met you last month when you were out here having a smoke. How are you, Soledad?" The voice put such emphasis on her name it made Soledad suspicious, as if the woman were a stranger trying to trick her into thinking they had met, or the way you use a child's name as if you are giving them a gift.

"I was doing great until you snuck up on me and killed my high," said Soledad. She turned to look at the woman standing over her. "Why do I only see you out at night?"

Alma Ruiz disliked direct questions. She had stopped caring about what other people thought or said about her a long time ago. But she didn't want to air her dirty laundry here in front of these women. No one truly cared what had happened to her, and she didn't feel like talking about the tragic and frustrating series of events that landed her a captive during the day and a nocturnal disfigured thing at night avoiding stares during her evening strolls.

Alma wavered for a few seconds until she saw the pathetic look on the women's faces. Alma couldn't assess if it was fear or empathy in their stares, but today's bad news weakened her previous resolve never to tell anyone her true story. She wanted to trust somebody again. Today's financial blow had deflated her, and she wanted to release all her pent up frustrations. She wasn't certain they would even understand.

Alma studied each woman, carefully summing them up quickly. Obviously, Soledad tried too hard to hide her age with makeup. Even in the dark, Alma could see Soledad's hideously long false eyelashes. All that camouflage made Soledad look older than she was. Alma guessed forty-three. All that hiding behind a mask might be covering serious character flaws, so she couldn't openly trust Soledad, but she admired Soledad's bravado. Clearly, Soledad was the informal leader of this group, probably just because she was the pushiest.

The chunky woman had a pleasant round face that looked like she had been crying, or perhaps she just had grass allergies. The young slender woman with her thick black hair in a ponytail had a forlorn and wide-eyed expression that reminded Alma of the dexterous spider monkeys in the Amazon rainforest, a place where she would rather be. A place she considered home and she missed so dearly. If only she could return, if only she had the financial means to return to its protective green canopy and its abundant psychotropic plants. Alma's sadness and the longing emanating from her seemed to pull her into the group, and the women went back to their conversation.

Soledad pointed to the round-faced women and said, "Margarita was just about to tell us about her boss, Judge Carrera, who has been rubbing herself. Come on, finish the story, Margarita."

Margarita blushed. She didn't think it appropriate to discuss her boss with a stranger.

She simply said, "I didn't say that, Soledad. It's just that lately Judge Carrera has been rubbing her breasts. I think that maybe they hurt her."

Soledad looked disappointed. All their senior employers had illnesses and she was sick to death of hearing about them; she had hoped the Judge's behavior might be a sexy story instead of a breast illness. Soledad concluded, "Margarita don't be so dull, tell us something interesting, please."

Margarita noticed all eyes on her. She got nervous with all eyes on her and her English got choppier, "Well, the Judge start with the breast rubbing business right after Claire gave her a massage a month ago. The Judge is so eager to see Claire that she ask me to call and make a second massage appointment in one week with Claire. "

Soledad brayed like a mule, and said, "Kinda kinky, I like it. Tell us more."

"I don't know what this kinky mean, but what I saw the Judge do next make me sad.She hold big bath towel wrapped like a baby and try to breastfeed the towel," Margarita answered.

Soledad rolled on the grass with laughter. Nobody else laughed. Margarita looked ashamed for revealing something so personal and unusual about her employer to a stranger. Ofelia decided to reveal a little something to help Margarita overcome her embarrassment. Ofelia said, "You know, La Linda acted even crazier than usual after Claire gave her a massage, too. All La Linda wants to do is dance flamenco non-stop. I have to put on her pair of red shoes, then the black ones, but then I have to change her dress to the one with the white polka dots to match the black dancing shoes."

"Boooring story," shouted Soledad. "Who cares how many times you change La Linda's clothes or her diapers, for that matter? She'll never dance in front of an audience again. Period. There's nothing intriguing about it. Come on, give us some dirt."

Ofelia looked offended. She said, "Why you so mean, Soledad? I always keep La Linda very clean, she not dirty." Ofelia glanced at Alma, and said, "My boss was a very famous flamenco dancer, the best in the world."

"I see, but what unusual behavior has she been displaying after Claire gives her a massage?" asked Alma.

Soledad chimed in. "Yeah, tell us something titillating. Is that the right word, Dr. Ruiz?" Soledad put special emphasis on the name. It was part payback for the way Alma had first addressed her, and partly to let Margarita and Ofelia know that Alma was a professional and not a caregiver. Not one of us.

Alma answered, "Yes, it is the correct word. But I'm more interested in the behavior displayed by La Linda, as you call her. What does she do after her massages?"

Ofelia chose not to answer her question. La Linda shouldn't be the brunt of their jokes tonight. Ofelia turned the table and asked, "Dr. Alma, what kind of doctor are you? And what happened to your face?"

If the night hadn't been so dark, the women would have noticed Alma's eyes narrow and her grimace contort angrily. She hated questions like these. She hated the first one the most because they weren't really asking her what kind of doctor she was; they were asking the relentless question of an adopted child's life: who are you? But it always sounded to Alma more like: who the hell are you, and what do you think you are doing here, what gives you the right to ask a medical question, what are your credentials? Why did she always have to prove she was a credible human being? It seemed unfair, but Alma answered anyway. If they wanted her to turn on the doctor, she would oblige them.

"I'll answer your second question first, although I find your approach very blunt and rude. I had Bell's palsy, which is an idiopathic, unilateral, facial nerve, paralysis. It is a paralysis of the nerve that supplies the facial muscles on one side of the face. The cause of facial nerve paralysis is often not known, but is thought to be due to a virus. The facial nerve is the 7th cranial nerve. As you can see from my distorted face, I am among the 10% of the people who do not recover. As for your first question—"

Ofelia quickly added, "You are a doctor. I'm sorry that I was so rude, Dr. Ruiz. I should leave now."

"Please stay, you didn't mean to hurt me. But please tell me more about La Linda. I'm a doctor, after all. Maybe I can help."

"Oh, yes. That is nice, Doctor Alma. Well, after Claire gives her a massage, she tells me she hears a guitar playing the most magnificent flamenco music she has ever heard. She hears a man singing a mournful song; a song so strong and deep that it seems to come from one thousand years ago. La Linda starts humming the tune and clapping the *compás*, and then she shouts, 'Must dance faster, I can't keep up with the guitar, must dance faster,' and then she hit me with the tambourine or a stick or whatever is near her. La Linda is like a crazy woman wanting to dance faster to the beautiful music only she can hear."

Soledad said, "Gotta put her in a home. She's gone loony. And you need to get another job tomorrow. I like Margarita's story better. So how long did Judge try to breastfeed the towel?"

"I feel sorry for the Judge," says Margarita. "She never had any children, not even a husband who beat her. I heard her whispering to the towel and talking in Spanish to the towel baby. She say, 'Mi *hijita, toma más leche.*' She want the baby daughter to drink more milk and then she sing a lullaby. I didn't even know the Judge speak Spanish. Her family came from Mexico when California still belonged to Mexico. Wasn't it one hundred and fifty years ago?"

Soledad chuckled and said, "Big deal, Dr. Nunez is going around writing Spanish poetry or stories or something like that. He tries to hide the notebook, but I looked at it and it is not written in English and it's not medical stuff. I think he is falling in love with Claire and is writing her love stories. My Spanish is not that good, but I read *amor* this and *amor* that. That means love, right?"

Both Margarita and Ofelia nodded, yes.

Soledad continued with her story. "Dr. Nunez can't wait for his massages either. He made me order some poetry books for him online because he can't see the screen so well. Yep, he's in love with Claire. He loves the verbena oil she uses in her massage."

"Yes, that is the oil that La Linda loves, too," said Ofelia.

Margarita agreed that the Judge started behaving oddly after Claire used the verbena oil.

Soledad tried to jump up, but was too wobbly from her joint. She waved her arms frantically at the sound of a vehicle, and said, "Oh, there goes Octavio driving down the hill. I wanted to stop him and ask him to recommend some good herbs for my sore back. Better yet, I was hoping he would offer to rub my back. You never know, a little back massage might lead us back to the future." Soledad laughed at her own inane movie allusion that flew by all the other women.

Alma added, "Octavio does know quite a bit about medicinal plants, but he didn't want to talk to me the few times I tried. On several occasions I have seen him loading some plants from Mrs. Dougherty's greenhouse. What does he grow there and why can't he do it during the day?"

Soledad felt a tinge of jealousy. Perhaps Alma also had her sights set on Octavio and she would seduce him one late night. She felt that she'd better make a move for Octavio quickly or she might lose him to one of these lonely women. Instead of playing it cool, she demanded, "Alma, if you're a doctor, what do you think is making our old people act so unusual lately?"

"I would have to meet them to determine their conditions. I'm not your usual doctor. I'm more of a, uh, a holistic doctor—"

"Why are you changing your tune, Alma?" asked Soledad. "You told me you were a geneticist or something like that. Then three weeks ago you told me you were a botanist. Now you're a what?"

Alma didn't recall exactly what she had told Soledad on previous occasions. She assumed that Soledad loved gossip and nothing else, so she had exaggerated about her professional background a tad here and there, but her basic back story was roughly, give or take, more or less, approximately, precisely what Soledad had just said.

❖ ❖ ❖

Alma Ruiz had spent thousands of hours, or at least that was how long it felt to Alma, doing genealogical research on her own family, both her adoptive parents and her biological parents. She had been raised in a strict Mormon family and she had learned the importance of knowing her ancestry. She found that her adoptive parents had already done their genealogical research for her and were trying to ram their Irishness down her throat. They told her all the things good adoptive parents are supposed to say, that biology didn't matter at all and that she was as much a part of their family as anyone else. But their obsession with their own genealogy gave them away. They held their connection to their own ancestors as extremely important, and then told her she could be Irish too because she belonged to them. But it didn't fit. The marrow in her bones would never be Irish. Her biological parents were from Latin America and Spain, or some such warm exotic places.

Throughout her college years in the mid 1980's Alma dedicated hours and hours looking at microfilm and then microfiche birth and death records for her birth parents. She never did find the ideal parents she had hoped to locate: lofty academics that had experienced a passionate love affair that had resulted in her birth. She fancied an Abelard and Heloise intellectual and physical love between her scholarly Peruvian mother and her academic advisor from the University of Salamanca who had been in Lima on sabbatical. All her research led to dead ends, and so she substituted the genealogical discoveries about others into her own autobiography. The more she embellished her ancestry the more others became interested in her life. Her tedious and ordinary life as one of thousands and thousands of state college students became gilded by her new person; her new ancestors.

Alma changed her major from biology to history to Spanish, and finally to botany. Her academic roller coaster did not make any sense to her parents or academic counselors, and frankly her low grades reflected her lack of interest and performance in any of these subject matters. They shouldn't have been surprised. You have to first know who you are to find your passion in life, and Alma still didn't know. She wasted eight years and still was nowhere near receiving her Bachelor of Arts degree. She made a little extra income by completing genealogical studies for busy professionals or wealthy yuppies wanting to find out more details about their roots.

Alma Ruiz never found her authentic self; she simply grew angry in the looking. In time, she discovered that her extensive vocabulary and middling knowledge about a variety of subjects led others to apply their own assumptions to her that she was a graduate student in history or genetics. Alma was not a con artist though, she was a cipher. She treasured the high esteem others showed in her shallow renaissance abilities. She stored their perceptions in her internal treasure chest against the day she might open it again and find something true about herself.

Alma dropped out of college in Southern California and floated from administrative job to clerical job and from one college to the next. She only felt at home in an academic setting, so she stayed there in underappreciated support roles. She never received any glowing praise from her superiors; nor was she ever terminated. Nonetheless, her supervisors were generally relieved to get her out of their research labs, since this is where she had found her niche. Many of her supervisors found her obsessive posturing disturbing, and at least on one occasion she was warned not to try to pass herself off as a doctoral candidate in genetics.

Eventually, in the late 1990's, Alma made her way down to Peru with an ethnobotany research team from California. She had exaggerated her credentials to the extent that the project manager, Dr. Yepez, had been delighted to hire Alma whom he believed to be a mature and overqualified administrative assistant fluent in Spanish and Kichwa, and with a working knowledge of the Amazonian indigenous dialects. He felt that the mundane administrative aspects of his research were handled superbly by Alma, and he left her unsupervised.

Dr. Yepez had just turned sixty-one and he had to publish again or truly perish from academia. His anxiety over his impending retirement without the kudos he had hoped to achieve added to his stress and only served to make him look ten years older than his actual age. Dr. Yepez spent his time hobnobbing with the Peruvian researchers in case they revealed some new and interesting hidden gem that he could polish into a scholarly text that would earn him his last academic hurrah. Alma thought that since she was 28 years younger than Dr. Yepez she might seduce him and convince him to include her name in his publications. Her ungroomed and squat appearance had never attracted many men, but Alma was certain that her youth alone would entice Dr. Yepez. By the time she made her move on Dr. Yepez he was romantically involved with a local woman barely twenty years old. Dr. Yepez caught on to Alma's seduction plan and he retaliated by not showing up to his office.

Alma was only happy to fill the void left by Dr. Yepez's absence from the office and soon she was back to her old self-aggrandizement mania. In some expat circles in Cusco she titled herself as a doctor of holistic medicine, which was not quite the credentialed and licensed doctor of natural medicine or doctor of integrated medicine, but it suited her fine. What Alma failed to recognize was that most people truly did not care about her phony license or credentials—she was simply the clerical person who staffed the office; and moreover, a dull conversationalist who was plain unattractive in every sense of the word. All her words fell on deaf ears, and she was only famous among the American ex-pats for clearing a cocktail reception group in a matter of seconds.

❖ ❖ ❖

Alma decided that a good defense against Soledad's accurate observation about her many past careers was to obfuscate the entire matter. Alma would enumerate her false academic titles and experiences and exaggerate her pseudo-research to the extent that crafty Soledad would never question her again. She needed to shut her down. Alma responded to Soledad's question about her professional background by saying, "In fact,

Soledad, I commend your sagacious understanding of my career path. My degree in Ethnobotany led me to focus further on Botanical Medicine and Herbal Studies. My publication on Clinical Pharmacology and Toxicology is still used by many institutions, as is my ground-breaking work on Tissue Mineral and Heavy Metal Hair Analysis. Which by the way, I would like to offer my services to you any time you aren't feeling well."

"Yeah, ok, whatever," replied Soledad, waving her hand in the air to stop the flow of Alma's words. "How about assessing the massive headache you just gave me with your medical mumbo-jumbo?" Soledad found herself once again, not giving a damn. "You should come and talk to my old Doctor Nunez about what is making his head cuckoo so that all he wants to do is write love poems in Spanish to Claire."

Ofelia chimed in. "*Ay,yayay*, I would love it if you could cure La Linda from hitting me all the time. The only time she is calm is right after Claire massages that nice oil on her poor legs. Ay, *pobrecita* La Linda."

Alma's face lit up. Among these needy women she really could have maximum impact. She could be a real doctor as far as they were concerned. She would be able to direct them in the same manner that all the Ph.D.'s and M.D.'s treated her as a simpleton who photocopied and sent emails for them. She would have to look out for Soledad, but that wouldn't be too hard. Despite never having earned any of the diplomas or taken the courses she'd just reeled off, she had learned quite a bit from all her previous jobs, and she was ready to help their elderly charges. Alma needed an income now, and these elderly folks still had money stashed away. And these women, they were the keys to those houses and those people.

Alma leaned over and attempted to pat Ofelia's shoulder, but her insincere grimace made Ofelia shudder. Alma said, "Don't worry, Ofelia. I will determine which modality will alleviate La Linda's condition. You let me come in and talk to her, and we'll see how I can cure her."

Ofelia was stumped. How could Dr. Alma cure La Linda? It was simply impossible. She quietly added, "Yes, Dr. Alma, God willing."

Soledad yawned at the pious reference. "Spare me the religious bull, would ya, Ofelia? Jesus, you're blinding me with your halo, just like Yolanda and Fatima. Has anyone seen those two goody-goods?"

Margarita answered. "I just saw them this week on different days. They should also talk to you, Dr. Alma. If you think that my story about Judge Carrera is unusual, wait until you hear about Yolanda's story about Mrs. Dougherty and Claire's oil massage; it's a real floozy—"

"You mean doozy, don't you?" Soledad said. Then she started singing: "I like to be in America, OK by me in America, Gotta learn English in America, Very big deal in America!"

A voice rang out from the dark. "Is that you singing in the fog, Soledad?"

"What's it to you? Who is it, anyway?" replied a sullen Soledad.

"It's Claire. Are we singing show tunes? How fun!" Claire cleared her throat and belted out a tune: "'I'm singing in the fog, just singing in the fog, what a glorious feelin'.' Why aren't you all singing along? Did I crash the party? I was just out for a walk." Claire was dressed in a pastel track suit, and unlike Alma did not hide her graceful face with its hood.

Ofelia was quick to respond. "Oh, not at all, pretty Claire. You have a beautiful voice! We just don't know the words to the songs."

Margarita added, "Yes, we are cueless."

"CLUELESS," shouted Soledad. She added, "Never mind. Claire, your ears must have been ringing; we were just talking about your magical massage oil. It's transforming our elderly bosses. Some of them are changing in very unusual ways. Tell her, Margarita."

"No, it is not polite to talk about the Judge. She was a very serious judge and very well respected," answered Margarita.

"What's wrong?" asked Claire. "I thought they liked the verbena oil."

"Maybe they like it a little too much," said Soledad. "Ofelia, you tell Claire about La Linda."

"Okay. Ever since you started massaging La Linda with that verbena oil, she hears a man singing a flamenco song so pure and forceful that she wants to dance for eternity."

"Is she in pain after I massage her legs?" There was panic in Claire's voice and she seemed truly worried that she had done something to harm her clients.

Ofelia shook her head, no. "Ay, no, Claire. She loves your massages. It's just that she wants to dance so badly, it breaks my heart and it exhausts me."

Since the women had forgotten to introduce Alma to Claire, Alma did it herself. "Hi, Claire, I've heard wonderful things about you from our friends here. I'm Dr. Alma Ruiz." Alma extended her hand and moved toward Claire, whose startled reaction to Alma's disfigured face angered Alma.

"I apologize for my reaction," whispered Claire to Alma.

"Don't worry, it's common. I was just telling the others here that I had Bell's palsy, and I never recovered. What can one do? Even someone in the medical field, like me. The one positive to come out of this disfigurement is that it has made me infinitely more intuitive about my patients' illnesses and concerns. I take the time to analyze the psychological, physical and social aspects of the entire person. In fact, I wrote one of the first scientific papers in which I posited that disease is a result of physical, emotional, spiritual, social and environmental imbalance. By the way, I admire the treatment that you provide to your elderly patients."

"It's just various types of massage therapy, that's all," said Claire. "I don't have a medical degree or anything."

"Well, the massage therapy in conjunction with the aromatherapy that you utilize appears to have triggered vibrant memories for your clients, right?" asked Alma.

"They have shared some interesting observations, but I'm not at liberty to discuss my clients," answered Claire. "I don't call them patients."

"Of course," said Alma. "You're absolutely correct. But it's been my experience that if you follow every letter of the law as it applies to needy patients without following your heart and your instinct, then many patients suffer, don't you agree?"

Claire looked as if she were going to be sick. The blow of such a brutal truth made her queasy. If she had only intervened earlier with Phil's deteriorating nerves, perhaps she could have forced his insurance to approve different therapies. As it turned out for poor Phil, his patience with the snail-paced medical insurance approval process allowed his nerves to degenerate into total paralysis. By the time his medical insurance approved the studies that were needed to confirm ALS, Phil was on a feeding tube blinking his unending love for Claire as he gasped his last breaths of life. Claire broke down crying at the memory of Phil's anguished and frantic eyes as they practically jumped out of their sockets while he gagged to death.

Ofelia knew about Claire's beloved Phil, and she cried along with Claire. Margarita wrapped her plump and warm arms around both women and hummed *Los Pollitos*, a Spanish lullaby. Its last stanza made Margarita feel protective of her friends. She sang:

Bajo de sus alas, acurrucaditos

¡duermen los pollitos

hasta el otro día!

Cuddled under her wings

Sleep the little chicks

Until another day!

Soledad rolled her false eyelashes up at the moonless sky in disgust at the melodrama. These wimpy women ruined her high and she was fuming mad.

Alma, on the other hand, saw an opportunity to ply these broken-down women for information about their elderly employers and mine them for money, substantial money, which would allow her to return to Peru and set up her own research institute.

Alma jumped into action. She didn't want any of the women to compose themselves. She forced her voice to falter in false sympathy. She said, "It just breaks my heart when I realize all the pain you've all gone through. My paralyzed face is nothing compared to the grief you've had to endure. Let me help you carry your burden. Claire, what can you tell me about your clients that would enable me to help them cope with these changes you are seeing? Let me help you and them."

Claire was beginning to regain her aplomb, but she saw a teary eye in Alma's twisted face. Surely someone who had to witness such paralysis daily would know about helping others. She decided to trust Alma because she displayed a wary perspective on the medical system. A system Claire held in the lowest regard after its mismanagement of Phil's degenerative disease. Claire said, "Why don't we ask Ofelia about Judge Carrera. From what she told me at the Judge's house, it seems that the Judge has been cuddling towels as if they were infants, is that right, Ofelia?"

"Yes, she tries to give the towel baby her breast milk. She, *ay,* I'm embarrassed to say it. Well, anyway, the Judge say to the baby: 'I never let them kill you. I killed my brother and I killed my enemies, but I never let them touch you. *Jamás,* never."

"Is she angry and confused when she says this?" Alma asked.

"Yes and no. She sound more, how do you say it, more defiant. But when I say, 'Judge Carrera, please calm down,' she looks at me and her eyes all glassy. She say: 'I am a warrior, I am nun, I am not afraid of anything. If they touch my baby, I kill them.' And she say all this in perfect Spanish, like long-ago Castilian."

Alma blinked. "Who does the Judge say is going to kill the baby?"

"She doesn't say," answered Margarita, "She just cradles the towel baby and doesn't let me take the rolled up towel away from her."

CHAPTER FIVE

Cusco, Peru

1623

Sister Clara

Drawn by A. Fredericks. Engraved by George T. Andrew, circa 1884

Cusco, Peru
1623

The nuns of Santa Catalina convent in Cusco took great pride in the thick walls of their church and cloisters. They stood prominently on the massive stone foundations of the ancient Inca *acllahuasi*, the Inca palace for the brides of the Inca sun. By the inordinate swagger of the Spanish nuns, one would think that they had quarried and carried the polygonal carved stones with their own delicate alabaster hands. On the contrary, it had been the bronze hands of the *acllas*, or brides of the sun, that had maintained the beauty of the interior of their *acllahuasi*. The *acllas'* days, months, and years of living in this structure were preordained by the timeworn rituals that had preserved their traditions unbroken until the Spanish conquered their Inca Empire and built right on top of the same walls. That had been in 1533, but by 1623 it was the Spanish nuns who maintained a tight control of their convent in Cusco, the former seat of the Inca world.

The Spanish nuns of Santa Catalina entered the convent with ample dowries, numerous servants, and inherited jewels, books, fine art and other treasures. Once inside the imposing walls, the cleverest among the nuns rose to positions of power. Some preferred to rule over fellow nuns and became strict administrators, others chose to spend their days in the fine arts, and the most astute of them all controlled the finances of the entire convent.

Abbess Inés de Jesús rose to power by her deft handling of the purse strings of the convent. She amassed the nuns' treasures like a greedy pirate, grew their co-mingled funds in ingenious ways, and became a cunning banker to the citizens of Cusco. Her discretion about who owed her what amount was beyond reproach, but her retaliation on any welcher terrified even the boldest of the merchants. The Abbess exercised unbelievable speed in seizing the collateral property of a debtor. She knew people in high places, people who could arrest anyone, people who could make a swindler disappear forever. She liked to make men disappear to illustrate to society how it felt to make a woman disappear into the life sentence of a convent. The Abbess reveled in knowing the extent of her punitive tentacles into Cusco's elite society.

Members of the upper crust dumped their excess daughters, sisters, and widows into Santa Catalina. The Abbess imposed a sliding scale dowry that each family was obliged to pay before she allowed their surplus female members to join Santa Catalina. She leaned heavily on the Spanish elite to pay a bonus, usually by deeding property titles to the convent, plus additional rental income on farms and plantations. The Abbess maintained a skilled *quid pro quo* with the elite families. In exchange for an extra dowry, the families could rest assured that their spare girls would be wearing the noble black veil, plus the Abbess would allow the novices to bring their retinue of servants and slaves into the convent. During her negotiations with the patriarch of each family she would let it slip that if the dowry were not increased, then their daughter would have to room with the white-veiled, mixed race, *mestiza,* nuns. The patriarchs reluctantly forked over a larger dowry along with their leftover daughters.

The Abbess applied an alternate tactic with the few remaining daughters of Inca nobility. She would accept a handful of such princesses as long as their dowry was laden with silver and gold. In tempting their families to intern the princesses at the convent, she would allow the novices to burn coca leaves as offerings to the watermelon size polished stone that she kept at the entrance to the Santa Clara church. The oval shape of the stone was an Inca symbol of divinity. The Abbess recognized that the Holy Office of the Inquisition would torture her for her heretical inclusion of the egg shaped rock, but the Abbess regarded it more along the lines of a golden goose that would fund her orphanage in perpetuity.

The Abbess's steely character had but one weakness: she fell in love with every infant that was left at the convent's doorstep or that was born to one of the *Kari shina* novices. One never to interject a Quechua word in her conversation, she allowed this one word in her lexicon. *Kari shina* meant more than a lazy woman with no morals; it meant "man-like behavior." And no one disparaged men more ardently than the Abbess. To be called a *Kari shina* was tantamount to emotional banishment from the convent.

◈ ◈ ◈

The piercing cries of a newborn infant woke the nuns of Santa Catalina at an odd hour: sometime between Lauds and Prime. The Abbess deduced that whoever was leaving the baby at their gates was waiting for dawn so that the infant would not be left out too long in the frigid Andean air of Cusco. "At least they have a semblance of a human heart," she said out loud. Often times the infants were half frozen by the time the nuns noticed the bundle in the basket. The Abbess waited for the usual bustle and running feet of the sisters designated to gather the basket and comfort the infant. This morning, however, the baby's cries came from within the interior of the convent, and this alarmed the Abbess, as unlike in recent times, there were no pregnant women among them. "Do not touch that baby!" she screamed into the central courtyard of the Spanish-style convent. Her voice echoed throughout the convent and instilled fear into novices and elder sisters alike. "I will not hesitate to inflict severe corporal punishment on the sister who dares to defy my orders," she hollered as she quickly dressed. The convent shook as if another Andean temblor had struck. The nuns knew the Abbess complied with her punishments, which ranged from subjecting them to eat nothing but old bread and water to the more severe twenty lashings and banishment.

The sacrist nun ran with the keys to all the buildings jangling from her key holder as if trying to muffle the infant's cries. She stood at attention near the Abbess's door. "I am ready to serve," she said in her naturally deep voice.

"Me too," chimed the gentle infirmarian nun as she ruffled through the first aid items in her basket, taking a quick inventory of what she might need for the baby, or God forbid, the mother who had just delivered the infant.

The Abbess stormed out of her eight-room cell and slapped the sacrist across the face. "Your habit is disheveled and you look sleepy." She struck her again on the other cheek. "Now you're alert, aren't you?"

"Yes, Abbess," whispered the sacrist.

The infant's cries led to the cellarium. The sacrist panicked. "Oh, sweet Mother of God, it can't be possible. I locked everything up. There is no way that a baby could have gotten into the storehouse."

"Open the door," ordered the Abbess. "I'll be the judge of what has happened, and I will castigate those responsible."

The minute the Abbess laid eyes on the whimpering newborn she felt an intense love for the child. She didn't allow the nurse to pick up the child. In fact, she elbowed her out of the way and rushed to the infant first. Quickly, she peeked to confirm the child's sex. She heaved a sigh of relief.

* * *

The Abbess hauled the infant and the nurse to the infirmary. She said, "I do not want anyone to know a thing about this infant. Not its sex, not its skin color, not about who is nursing the baby. You are to remain silent at all times until I tell you to speak, do you understand me?"

"Yes, Reverend Abbess," said the nurse.

She wacked the nurse squarely on the lips. "Did I command you to speak? I am your judge and your commander; don't ever forget that."

Once the nurse nodded appropriately, the Abbess cooed and held the infant as gently as a fragile cattleya orchid. "You're my new baby angel, aren't you?" She inhaled deeply of the baby's breath. "Ahhh, fresh mother's milk," she exhaled as if she had uncovered a secret in the scent of mother's milk. "You will never worry a day in your life," she whispered to the baby. "Your mother Abbess will protect you and keep you from harm. I will never judge you, for you are an innocent victim of one man's sins. I will find him and I will not wait for the Cusco magistrate to eke out his punishment; I will sentence him harshly." She kissed the infant's clenched fists and buried her nostrils in its neck. "Yes, indeed, that is the tang of mother's milk that must have run down from your bitty mouth to your teensy neck. I'll sniff out who your father is, and he will only smell the rotting soil of the graveyard." The infant's sleepy head rested on the flat chest of the Abbess's linen gown. The Abbess gazed down with glassy eyes and said to the baby, "You will stay with me as my own child in this convent and you will be my precious doll."

The Abbess had held dozens of infant girls in her arms. She cuddled them and loved them and nurtured them. These angelic gifts from our Heavenly Mother became her daughters and she dedicated her life to them. Most of the babies left at Santa Catalina were *mestiza* girls born out of wedlock to an indigenous or *mestiza* woman. Their Spanish fathers left them at Santa Catalina so that they would undergo a Hispanization process, but more importantly, so that they would be out of sight and out of mind forever. The Abbess would squeeze the fathers for as much dowry as possible, but it never amounted to the largesse that a Spanish family would provide to erase an illegitimate Spanish daughter from their family tree. The Abbess complied with contempt, never forgetting to extract as much money as possible from these families at the very onset lest they never remember their angelic daughters again.

❖ ❖ ❖

The Abbess knew that as long as the civil authorities remained content with their understanding that Santa Catalina was a solemn and charitable convent, they would never interfere with her huge household. In 1623, Santa Catalina housed over 100 nuns and 150 others, such as orphans, the handful of the remaining Inca princesses, *mestiza* girls being trained to become more Spanish like their fathers, and the retinue of servants and slaves that did all the work in the convent's orchards, gardens, and textile workshops. (Unlike her predecessors who had allowed an Inca princess, Doña María Cusi Huarcay, to be taken in and out of the convent while the elite Spanish and the crown decided over a thirty-year period who could marry her and her vast wealth.) No, the Abbess would not tolerate such disrespect of one of her charges, and thus she kept a tight grip on all matters within the walls of the convent.

She walked a fine line between asserting her independence from the crown and the meddlesome priests, and administering a bustling and economically successful convent. She knew that money made the world go round, and as long as she kept the elite happy financially, she was free to do as she saw fit. What she wanted was to create a disciplined heaven on earth for the unwanted girls that were left at her doorstep, and she never wavered from this goal.

Above all, the Abbess knew that her most avid supporters were the merchants and entrepreneurial elite whom she, in return, supported with her own ingenious financial schemes.

Never one to shy away from resolving any problem with a corresponding fiscal response, the Abbess's knowledge of Castilian law superseded that of the crown's attorneys. She out-maneuvered them with her well-structured mortgage-lending operation that adhered to the laws banning lending at interest. In the case of Don Rolando de Celaya, whom she needed to help her strong-arm the abusive husband of Rosa Delgado, she advanced him 1,400 pesos but demanded collateral of his sugar-producing estate. When Don Rolando did not sufficiently deter Rosa's husband from trying to forcefully extricate his wife from the convent of Santa Catalina, the Abbess started foreclosure proceedings on the sugar estate of Don Rolando, and lo and behold, Rosa's husband mysteriously drowned in the Urubamba

River near Don Rolando's estate. The drowning brought a harmonious conclusion to a tragic marriage.

With the arrival of this last infant, whose pearly white skin and downy auburn hair proclaimed Spanish ancestry, the Abbess aimed to line her coffers and pick the pockets of all her Spanish debtors, not only for additional financial support for all her orphans, but for information about the Spanish father of this innocent child. She relished the thought of administering this deadbeat father's final terrestrial judgment.

The Abbess handed the baby over to the nurse, and reprimanded her again just in case she had any disobedient thoughts. Obedience and chastity comprised the only two evangelical counsels the Abbess adhered to. She overlooked the third counsel: charity or poverty, since she was far from leading a perfect consecrated life. Poverty had no place in the running of a convent with so many mouths to feed for many generations. She ran a family of over 250 members, she was the executive of many business enterprises, she held the property deeds to dozens of properties, and she planned financially for the future in a more precise manner than any man.

The Abbess commanded the nurse, "Not one word, not one nod, nothing—to anyone. You are now made of the same stone as the foundations of our convent: strong, yet silently keeping many secrets. I'm going to dig with a vengeance until I finally get to bottom of this abomination!"

In short order and with total lack of respect for every female in the convent under the age of thirty-five, the Abbess inspected them closely to verify that the mother of the infant was not one of her charges. Once this unpleasant matter was resolved, the Abbess cleared every visitor from the *locutorio*, the waiting room. From behind the iron grill room divider, she practically growled for everyone visiting the nuns to clear the area. She then yelled at the majordomo, "Bring me Francisco Muñoz and Simón Alfonso immediately."

◼ ◼ ◼

The two degenerate gamblers dropped their lackluster card game, took one last swig of strong *chicha,* and rushed to Santa Catalina. Before stepping out onto the steep and narrow street of San Blas, the majordomo instructed them to cover their heads with the large hats he brought along for them, and handed them old capes to cover their soiled Spanish garb. All three stayed close to the Inca stone walls that lined the streets, their faces hidden from busybodies interested in the majordomo's latest foray into their bustling neighborhood. The majordomo was not only a skilled henchman, but a former Portuguese spy the Abbess had nursed back to health years ago while the authorities hunted for him for being a heretic—a Jewish *converso* secretly practicing his religion. The Abbess let him recuperate from his stab wounds near the convent's pig sty, but after she removed his infected eyeball, she had seen a certain amount of good in his bad eye, along with the necessary evil she needed in a trusted majordomo.

The henchman touched the handle of his sharp dagger and said to the gamblers, "Respect the Abbess at all times or you'll end up chopped up in the swine trough."

The Abbess didn't bother greeting the men. She dangled a purse coin, and said, "Some poor woman gave up her Spanish infant this morning. Don't lead me astray or it will be your last day on this earth. Who did this?"

"We do not know anything about a Spanish baby. Are you sure the baby is Spanish, could it be a common *mestizo*?" said Simón.

The Abbess delicately put her hand through the iron grill and forcefully grabbed Simón's hand and yanked it onto the many nails that protruded from the iron grill separating the nuns from their visitors. Simón yelped like a wounded dog, but managed a quick response. "There was a murder last night near San Francisco Church perhaps that had something to do with a baby."

The Abbess pitched a silver coin to Simón, who caught it with a bloody paw but with the agility of a *callimico* marmoset. "Continue, speak quickly but don't leave out any details," commanded the Abbess.

Francisco took over the description of the murder in his breakneck-speed Andalusian Spanish. Without stopping to catch his breath he said, "The hairy gambler, El Cid, stole four gold coins from a Basque lieutenant at our gambling table, they exchanged blows inside the gambling house, but when we all left, El Cid waited in hiding near the doors to San Francisco Church ready to attack the Basque. I heard El Cid say, 'You dog—still alive?' and then I heard a woman's voice cry out, 'It's your own infant!' The Basque pulled out his sword and stabbed El Cid, but El Cid and his accomplices stabbed the Basque; now El Cid is dead, the Basque is near death in the cell of Friar Martín de Aróstegui, his fellow Basque, at the Franciscan monastery. You know how clannish and proud those Basques are as they yap secretively in their convoluted language that no one else understands. And yes, I did hear a baby wail bloody murder at the end of the fight. And no, I did not participate in the fight because my hands were occupied with a warm-blooded *mestiza*. End of story. Fling me the rest of your coins, beautiful Abbess!"

She threw a couple coins at the feet of Francisco, who had to bend down to pick them up.

The Abbess nodded to the majordomo who pulled out his dagger and held it at the nape of Francisco's neck, ready to jab it in. The Abbess commanded, "Look up, and listen carefully. Francisco you stay here and tell me everything you know about El Cid and this Basque soldier; and you, Simón, go over to the Franciscan monastery, and if the Basque is still alive, find out all you can about the baby." She hurled two coins to Simón who caught them mid-air and ran out of the *locutorio* dripping blood from his injured hand, but grinning at the spirit of the dauntless nun.

The Abbess paced on her side of the iron grill. Once her prosecutorial mind was in gear, she proceeded with a series of questions. She asked, "Did the woman speak in Castilian, Quechua or Basque?"

"Castilian, of course. I only know how to give commands in Quechua, and I only curse like a Basque sailor. Proceed, sweet lady." Francisco's impertinent answer was received with a blow to his ear. As he jumped up to strike back at the majordomo, the Abbess threw another coin at him.

"You will stay seated and you will give me a full descriptive response. Next, did you see the woman's face or attire?"

"You're not going to like my answer," said the lecherous Francisco, smiling.

"Answer now and be precise!"

"Yes, Abbess. The moonlight illuminated the woman's breasts and they were as milky white as the milk she was feeding her baby, so I did not see what she was wearing." He winked at the Abbess, who in return winked at the majordomo, and Francisco's forehead hit the wooden floor with a loud thump. The majordomo kept his heavy foot on Francisco's back and his sword ready to strike.

"Who was the woman addressing when she said, 'It's your own infant?'"

"May I clarify something? And may I sit down?" asked Francisco.

"Yes and no. Continue."

"The woman spoke a couple of minutes before El Cid and the Basque fought. She was trying to hide in the shadows of the wooden doors of the church, but the infant started crying, that's when she sat down on the steps and whipped out her, uh, that is to say, that is when she fed her infant. Naturally, I had to stare." Francisco paused since he felt the majordomo's foot press down forcefully on his lungs and ribs. "The woman was singing a lull-aby to the baby, in Castilian," he quickly added. "Then, out of nowhere comes the Basque lieutenant and sneaks up so close to the breastfeeding woman that I thought he was going to drink the, uh—that is to say, that he was close enough to touch her, uh—infant." Francisco felt the majordomo release his weight from his back.

The Abbess continued with her questions. "What did the Basque do at that exact moment? Did he and the woman exchange any words?"

"It was a moonlit evening, and the woman never took her eyes off her baby. The Basque spoke to her in a delicate voice, he said, 'I am a warrior, but I am a nun.' I thought I heard the wrong thing, but like I said, I was preoccupied. Then the Basque stared at the baby with the same watery eyes as the woman. The Basque took a deep breath of the baby's open mouth and smiled like a mule. Finally, the woman looked straight into the Basque's eyes and said, 'If they touch my baby, I will kill them.' The lieutenant replied, 'I will never let them kill the baby. I killed my brother and I killed my lovers, but I will never let them touch the baby. *Jamás,* never!'"

The Abbess's legal and financial mind was addled. She couldn't add two and two together. She had hoped to demand an immense dowry from the Basque lieutenant, assuming he was the father. And as all Basques claim titles of nobility, she would start the bureaucratic proceedings for additional funds from the crown. The prowess of the Basque ship owners and sailors had transferred handsomely to entrepreneurial skills in the cities of the Viceroyalty of Peru. But Francisco's description of the lieutenant's behavior confused the Abbess; it simply was not manly. On the other hand, if El Cid was the father of the infant, she would go after his estate, but a common gambler would not have amassed a fortune. She would have to find the Spanish woman's family. She hated damaging the mother of the child, but she had to think of the infant's future. She would coerce the mother's family into paying for the Abbess's silence. Yes, this would be her plan. She commanded, "Tell me the rest of what you saw and heard."

"The woman screamed when she saw El Cid lunging with his sword toward the Basque and the baby. At that point, I was ready to jump in, but the woman screamed, 'It's your own infant!' and all hell broke loose. In a matter of minutes, several men were on the ground bleeding and the woman and baby were gone."

The Abbess threw the coin purse at Francisco, pursed her lips, and blew air calmly at the majordomo. She was through picking Francisco's memory for any useful information. The majordomo understood her command. It meant: execute the final blow outside the convent walls. They didn't call her the final judge for no reason.

The fast talking Andalusian gambler was never seen again in Cusco, but Simón returned in record time to Santa Catalina to collect more coins for his information. He panted and said, "Dear Abbess, it appears that the Basque lieutenant is a woman.

She, I mean to say, he is a soldier who has killed dozens in the wars, but he confessed to being a woman, a former nun from the Basque country, who came to the New World dressed as a man. Apparently, his name is Catalina de Erauso, and she is a decorated military man."

The Abbess was temporarily stupefied but she did not reveal her shock. Instead she calmly asked, "Who confirmed that the lieutenant is a woman?"

"Good question, why didn't I think of it?" asked Simón.

The Abbess struck the iron grill with a wooden rod; both Simón and the majordomo jumped at attention. She said, "Let me rephrase my question: Has the Bishop confirmed that the lieutenant is a woman?"

"Yes, siree, he is. He is at a nunnery in Guamanga, and two old ladies took a good look at his privates and confirmed that he is a woman. His Eminence received the news, and he has forgiven the lieutenant. I'll be wantin' my coins now, your Abbessnence, and by the way, where is Francisco?"

❈ ❈ ❈

The Abbess smiled for the first time in twenty-four hours. The bells rang in the convent for the prayers of Vespers. She had to rush in and lead the prayers. She had to thank the Blessed Mother for giving her a perfect Spanish daughter, a daughter who would grow up to be the judge and administrator of the human and financial treasures enclosed in Santa Catalina.

She chuckled at the thought that by now her innocent infant daughter would be on her schedule of suckling fresh mother's milk from one of the *mestizas* kept in the convent just for this type of motherly duty. The Abbess felt a pang so deep in her chest that it seemed to hurt the marrow of her bones.

The Abbess had a profound desire to nurse the child. She recognized the futility of this desire, but at least she could nuzzle with her new daughter and tickle her chin as the nourishing milk trickled from the corners of her upturned Cupid lips.

The Abbess puckered her own lips and blew once again in the direction of the majordomo. The majordomo understood instantly what he had to do to Simón, but Simón's cheeks blushed a crimson red at the thought that the ornery old Abbess had just blown him a kiss.

Los Feliz
April 25, 2011

During the next week Alma ingratiated herself with Claire by purposefully running into her as Claire carried her heavy massage table from one elderly client's home to the next. As much as Alma dreaded revealing her twisted face in the daytime, she now donned an oversized grey fedora and a hoodie and designer jeans, in hopes of blending in with the hipsters who were moving into Los Feliz. She completed the cool independent look she hoped to exhibit to the world by accessorizing with large retro sunglasses, and walked around at daytime on the Los Feliz streets where Claire's clients lived.

Alma was uncomfortable out and about, but she kept all her senses on alert for clues as to when Claire saw which client. More significantly she tried to detect Claire's vulnerabilities as they briefly chatted on the driveway or street in between Claire's appointments. Alma didn't follow Claire from appointment to appointment, but over the course of one week she managed to coincide taking a walk around the streets where Claire had appointments. Alma wanted to move swiftly and get her hands on the old people's money, but her impulsiveness had gotten her into trouble many times in the past. This time, she had to negotiate a fine line among the well-intentioned Claire, the old people whom she had not yet met, and the caregivers. She needed to convince all three groups that what she was about to propose was logical and necessary for the elders' well-being, and she had to do it in record time or she would be thrown out of her own house; she would be totally destitute.

Alma walked with her ears perked up like a Doberman pinscher waiting to attack. She'd made a preliminary assessment of Claire's personality based on the brief conversations the two had had out on the driveways of Claire's clients' homes. Claire was someone who saw herself as cheerful, helpful, and kind, but Phil's death left her depleted of those traits. The couple of times that the caregivers have gathered outside Dr. Nunez's house, Claire stopped by and chatted amiably and candidly with all of them, Alma included. The caregivers trusted Claire, and now some of them trusted her, as well. Alma decided that today was the day she must put her plan into action.

As Alma strolled down one leafy street, she stopped in her tracks. She heard flamenco music escaping boisterously from the wrought iron window grill of the spacious Spanish Revival house. The side window was barely visible through two old cork trees whose thick bark had never been harvested. Alma bent down to tie her track shoes a few times as she waited for a clue. She heard a women's shrill voice shout, "Alé, guapa, alé!" Clearly the woman was cheering another woman. The constant clacking of shoes onto a wooden floor picked up speed and intensity as the music reached a crescendo.

"Alé, La Linda, alé!" shouted another woman, followed by the sounds of items being thrown against the walls, the wooden floor, and even the open window. Alma heard the sweet voice of Ofelia say, "No, this is too much, La Linda. Please take it easy. I go outside now; I'm exhausted."

Alma saw Ofelia walk out through a side door and she called out to her. "Hi Ofelia, what wonderful music were you listening to?"

Ofelia waved back but she appeared to be crying. Alma rushed to her side and said, "Dear Ofelia, what's the matter?"

Ofelia shook her head, but couldn't answer. Alma stayed by her side and said, "Why don't you stay out here and I can go in and say hello to your employer? Just until you feel better, ok?"

A woman's voice shouted out, "Ofelia, hurry up in here, I must practice an *alegría!* Ofelia, answer me, I hear you out there!"

Alma seized the opportunity and called out, "Hello, La Linda, I'm Dr. Alma Ruiz and I hope you don't mind that I was admiring your dramatic dancing. I'm a huge fan of yours."

La Linda quickly responded in a remarkably strong voice for a woman her age. "Why thank you, Dr. Ruiz. You're so kind to say so, but surely you couldn't have seen me dancing since I have privacy sheers on all my windows."

"You're so right, La Linda. I guess I was reminiscing about your past performances that I saw as a child, I mean as a younger person. You were, and continue to be, a remarkable dancer. You will go down in the history books as a *bailaora par excellence.*"

"From your lips to God's ears, Doctor Ruiz. You're obviously an *aficionada* otherwise you would have not called me a *bailaora.* So, thank you, Doctor—"

"Please call me Alma. I would love to come in and chat with you while Ofelia gets some fresh air, would it be all right if I came in?"

"Alma, you are too kind. But, alas, I'm an old-fashioned *bailaora*, and I do not have my stage makeup on. Why don't we just talk through the window grill, like old friends and lovers used to do in old Seville? Have you ever been there?"

"Yes, many years ago. Did you like to perform there?" asked Alma. She was banking on the fact that the old lady was dying to talk about herself *ad nauseam*, and would not ask her any details about Seville, a city Alma had never visited. Alma noticed the same long-winded, self-absorbed characteristics in La Linda as those of her old Granny years ago. Every day her grandmother used to recall some long ago feat that Alma was certain had never occurred in quite those vivid details. The older Granny got, the better she was in her own mind, and the more desperate Alma had become to get the hell out of Granny's house. Granny was now dead and had left her small Los Feliz house mortgaged to the hilt.

⊞ ⊞ ⊞

La Linda's answer shocked Alma back to the present. La Linda said, "Not only did I like to perform in Seville and in all of Andalucía, but I plan to perform there in September. That's why I'm rehearsing feverishly." Her voice escalated to a booming crescendo. "There's an old song that I'd like to revive, to give my fans something totally new. They'll think it is something new, yet I know it is ancient. It is pure flamenco or as we call it: *cante jondo*. This age-old sound is like the kind of passion that emanates from the core of who you truly are, from the depth of the marrow of your bones. It's just that, I'm not sure that I have all the passion for this, I'm missing something. I-I-I think I can still do it, don't you?"

Alma couldn't see La Linda's face or body through the privacy sheers, but she detected an opening, a golden opportunity, to wedge her foot in the door of this not so confident *bailaora*.

"I'm a holistic practitioner, perhaps there are some therapies and a nutrition program that I could get you started on to revive your energy," answered Alma.

La Linda didn't answer. Alma let her chew on this possibility of renewed strength. Finally, La Linda shouted, "Ofelia, don't be so lazy, get back in the rehearsal studio, we have much to do."

Ofelia walked back from the rear yard with a small basket of figs. She said, "I am coming, La Linda. I'm bringing you some delicious figs that Octavio just picked for you. He's pruning some trees and he says hello and to take it easy. He says that the high mucilage content in figs helps to heal and protect sore throats. Do you know what he means by this mucilage? Anyway, I'll serve them with a slice of Manchengo cheese. You need to rest now. Cool down a little before Claire comes for your massage."

La Linda didn't answer; she was clapping rhythmically to a very complex sound in her mind. She stopped and asked, "Ofelia, please call Claire on her cell and tell her to bring her curative verbena oil."

"Yes, La Linda. I'll call her right away."

Alma jumped into the conversation before it was too late. "What is it about the massage oil that makes it so special? As a world-renowned artist, I'm sure you've experienced the best massage therapists in the world, so why is Claire's massage so special?"

Ofelia went inside and did not invite Alma in. Alma didn't want to leave; she had to find out why the old people craved Claire's massage. She persevered. "In my medical practice, I find that my patients instinctively know a natural healer, some even say that I am such a healer." La Linda did not respond, yet Alma could hear her adjusting items in her studio. "Do you think that Claire is a natural massage therapist, someone who can manipulate your muscles, connective tissue, tendons, and ligaments to enhance your health and well-being?" Alma rambled on.

After a few seconds of silence, La Linda whispered, "For me, her massage is a key that opens doors to a stage where I have never performed before. I hear flamenco music so authentic, so undiluted, that I never want to leave that stage. Except that the *duende* is there and that is a fact I cannot bear."

Alma had to select her question adroitly. She wished she had paid more attention in her college Spanish classes. What was a *duende*? If she asked La Linda this question, perhaps she would end the conversation. La Linda would figure out that Alma was not a true flamenco fan, just a wannabe. So she asked another open-ended question. "It must be an exhilarating feeling that you want to relive, am I right?"

"Yes, Claire's massages have always revitalized me, but ever since she started using her grandmother's Ecuadorian oil blend, the massages have become cathartic; they arouse all my senses. They take me back to an all-encompassing flamenco experience. The *duende* is there, but I cannot endure it."

Alma heard Ofelia enter the room. She tried to peer through the sheers, but they blocked almost everything; all Alma could make out was the outline of Ofelia's slim body and perhaps La Linda sitting down. Alma wanted to ask Ofelia the meaning of *duende*, knowing this fact would lead to the next question, but La Linda was in the room. Alma took a chance and said,

"What do you wish the *duende* would do?" There was no answer.

Alma gave this conversation her last and best guess. She said, "La Linda, when Claire massages you and you feel this intensity, do you wish the *duende* would leave you alone?"

La Linda cackled like a possessed witch. She said, "No, I want the *duende* inside me."

◈ ◈ ◈

The cryptic answer stunned Alma. While she thought about what to say next, La Linda and Ofelia were no longer in the dance studio. Alma assumed that Claire would be coming soon and she wanted to speak with her after La Linda's massage. She took the liberty of walking back to the rear yard to kill some time by talking to Octavio.

At a 90-foot distance she saw him squatting behind some dense shrubs. She wanted to sneak up to him to see what plants he had growing in the back. She had stopped him on a couple of occasions to ask about his plants and about his life back in Peru. She could tell that he was from the Amazon region, yet he insisted that he was from Cusco. Alma shared some of the research she had been doing while in the Amazon region, but Octavio dismissed her comments.

Today she would find out what plants he secretly grew in La Linda's yard. Alma was of slight built and with the rubber-soled shoes she was wearing, she was sure that she would not be heard by Octavio. Alma tiptoed from one large tree to the next, hiding for a few seconds behind the thick oak trunks. Suddenly she felt the sharp end of a pair of garden shears touch her back. "What is it that you want, Alma?" asked Octavio.

Alma froze in fear and confusion. Seconds ago she had just seen his shoes behind the shrubs, hadn't she? "Octavio, I didn't want to startle you, but it is you who has startled me! What plants do you have growing back there?"

Octavio opened and closed the shears and said, "Why don't you walk over there and take a look." He took another step closer to her with the garden shears leading his way. "You know all about plants, isn't that what you did in the jungle, as you call it?"

"Well, I am a trained botanist, but on that assignment I was more involved with the administrative aspects of our research," Alma answered.

"Ah, of course. So what brings you to the farthest corner of La Linda's property?" asked Octavio with a sly smile. "Perhaps you lost your medical marijuana and are looking for a free supply?"

"Oh, no, I have no use for any type of medicine."

Octavio touched her paralyzed cheek with a muddy finger and said, "Oh, is that so?" and he walked quickly to the front yard.

Alma felt tears of anger welling up in her eyes and she felt a twinge of pain on the nerves of her face. The insensitive doctors had told her that the sporadic twinges could mean that her seventh cranial nerve could be healing or it could mean that it was totally dying. What kind of answer was that from a medical professional? The doctor had said that from now on her condition could be characterized by unsynchronized facial movements, and something about synkinesis that could vary from severe to mild. Blah, blah, blah! Alma was in pain, her eyesight was deteriorating, her corneas dryer by the day, and she had to get back to the Amazon. She needed money, lots of it to get her research going, to pay her assistants, to be the lead researcher, to be somebody.

CHAPTER SEVEN

Seville Spain

1860

Illustration of man and woman playing a seguidilla.

Created by Dumas, published in L'Illustration Journal Universel, Paris, 1857

Seville, Spain
1860

"I don't care what or who comes near me, I'll cut them to pieces!" yelled La Andonda as she jabbed her knife in the air. All the drunkards at the *juerga*, the Gypsy get-together in Triana, on the wrong side of the Guadalquivir River, knew she meant what she said. Some pretty-boy count who was slumming with the Seville Gypsies had once made a pass at La Andonda. Before she finished singing her forlorn tune, she lunged at the count, sliced him, and went back to singing, while his friends dragged him away.

Tonight La Andonda was in a foul mood. She sang her heart out, she drank her moonshine, and she even cut herself, yet she didn't feel *duende*. La Andonda's extremely mercurial nature often impelled her to draw blood, more often than not, her own. It wasn't a bloodthirsty expression of lunacy. It was La Andonda's way of blood-letting for the beneficial effect of reducing the pressure of the accumulated injustice, resentment, and revenge she bottled up in her heart. All the Gypsies in her audience understood that she was sacrificing herself a drop of blood at a time. They were all at a breaking point themselves for the suffering of centuries of discrimination at the hands of the crown, the Inquisition, and now the government. Her audience clapped and shouted their encouragement: "*Ezo! Toma que te toma!*" But tonight the capricious *duende* was not touched by the trickles of blood and evaded La Andonda's performance.

La Andonda was the foremost *cantaora* during this legendary period of the flamenco *café cantante*, the singing café. In Seville 1860, the ruling café owner was Silverio Franconetti, whose nightly *juergas* were the talk of Seville. His amazing voice befitted the tragic *siguiriya* song style, and his showmanship attracted the big tipping nobles from all over Andalucía. Many of the nobles were the descendants of the Basque sailors who struck gold in the New World and settled in the warmth of Andalucía.

La Andonda detested Silverio Franconetti, as did many of the pure Gypsy flamencos whose art form Silverio expropriated and exploited in his popular café. Silverio's excessive theatricality and planning, which the Gypsies attributed derisively to his Italian heritage, enraged them. Flamenco was visceral, not a conscious art form. Silverio's Italian sensibility attributed his singing skills to the grace of the angel of music and not to the dark *duende*, the *duende* the Gypsies beckoned. Between an angelic muse and a foreboding *duende*, the Gypsies would always clamor for *duende*.

Silverio's premeditated character was poison to La Andonda. And when La Andonda hated a man, he'd better watch his back. In this flamenco milieu of love and hate, rich and poor, strong liquor and sharp knives, La Andonda was feared like no other. Unlike her contemporary women singers, María Borrico, The Little Donkey, who brayed and charmed her audience, or Tía

Sarvaora, a supreme artist of the ancient *tonás* genre of song, La Andonda's voice was unbridled fire; pure energy.

La Andonda discovered that her fellow singer, Diego El Fillo, had begun to despise Silverio, and would rarely sing at his café, no matter the salary. She paid El Fillo a visit. She cornered him in his own house and said, "You have a voice that is truly as sharp and painful as a stab from my knife. Teach me some of your songs. Now."

El Fillo was thirty years her senior, but he saw in her a Gypsy woman who would not take no for an answer. One look at her dusky skin and ebony hair, and there was no doubt that her Gypsy ancestors had traveled from India to Egypt and landed in the south of Spain. Besides his desire to touch every part of her bronzed skin, he was excited by her threatening nature.

⊠ ⊠ ⊠

Over the course of their travels throughout Andalucía, between the harvest of grapes in Jerez in September and the olive harvest in Jaén in March, El Fillo taught her everything he knew about singing and desire, and La Andonda became his willing pupil. She also became his wife, but their marriage didn't meet La Andonda's fiery passion. She burned up old El Fillo in no time. Perhaps it was the abundance of the harvests that planted a seed of insatiable urges in La Andonda. Her hungry eye began to turn to El Fillo's young relative, Tomás El Nitri, whose reputation as a compelling *cantaor* was matched by his off-stage tight-lipped demeanor. His silence intrigued La Andonda; she wanted to test for herself if still waters did indeed run deep. In keeping with her tempestuous nature, La Andonda betrayed El Fillo by passionately seeking out Tomás El Nitri.

La Andonda searched for Tomás from harvest town to wine festival. When she caught up with him, she said, "Tomás, let me tell you how I just rescued your uncle or cousin or whatever El Fillo is to you."

Tomás always saved his voice for singing, so he just nodded. She was speaking at lightning speed, in the Andalusian manner, but Tomás was blinded by the flicker from her eyes and the scent of verbena and cinnamon in her hair. La Andonda pulled up an old stool and said, "We were returning from the horse fair at Zafra and old El Fillo couldn't make the river crossing. He sat on the riverbank and cursed at it. A lot of good that did. Let me have a swig of your *aguardiente* and I'll tell you the rest," she demanded. Without saying a word Tomás handed over his liquor, and she downed half the pitcher and continued. "I picked up his scrawny ass and carried him across the choppy river and into an inn. I left him there. El Fillo's voice cries out about the nothingness of life, but I want to seize life. I want to feel it deep inside of me." She grabbed Tomás in such a way that he understood her razor-sharp meaning. He moaned in anticipation as she ran what was either her sharp fingernail or a dull knife from the nape of his neck down his spinal column. He didn't care which one it was as long as she kept panting in his ear. With her other hand La Andonda deftly maneuvered him to a bale of orchard hay and mounted him next to the grey Andalusian horses. Mutely, but with all his potency, Tomás complied.

Tomás and La Andonda sent sparks flying in the Gypsy world of Seville. La Andonda didn't care who she took him away from. He was hers and that was that. El Fillo saved face by returning to Seville. People urged him to cut her down, but he refused. What they didn't understand was that El Fillo had been feeling close to death for quite some time. La Andonda had stormed late into his life and resuscitated him, and he was grateful for the hot breath of life she had temporarily given him.

La Andonda sang with immense intensity after commencing her love affair with Tomás, and depending on how she felt on any given day, she either sang of abuse or verbally abused her many detractors. She stood in front of her audience and took command of the scene. She didn't need guitar accompaniment or dancers; she did it all with her throaty voice and her ready knife in hand. She belted out:

Whichever man gives me cause

May they fatally knife him!

Everyone knew that she was being coy because she would never wait for anyone else to knife her enemy—she would rise to that challenge, drunk or sober, and relish the occasion. La Andonda did not believe in doing anything by proxy. She demanded to feel her blade cutting skin. Cowardly substitutions were best left for the soft nobles and their field of honor duels in which neither the combatants nor their trusted seconds were willing to risk their lives. La Andonda, like all the Gypsies, lived by the code of blood for blood.

After one particularly raucous evening, El Fillo's brother, Juan Encueros was found murdered. La Andonda went to find El Fillo, and located him on stage. She was foaming at the mouth with anger. She screamed, "An eye for an eye! You must find the murderer and destroy him."

El Fillo was in the middle of a song and he continued wailing until a man in the crowd yelled, "It was Silverio who killed your brother!"

El Fillo continued wailing. He changed the lyrics he was singing to crow boastfully about how he would annihilate his brother's assailant, but in the end he did not seek revenge for the murder of his brother, Juan Encueros. For over sixty years El Fillo had burned the candle at both ends and he didn't have any flame left to hunt anyone down; not Silverio, not Tomás El Nitri, and certainly not La Andonda.

No one could confirm if it was actually Silverio who murdered El Fillo's brother, but the Gypsies hardly needed an excuse to despise Silverio more, and their rancor for him increased. And as Tomás grew to detest Silverio, La Andonda began to love Tomás more and more. In her view, her enemy's enemy was her friend. To inflame matters, in the ever growing world of the flamenco *café cantante,* Silverio's voice began to be compared to that of Tomás El Nitri. Tomás even won the prestigious Golden Key of the *Cante,* yet it was Silverio who hogged the limelight.

Tomás was pure Gypsy and he refused to sing anywhere near Silverio. He avoided Silverio at all costs since it seemed certain that La Andonda would soon attack Silverio no matter the repercussions. When they weren't singing or making love, La Andonda busied herself sharpening her assortment of knives and daggers. Periodically she would cut herself offstage. Tomás figured she had her secret reasons for her self-inflicted wounds just as he kept his mouth shut in order to contain the tuberculosis inside him. Never one to speak an unnecessary word, Tomás gathered their belonging and he and La Andonda traveled all over Andalucía attracting aficionados to the pure and ardent flamenco they sang. He didn't want to tame her or keep her in a cage, he simply wanted to let her be her belligerent self without incurring the wrath of Silverio's many defenders.

When they sang, their fellow Gypsies experienced a fervent sensory moment. Their ears exploded with sound, their mouths watered with anxiety, their eyes cried anguished tears.

Tomás sang as if strangling his voice in the throat. He elongated a series of introductory *ayes* into a single syllable; holding on to it for dear life. Unlike Tomás, La Andonda did not hold any anguish inside her. She strutted on stage with a violent scowl and a menacing dagger. She howled and moaned and caressed the lyrics as if grinding glass in her mouth. The audiences accompanied La Andonda and Tomás El Nitri with complex clapping patterns, and they shouted *jaleos* of encouragement. Their fellow Gypsies acknowledged that Tomás and La Andonda's deep song, their *cante jondo,* erupted from the depths of the ancestral memories buried in their bodies. The songs they wailed were the collective agony of all of their forbearers.

▦ ▦ ▦

In 1610, along with the expulsion of the Moors from Spain, the Council of State wanted to also expel the Gypsies. Unfortunately for the crown, they could not use the time-tested method of forced conversion to Catholicism, as they had done with the Sephardic Jews and the Moors, as the Gypsies were devout Catholics. The crown dropped the expulsion solution, but they forced the dispersal of the Gypsies to other cities in the realm.

By 1633, the Gypsies were forbidden to speak their language, to trade in horses, and to associate with other Gypsies. The laws of forced assimilation became more and more draconian from 1695 to 1746, ultimately leading to the general internment of 1749, and to the truly heinous policy of removing Gypsy children from their parents at birth, and to branding older Gypsies like cattle.

Despite the efforts to exterminate the Gypsies, they survived in Spain, and in particular, they remained in their ancestral home of Andalucía. Among their fellow Gypsies, La Andonda and Tomás El Nitri continued with their outcast way of life. They exulted in a passion for living in the moment, a devotion to their cult of honor, a disdain for bourgeois values, and above all, mistrust for the *payos,* the non-Gypsies.

La Andonda's renown as a singer of *soleares* was without equal. Her four-line stanzas could range from the frivolous to the tragic. She was known to aim her knife at a man in the crowd and the audience howled knowing that the upcoming *soleá* would be one of a love lost or a love betrayed. She scanned the audience with her piercing eyes. In her inebriated state she sometimes thought she spotted the corpulent body of Silverio in the crowd. She jumped off the platform and chased her invisible fat enemy. She craved the satisfaction of an eye for an eye, a tooth for a tooth, and a pound of fat flesh.

Despite her bellicosity and bloodlust, La Andonda could have moments of gaiety and humor, which left the audience weeping with laughter. But Tomás carried the burden of his people at all times. Besides his genetic melancholy, his tuberculosis worsened. His normally reserved character masked this torment in his life, but on stage, Tomás released his pent-up voice and transformed into a commanding interpreter of pain. He called out for *duende* by raising his arms and clenching his fists as if he were clawing himself. The veins in his neck bulged with the affliction of his ancestors. While he sang a tragic *siguiriya,* an image formed in his mind. He saw himself manning the galleys, as the crown had often forced the *gitanos,* the Gypsies, to do. He rowed until his skin and muscle disappeared. The wood of the oar scraped the bones in his hands, but he continued rowing until there was nothing left to his hand but the gel of his marrow. His voice, always hoarse, wailed and growled above the crowd. He proved that pure flamenco should cause pain, not joy.

His one source of happiness was La Andonda. The audience's admiration for her, and the love he felt for La Andonda, was more than enough for Tomás. He could live with his melancholy and the blood in his cough and the pain in his heart, as long as La Andonda's constant chatter filled his ears. One evening in Cádiz, she said, "Tomás, next week we're heading back to Seville. Do you think that we should stab Silverio as he leaves his café or as he stops to chat with his buddy at Café del Burrero?"

Tomás shook his head no. La Andonda said, "You're right, we should wait until Silverio is alone. I'm going to pierce him so deeply; I'll leave my dagger inside his blubber."

Tomás did not have the courage to tell her that Silverio had escaped on a ship to South America months ago. He had lived in Uruguay as a young man, and now he was hiding out until the authorities forgot about the murder of Juan Encueros. Instead of answering La Andonda's crazed questions, Tomás took her hand and walked slowly through the narrow streets of Cádiz's San Agustín neighborhood, past the church built by the Berástegui clan of Basque sailors from Guipúzcoa, past the plaza where his ancestors were sentenced to row perpetually in the galleys, past the open windows where mothers sang Gypsy lullabies, and he and La Andonda headed to their next performance in the Gypsy quarter of town.

Tomás, in his usual silent way, was resigned to their fate. He had protected La Andonda the best he could, but she was a wild Gypsy woman. Even if Silverio escaped her dagger, her inherent bloodlust would eventually drive her to some violent end.

Their performance that evening was one that Gypsies would talk about for generations. The fans went wild with *duende* at Tomás's raw energy and the depths of his sadness. La Andonda sang an accompanying lament while holding a dagger to her own throat. The *duende* inside her was insatiable and she downed a clay pitcher of moonshine. Her love for Tomás and her hatred of Silverio threatened to possess her entirely, but Tomás's soaring anguished cries kept her tethered to the earth. He sang like he'd never sung before, his eyes shining with love for La Andonda and pain for his people; he sang until his voice dwindled to a mournful croon. By the time anyone noticed that Tomás was no longer singing, he had choked to death on his own blood. *¡Olé! gitano, olé!*

CHAPTER EIGHT

Los Feliz

April 26, 2011
...and Andalucía, Spain 1623

MOSQUE, CORDOVA.

La Mezquita

Engraving, 1890

Bigstockphoto.com

8

Los Feliz
April 26, 2011

The smells and warmth of a day of cooking from a world far away rushed out to greet Alma and Claire from behind Mrs. Hamieh's wood-carved Moroccan door. The woman was diminutive and had to stand on the tips of her pointy-toed slippers just to give Claire a hug. Then she laughed, and clapped her bony hands together making a small cloud of flour appear from thin air. She was like a carnival this woman, joy embodied.

"It's so much fun to open my old door from Marrakech very, very slowly as if it were the entrance to a prehistoric cave," she said. She giggled like a mischievous pixie. "People step back with fear expecting a giant *jinni*, but it's just little old me." She ran back inside and beckoned for the other women to follow her. "Come in my dears, we just finished making the most delicious sweets for my sweets." She laughed and grabbed Alma and Claire with her tiny, sticky hands. Her smile lines—no one would dare call these wrinkles—radiated from the corners of her twinkly amber eyes and creased her entire face. On her cheeks were traces of the powdered sugar she sprinkled on the honey and pistachio filo dough pastries.

Clare and Alma followed Mrs. Hamieh into her kitchen with its mosaic tile walls and oversized stove. The smell of argan oil and sweet honey permeated the air. Mrs. Hamieh handed Claire a covered plate of baklava and said, "Precious girl, I'm so glad you are here. These are for your grandmother to thank her for the oil she blended for my massage. My arthritic hands feel like new." Mrs. Hamieh raised her hands in the air and waved her knotted fingers into aerial pirouettes and snapped her fingers as if she had miniature cymbals attached. Impossibly, she undulated her hips and shoulders like a belly dancer and when she clicked her fingers together they rang like bells. Claire and Alma's mouths fell open in unison, and Mrs. Hamieh bent over laughing uncontrollably.

In her melodic, Middle Eastern-accented English she practically sang over her shoulder, "You can come out now." Fatima peeked out of the butler's pantry where she had been hiding, still striking the *sagat* cymbals on her fingers. "We got them good!" said Mrs. Hamieh. Fatima's laugh was guttural but it harmonized with Mrs. Hamieh's high-pitched giggles and the brassy finger cymbals. These two were pulling pranks like school girls. Fatima's wide smile showed off her gold-capped front teeth that on this day made her look like a friendly genie. She said, "Mrs. Hamieh loves to play jokes, and I am her sidekick. We are partners in crime."

Mrs. Hamieh scurried over to Fatima, hugged her and said, "Happiness is no crime, Fatima, and you are no sidekick. You are a sous-chef and my fellow frolicker." Mrs. Hamieh put so much emphasis on the title sous-chef that Fatima actually blushed. Quickly, Mrs. Hamieh the pixie rushed back to Claire and held her hands. She said, "In all seriousness, please tell your grandmother something important for me. I dreamt of amber-gris, the essence of perfume, and lo and behold my dream came true. Your grandmother's oil has done me so much good."

Fatima added, "We've been cooking like lunatics since her last massage. Look at all this food. Mrs. Hamieh had a dream of a new moon and this means hot bread coming from the oven, so guess what? We also have warm bread."

Mrs. Hamieh took a few hesitant steps up to Alma; she appeared to be sniffing the air for an unpleasant odor. Finally, she said, "What is happening to my manners? Excuse me, but who are you, my dear?"

Alma was clearly embarrassed by Mrs. Hamieh's sniffing her like a dog. She stammered, "I, I, I'm Doctor Ruiz. Your house is beautifully decorated. What remarkable carpets and wood tables. They're inlaid with mother-of-pearl, aren't they? I feel like I'm in an old *riad* hotel in the *medina* of Marrakech. I was there doing some research on the benefits of argan oil many, many years ago, before argan oil products became trendy in the United States. I would love to have a taste of the baklava you made, may I?" Alma was nervous and spit her words out too quickly. She ended up sounding like a name dropper who was trying too hard.

Mrs. Hamieh recalled her dream of last night. She was chasing a mouse through her house, just one solitary mouse, a mouse who was trying to look like a welcome guest in her home. The mouse had defecated near her well-stocked pantry and she had wanted to smash it. To dream of a mouse in one's house means a dangerous woman will enter.

Mrs. Hamieh did not respond to Alma's claims about having visited Marrakech. She was certain her dream mouse now perched on the kitchen stool stuffing its hideously twisted mouth with her desserts had never visited the historic Red City. It would not have appreciated the architectural features of the *riad* with its focus on the central courtyard full of zesty lemon or orange trees and gurgling water features. Had she not been revived by Claire's bewitching massage oil, she would not have been alert enough to remember her lucid dream about the mouse. Today the pantry in her brain was organized as if for a huge family feast, and Mrs. Hamieh remembered everything.

Claire took a bite of the baklava and said, "This is heavenly, Mrs. Hamieh. Is this from one of your secret recipes, too?"

"Yes, sweetheart, but they're no secret—I share all my recipes. It's just that they are all so time consuming no one wants to follow them anymore. Look at all the spice jars we have out on the wood block island. We used every single one of them for today's recipes, and look at how easily I can open and close the jars." Mrs. Hamieh proceeded to twirl caps on and off from various bottles and jars as if in a whirlwind. She said, "Your grandmother is a magician with her oil blends. Fatima tells me that Elena Dougherty is feeling so much better, too. She tells me that even Judge Carrera has been behaving very motherly toward Margarita, right Fatima?"

"Oh, yes," Fatima said. "She's even been driving her to English as a Second Language classes in Hollywood so she can improve her English. Except Margarita does not like the way the Judge drives. And Soledad was telling me that even grouchy Dr. Nunez has been reciting poetry."

Mrs. Hamieh said, "Your grandmother has been given a noble gift and she is passing on the blessings to the rest of us. Did you tell me that your grandmother's name is Beatriz de Robles?"

Claire jumped off her stool at the kitchen counter. "That *is* her maiden name, but I don't ever remember telling anyone her name; everyone calls her Verito. It's a play on the Spanish word for truth, *verdad*, since my grandma always tells you the truth, like it or not. But how could you know her name?"

Mrs. Hamieh smiled in her impish way and kept on humming a desolate tune. Fatima spoke up above the humming and said, "Mrs. Hamieh speaks a lot more Spanish than you realize, she even dreams in many languages. And she believes in the importance of interpreting one's dreams. She said that in her dream she knew a woman named Beatriz de Robles many, many years ago. Anyway, I like it when Mrs. Hamieh helps me to interpret my dreams."

Mrs. Hamieh said, "On the contrary, Fatima, you are the best interpreter of your own dreams."

"Yes, you did tell me that. But since today is not Tuesday or Wednesday and it is still morning, can you please tell Claire about Beatriz de Robles?" Fatima looked over at Claire and added, "Those are some of the rules you have to follow if you are going to interpret your dreams. Oh, and another important rule, dreams of liars never come true."

Alma tried to make herself disappear into the cabinetry. She wanted to stay and hear where this dream conversation was leading. In a matter of days she would be following her own dreams. In the meantime, she would sit on the kitchen stool and listen to this hogwash. Since Alma kept her sunglasses on inside the house she was able to surreptitiously assess how much money the more transportable antiques in Mrs. Hamieh's vast living room would bring in. She took inventory: French mantle clock, gilded, bronze with black Roman numerals and Arabic five-minute markers—$25,000; painting of a Moroccan woman in a canary yellow caftan, Matisse—millions, even with a shady provenance.

※ ※ ※

With every conversation Alma had with each of the caregivers she gleaned valuable financial information about each of their rich employers. She knew that old Dr. Nunez kept gold ingots in a safe he called Fort Knox. Soledad knew the combination but not the location of the key to the steel closet door where the safe was hidden. Alma knew Mrs. Dougherty was naively generous and signed checks to any sappy charity that came her way. Although Yolanda did tell Alma that Mrs. Dougherty's attorney daughter had placed a maximum limit on her mother's ability to write checks. And only that morning Alma had seen the deserted priceless Hispano-Suiza waiting to be torpedoed out of that crazy La Linda's garage. Alma just had to fine-tune the details of her plan. It was important to entice the elderly to hand over some of the assets willingly. That way, if she was caught, the issue of stealing would be cloudy, a misunderstanding due to the failing memories of the elderly.

Alma could still hear the voices of those snobbish academics at the research lab. It was always "be careful with the data collection," or "don't fudge the data results." Well, she certainly got even with their precious data when it all went up in flames. Alma gulped at her water, feeling feverish at the memory of the fire. She hoped Mrs. Hamieh would tell the story of Beatriz de Robles right away before she ran out of excuses to be there. It was sweet Claire who spoke up first, always so concerned with the privacy of her clients.

▨ ▨ ▨

"I would love to hear the story," said Claire. "But I am here to give Mrs. Hamieh a massage, and Alma just helped me bring in the massage table, so I think she is ready to leave…"

Claire was being paid and didn't want to waste her client's time or money. Sweet and ethical. Alma could barely stand it. Fortunately, Fatima remained clueless, did not read Mrs. Hamieh's reluctance to tell the tale, and said, "Claire, if you

have the time to stay, Mrs. Hamieh and I have the whole afternoon free, don't we?"

"Indeed we do," said Mrs. Hamieh. "The dream about
Beatriz de Robles popped up when I was wide awake after
a massage. I normally don't like to discuss such intense memories. I mean dreams. Oh, what's the difference? But I think it is
appropriate for me to talk about Beatriz de Robles because
it advocates being a virtuous person. One should never recount
a bad dream or a nightmare, you know."

Claire did not want to upset Mrs. Hamieh's happy mood.
She had an awful feeling about the coincidence between her
grandmother's name and Mrs. Hamieh's wide-awake dream.
And what was a wide-awake dream? A doctor might dismiss it as
a fantasy, a delusion, or worse, a hallucination. Claire's grandmother often talked about her ancestors in the present tense as
if they were in the same room. These were the types of cultural
idiosyncrasies that made Claire cringe around her All-American
friends. During a recent get-together with some girlfriends at her
house in Echo Park, her grandmother had walked into the
hillside patio and said, "Isn't it just like my great-great-grandmother to come by and visit right now? She loves a good chat
with girlfriends."

Claire's girlfriends reacted with pity—it was obvious Verito
was going bonkers. Anything unexplainable from an old
woman's mouth was dementia, Alzheimer's, or a "senior
moment." What would have been worse was if Claire had admit-
ted to them that she had also felt the warm presence and detected the faint violet scent of her maternal ancestor from 1855.
Rather than explain this phenomenon, she went along with all
the sighs of sorrow from her girlfriends and their nods of understanding. Claire recognized that Mrs. Hamieh had the same
ancient Mediterranean sensibility to the unknown peregrinations
of the souls of the departed, so Claire accepted the fact that
Mrs. Hamieh was going to tell her the inevitable.

⊠ ⊠ ⊠

Mrs. Hamieh would have liked to chase the rodent sitting in her kitchen out of the house, but her own proper upbringing would not allow her to do so. She tried to analyze the lesson that she was being taught at that instant; and there was a lesson, of that she was certain. She designed a mental diagram of all the possibilities being presented to her that moment in her own kitchen. In the first column, there was the unwanted dangerous woman acting like a righteous church mouse. On the second column, there was the angelic and doleful young woman who was there to help her feel vibrant again. Crossing the diagram at a pure right angle was the gold-toothed, former Zapatista rebel turned culinary genius who had become not only her sous-chef but her goddaughter. Finally, on the plane above the intangible diagram floated the blissful oil whose properties had resurrected dreams of an ancient world.

Mrs. Hamieh had to proceed with telling the tale, and like Claire's warm massage oil, she would let the tale penetrate whatever pore it could find. She would let her story take its own course. It would go in and out of dead-end alleys and seemingly narrow paths leading to luxurious *riads*. She would turn the rusty hand knocker in the shape of a hand and step into the safety of the *riad* and climb its multicolored, geometric, tile steps where she would have a wide vista of the *medina*. She would tell her tale with all the details so that her listeners could mine for their own bejeweled memory.

Finally, Mrs. Hamieh would rest her eyes on the massive stork nests at the highest towers of Marrakech. Her recent dreams had already foretold the direction she would take for herself, but it would be up to her three listeners to interpret this dream any way they chose. They would see for themselves if the storks were flocking together or if they scattered. Then each woman would know in her own heart and mind, in her own bones, what was good and what was evil.

Claire said, "Mrs. Hamieh, I have two hours before my next appointment, so I would love to listen to your dream."

▣ ▣ ▣

Mrs. Hamieh suddenly looked fatigued and sat down on her down-filled velvet divan. Her mien was such a departure from the joyous pixie who had greeted them at the door. Claire wondered if she was merely curious because of the mention of her grandmother's name. Mrs. Hamieh began her story and said, "I knew Beatriz de Robles many, many years ago—"

Claire asked, "Did you meet grandma in Ecuador?"

Fatima interjected, "It is better if you allow Mrs. Hamieh to tell the entire story without interrupting her. That is how I finally found out that one of her dreams had predicted I would come to work with her. Mrs. Hamieh dreamt of someone giving her a mother-of-pearl comb with the number fifteen on it. At that time I was still up in San Cristóbal de las Casas, you know it is in the highlands of Chiapas, Mexico. I was carrying my machete and wearing a mask. My job was to stop the traffic on the highway leading into our village and then to hand out our written communiqué so that foreign tourists would tell the world about our plight. I never thought that I would end up getting trained as a chef in Los Angeles, but Mrs. Hamieh saw it all in her dream. The mother-of-pearl gift meant that she would get a servant, and the number fifteen meant that justice would be restored. She says I am her helper, not a servant, and she's training me as a chef and now great things will come my way. Listen to her dreams with your ears and your eyes and your heart. And please eat, because the sumptuous taste of our food will transport you to her dream world."

As if she were in a hypnotic trance, Mrs. Hamieh lounged on her emerald divan momentarily immobile, and then she spoke softly and deliberately. "I knew Beatriz de Robles during the sorrowful times. The Spanish Inquisition had expelled all the Jews, Muslims, and others they deemed heretics from their shores, but many of us children stayed behind in Seville, or we hid in the mountains and caves with other Moriscos. This is what they called us: Moriscos. We felt Spanish, we sang such beautiful songs in Castilian, but we also danced in the Morisco style at our *zambras* and *leilas* music festivals. You liked how I danced, didn't you?"

All three women nodded, yes. Mrs. Hamieh continued speaking. "We have been famous dancers since the time of our Phoenician ancestors who inhabited the south of Iberia in 1104 BC. Just think how long ago that was? The fortunes of Gadir, that's what Cádiz was called then, have swelled and recessed with the trade routes of the Mediterranean. We were conquered by the Romans, the Visigoths, the Moors, and Alfonso X of Castile, but the one constant that withstood the test of time has been the acclaim of the female dancers of Cádiz. Did you know that the decadent Romans dared to call us the wanton dancers from Gades, their name for our city, for our excellent undulating movements and the melodic strikes of the finger cymbals? They judged us harshly, but they couldn't live without our dancers. They even abducted the most prestigious dancer of that era, Telethusa. One day she was dancing in the cool breezes of her Cádiz home and the next she was thrust into the swelter of Rome. Can't you just imagine the grief of that lonely abducted girl?"

Fatima handed Mrs. Hamieh a cup of mint tea. Mrs. Hamieh had so much more to get off her chest. She said, "Let me get back to the last time I saw Beatriz de Robles."

Claire asked her, "Mrs. Hamieh, what era are you talking about now?"

Mrs. Hamieh plowed on. She said, "Over 300 children were left in a warehouse in Seville on December 10, 1609 while our parents were forced to board the ships owned by Basque sailors who took them and dumped them on the shores of Berbery. Can you imagine on that day alone 18,000 Moriscos left our cherished Al-Andalus? Altogether over 300,000 Moriscos left during the expulsion, but we were no more welcome on the Berbery Coast than on our own land: Spain. Can you believe that some Moriscos even took the treacherous journey back and snuck into Spain? Our love for our homeland was so great. You know we tended the land and grew such divine pomegranates, oranges, and figs in Spain. The entire mulberry tree and silk worm production was our specialty. Fatima, be a dear and pass the savory fig *amuse bouche* to our guests." Fatima did as she was told and even added her own flourish by placing a linen napkin on her left forearm.

Mrs. Hamieh took a very, very long and tragic Moorish sigh and continued. "Anyway, Beatriz thought her parents had received exemption by royal dispensation to stay in Spain, but this was simply not the case. Poor Beatriz kept on looking for them until the brotherhood of the *Cofradía de los Niños Perdidos* transferred us to the convent of the Sweet Name of Jesus in Seville. I never looked for my parents because I myself had closed their lifeless eyes when they attacked our Moorish quarter. So I didn't hang on to any false hopes. In many ways, I was the lucky one for I knew I would never see my parents again."

Mrs. Hamieh downed her second cup of mint tea. She said, "When we were in the convent we came to realize that this was established as a convent for prostitutes. As little girls we played with the head coverings of the older girls because they had a shiny tinsel attachment to them. How could we have known that this was how the prostitutes identified themselves? Oh, my dears, the things we witnessed were just too horrific. The Spanish had massacred the Moriscos in Alpujarra near Granada in 1570, so I was always ready for my feet to feel the pyres of the Holy Office, not because I had done anything wrong, but simply because I was a Morisca. In time, Beatriz and I felt Christian enough, and we enjoyed the hymns and prayers. We survived our childhood."

Claire tactfully inquired, "So, Mrs. Hamieh, in your *dreams* the last time you saw Beatriz de Robles was in 1609?" She emphasized the word dreams so Mrs. Hamieh would calm down and realize that she was recounting just that: a dream.

"No, precious girl. I last saw her as the Inquisition paraded her down the otherwise beautiful streets of Seville in the auto de fe in 1623. Oh, how the Holy Office kept such an eye on us Moriscos. By then we were only 12,000 left. All of us were Christians by then, and believe me, we toed the line. They called us New Christians, and they wanted to make sure we would never revert. They had the most barbaric tortures for anyone accused of heresy."

Fatima exclaimed, "You don't have to tell me about torture. The massacre I witnessed as a young girl Chiapas in 1997 still haunts me!"

Mrs. Hamieh sat up and said, "Fatima, you never have to worry about that ever again. You are in your home now, and isn't it warm and welcoming? Even our enemies might feel at ease here."

Alma had tuned out Mrs. Hamieh's blather about 1609 and the Inquisition. She had used this time to devise a plan to move the Matisse painting, several carpets, and the mantel clock out of this house in five minutes flat. She had also been counting her liquidation assets from the other affluent homes, and she had come to the conclusion that she had to enlist Soledad's help so that together they could expedite this transaction. She smiled at Mrs. Hamieh as if she were looking at an old zoo animal on its last leg.

Mrs. Hamieh smiled back but the corners of her wrinkled little eyes did not light up, they scowled. She said, "It was so painful to watch Beatriz de Robles, who by then was a woman in her twenties, dragged down the street. She had married an Old Christian, yet she was accused of illuminism. Apparently, Beatriz claimed special religious enlightenment. She showed an overwhelming amount of emotion during Holy Communion, and she claimed that God loved her and favored her. At first, they humbled her by having her serve in a hospital for women. Years later, I heard they had burned her at the stake."

Mrs. Hamieh paused for a few seconds and finally said, "They said that Beatriz de Robles, like so many Moriscas, knew all about healing and love potions and predicting the future. She was an excellent cook, as were the many Moriscas who made a living by peddling food in Triana and the other crowded neighborhoods of Seville. The docks overflowed with men wanting to make their fortune in Peru and Nueva España. Why there were even women dressed as men who made the voyages as sailors! They were called *mujer baronil.* Can you imagine there were even dramas and poems praising these manly women? Beatriz was not one of them. She was known as *la mare,* which means mother in the *Gitano caló* dialect of the Gypsies, for she doled out maternal love along with her cures and ointments to the Gypsies who populated the busy docks along the Guadalquivir River. The *gitano* singers then as now will sing ferociously from the seed of their bones, so you can envision the rawness of their vocal chords at the end of a long night of singing! When Beatriz applied her poultices and ointments to the ailing Gypsies she absorbed a residue of the *duende* still throbbing in their bodies, and it filled her heart with fervor."

Hearing the word *duende*, Alma stopped counting her future treasures and paid attention. She was up to a gross total of 1.65 million dollars, but by the time she would have to split it with the fencers and the carjackers, and Soledad, maybe she would only net 20%. In the Amazon she could live on $330,000; she could be the director of her own research lab. But now even ditzy Mrs. Hamieh was referring to *duende,* and it appeared that her story had ended with the *duende* and fervor. The meaning of both wee words stumped Alma so she was forced to jump into the conversation before they asked her to leave.

"What an arresting story you've just recounted, Mrs. Hamieh," Alma said. "I only wish that I had interviewed you as an unparalleled research subject into my pioneer work on ancestral memory. Claire, do you remember you asked me for my expertise on involuntary autobiographical memories?"

Claire nodded yes and looked down at her watch. She noticed that Mrs. Hamieh's body was slumped as if in pain and anxiety, and Claire wanted to begin the massage. Mrs. Hamieh's blood pressure could peak unexpectedly.

Alma continued, "Well, after my work on that type of memory recollection, I received federal funding to research ancestral memories. Quite simply put and very apropos to Mrs. Hamieh's story, the ancestral memories theory postulates that our DNA is encoded with specific memories from the experiences of our ancestors. I would say that Mrs. Hamieh has just demonstrated the extent of the details that one can unintentionally remember going back many, many generations. In particular, our research indicated that mature subjects, those past the age of seventy, recalled the most vivid ancestral memories. Again, congratulations, Mrs. Hamieh."

All the reminiscing about the Inquisition's malevolence exhausted Mrs. Hamieh and she appeared to have dozed off on her divan. She had only told them a fraction of the horrors the

Moriscos had endured at the hands of the Inquisition and the crown in their precious Spain. She didn't have the heart to tell them that the crown paid a bounty for the capture of youngsters who were then sold as slaves or prostitutes for the brothels. She couldn't utter the pain and shame of her fellow cave dwellers who had been branded on the face so that everyone would recognize them as Moriscas.

Alma decided to summarize her theory quickly and get the hell out of the house. She had just come up with a stroke of genius to jump start her plan. She delivered her impromptu mini-lecture at full tilt, using impressive jargon. She said, "When one considers that involuntary autobiographical memories occur after receiving spontaneous sensory triggers and that most seniors recall events from their early adulthood, known as the reminiscence bump, then it is reasonable to assume that massage therapy facilitates those triggers penetrating deep into the cerebello-frontal pathways. Therefore, Claire, your clients have been retrieving remnant DNA memories from their long, long ago relatives. Keep in mind though, that my research on ancestral memory invalidates previous research labels or obsolete terminology such as *déja vu*, the uncanny, cryptomnesia, or personal and collective unconscious. Quite the opposite, what I have theorized and Mrs. Hamieh has clearly exemplified is that there exists a definitive genetic transmission of vast memory relics."

Neither Fatima nor Claire was particularly astounded by this supposedly new theory. In their cultures their deceased relatives and the specific details of their lives continued to be passed down from generation to generation. They didn't need scientific approval of such a genetic memory. They just assumed that in time science would catch up and label what others had already accepted as a universal phenomenon. The terms Alma used to explain her ancestral memory theory were confusing to the women, but in their cultures their ancestors' lives were often retold until present-day relatives felt they had known a great-great-grandmother's predilection for singing a particular hymn or her favorite dog's name from 1798 or even earlier. These things were not mind-boggling behavior. Naturally, elderly people recalled more ancient details because they had lived longer and had acquired the wisdom to interpret their memories and dreams. They were more perceptive and receptive to the mysteries of the human mind.

❖ ❖ ❖

Wisdom is what Claire's grandmother displayed with intensity as she listened and held the hands of the people who came to her peaceful Echo Park home for healing and empathy. Her grandmother had already explained to Claire the phenomenon that Alma called "ancestral memory." Grandma said it was a glimmer or sometimes a crimson streak of a shadow flowing from the miniscule spaces of the marrow of her rickety bones to every recess of her being.

"Can it happen to me? What if I don't like what my ancestors want me to recall?" Claire had asked grandma.

"Mi hijita, you don't have to worry about their shadows surging through your médula for you are still too young. The residue of our ancestors doesn't pulsate in our bodies until we are much older or until our soul has quaked with deep sorrow."

Claire's soul had been devastated after Phil's death just as Fatima's vital force was nearly extinguished by the waterfalls near the road she and her comrades blockaded regularly. Both women were not yet thirty, but through their intense grieving the traces of their ancestral memories had begun to flutter in their marrow.

For Fatima, the ripple in her médula began the day the bus driver was sick and tired of being stopped by rebels on his way up and down the road to San Cristobal de las Casas. He swerved to outmaneuver the masked woman stopping the bus with her machete. The bus driver and dozens of lives came to an end as their screams blended with the crashing sound of the nearby waterfalls. Mayahuel ran down the road away from the drowning screams. Her gold-capped teeth bit her lower lip, which had wanted to open up and cry out. Mayahuel tore off her mask and tossed it along with the machete into the rapids. As she ran away from the rushing river, the trail of paper communiqués flew by her like a tight flock of storks.

Mayahuel eventually divulged her anguished guilt to Mrs. Hamieh. In time, in the warmth of her kitchen, with the resuscitating sounds of Gnawi music playing while she learned the culinary arts, Mayahuel healed. One morning Mrs. Hamieh told her that in her dream Mayahuel should now be called Fatima, a name revered in both the Arab and Hispanic world.

◻ ◻ ◻

Both Claire and Fatima leaned over to see if Mrs. Hamieh was resting her eyes or if she had fallen asleep. Her well-being was what each woman cared for the most at that moment. Alma noticed their sincere gesture of concern for the old biddy. To Alma, she seemed like a lazy old bat that had fallen asleep upside down after her bogus story. Albeit the story had given Alma the hook she needed to get the wealthy seniors to willingly loosen their purse strings. Alma was itching to put her plan into action, yet she wanted to impress the other women with her perceptive and polite manners. She might need to pick their brains and their pockets in the near future. Alma said, "It's been a real pleasure spending time with you this morning. The food was truly inspirational, and I will never forget Mrs. Hamieh's story." Alma scampered to the door; she wanted to enlist

Soledad's help with her plan before Dr. Nunez finished reading his large print book.

Mrs. Hamieh opened her eyes and asked, "Do tell me, Dr. Ruiz, when you were in Marrakech, did you see any bird nests?"

Alma answered nonchalantly, "It was so many years ago, but I do recall that there were quite a few large stork nests made of sticks. They dotted the historical towers; the people had even built platforms for the stork nests. In fact, I was so touched by the foresight of the veterinary care in this venerable city since it even had a stork hospital going back many, many generations. The brass door of the hospital was quite notable in a city with the most impressive doors in the world. Why do you ask?"

Mrs. Hamieh thought that maybe she had judged Alma unfairly. Surely anyone who would remember such a detail as the brilliant brass door of the stork hospital could not be the evil mouse from her dream. Nonetheless, Mrs. Hamieh asked the critical question, "Alma, did you see the storks flocking together, or were they apart?"

Alma smiled her crooked and disingenuous smile and said, "Why they were like one big happy family flocking together! They are such large white birds, perhaps four feet tall, with pure white bodies and only the tips of their wings are black. Flying together they looked like a like puffy white cloud. Thank you for your hospitality, but I must return to my data collection."

Claire was already up and moving the massage table for Mrs. Hamieh. Fatima's golden mouth clenched. Her neck muscles tensed as she made eye contact with Mrs. Hamieh, who in turn gave her their silent sign. If the storks had been flying in a scattered formation then it would augur good news. It would mean that an absent family member would be coming back home. Seeing a stork eat a mouse would have been a compelling sign also. Alas, both women understood the adverse significance of storks flocking together. It meant that thieves and enemies were in their midst.

Fatima rushed to get Mrs. Hamieh and herself a cup of mint tea. She knew Mrs. Hamieh was as thirsty as she since Alma's covetous evil eye, her *mal ojo*, had started to dehydrate them both. Mrs. Hamieh had also noticed Alma's furtive glances at her Matisse painting, at her heirloom carpets, even at Fatima's devotion to her. Alma had repeatedly cast the evil eye on both women. Her desire to cause them harm emanated from her droopy eye to Mrs. Hamieh's entire house.

Fatima sat next to Mrs. Hamieh on the divan and they both sipped their tea without saying a word. They heard Claire's angelic voice call out, "Fatima, can you escort Mrs. Hamieh for her massage in the master bedroom? I just warmed her massage oil, doesn't it smell wonderful?

Fatima said, "Mrs. Hamieh, do you mind if I apply a few drops of the oil on my hands, I think Alma's *mal ojo* was directed at my hands; they are so dry."

Mrs. Hamieh lifted her own wrinkled right hand, palm up, and with her thumb and pinkie slightly extended. This was the same gesture she had made when Alma spoke of the storks in Marrakech. Fatimah mirrored Mrs. Hamieh's hand gesture with her own coppery right hand. The women smiled smugly knowing that their matching tattoos of a miniscule open eye in the center of their respective right palms would protect them. They sipped the last of the mint tea and placed their permanently tattooed amulets on each other's loving hearts.

Los Feliz
April 27, 2011

The excitement of finally putting together a concrete plan of action made Alma's face twitch spasmodically. She flew out of Mrs. Hamieh's house through the heavy Moroccan door and back to the reality of Los Feliz like a bat out of hell. She had to force herself to slow down and walk at a normal pace to Dr. Nunez and Soledad's house a couple of blocks away. She had ridden with Claire and didn't have her broken-down car with her. By the time Alma got to Dr. Nunez's side yard, Soledad was agitated and smoking a cigarette in her bathrobe. She tapped her ashes and said, "For someone with killer news you move like a garden snail. I'm going to get Octavio to flatten you. You should see the way he stomps on the snails." She demonstrated with one bare foot, the toenails painted metallic purple. "He shows no mercy. What's so important that you made me step out of my whirlpool bath?"

"You take a bath in the middle of the day?" asked Alma, incredulous.

"Hell yeah! I take a bath in the middle of the day. I also swim naked in the pool at midnight. Old Dr. Nunez had the whirlpool installed for his hundreds of aches and pains then decided he didn't like it. The jets aren't soft enough like Claire's hands. He'd rather have his sweetheart Claire. Anyway, that's what I read in his poem. He wrote: *mi amada*, so I asked Yolanda what this means and she said: my beloved. Claire's become the apple of his foggy little eye. What a crock!"

Soledad was getting loud and Alma was afraid she was going to draw attention. She tried to signal her to lower her voice, but this seemed to only make Soledad louder. Alma was thinking she would have to be careful with this one. Soledad was in many ways like a child. She wanted to have her way. She enjoyed using Dr. Nunez's toys for herself. And if given an order she was likely to do the opposite just to prove she could. "And get this," yelled Soledad. "The other day after Claire's stinky oil massage he refused a shower. He told me that he dreads getting into water ever since he abandoned his mermaid in Spain." Soledad slapped Alma on the back and let out a gut-splitting laugh. Alma jumped in while she could, both to quiet her conspirator, and to finally get some useful information about what the old man was dreaming about. It was Alma's first rule as a world-class liar. The more detailed the lie, the more people were willing to believe it.

"What did he say about the mermaid? How did he describe her?" asked Alma.

Soledad hee-hawed relentlessly. There was no shutting this woman up. Alma was beginning to reconsider involving Soledad. She had the potential to ruin everything if she continued to think this was a game. Alma didn't join Soledad in her laughter, she gave her the most serious expression her crooked face was capable of making. It finally made Soledad fall quiet.

Soledad took a drag on her cigarette and asked, "Have you been shrooming with Octavio or what? Didn't you hear what I just said? The man is losing it. He's talking as if he really knew a mermaid; as if he had been in love with an m-e-r-m-a-i-d! Doesn't that smell fishy to you?" Soledad broke up again.

Alma was losing her patience, but she needed Soledad's help. She would have to approach Soledad on her own terms. Soledad was not a woman who could be controlled, not because of some inner strength she probably thought she had, but simply because she was a big mouth. "Of course, you're so right, Soledad," Alma said. "The notion of an accurate memory about a real mermaid is preposterous. But that's exactly where we have the captivating possibility to make the money we both desperately need." That got Soledad's attention. "And deserve," she added for good measure.

"You may be stoned, but you're making perfect sense," Soledad said. "Let's hear it and make it quick before Dr. Nunez calls for me."

Alma took Soledad by the arm to a corner of the yard. She lowered her voice to a more appropriate register and said, "There is obviously something in Claire's massage oil and her massage techniques that is provoking these elderly people to have some astonishingly graphic memories."

"Like the stupid mermaid," said Soledad.

"Yes, which they want to keep reliving. That is why Dr. Nunez, Judge Carrera and Mrs. Dougherty, and even La Linda, can't wait to have another massage by Claire. For all we know, Claire might be drugging them, right?"

Soledad looked at Alma like she was crazy. "Are you kidding?" she asked. "That goody-two-shoe wouldn't hurt a fly."

"How can you be so sure?" asked Alma.

"She's always rambling about how her grandmother brought her back to life after her fiancé died, and how wise the elderly are. She actually loves these old farts," said Soledad.

Alma continued pulling Soledad gently by the arm around the yard. She kept physical contact and noticed Soledad had finally lowered her own voice to match the register of Alma's. For this to work, Soledad had to be able to see everyone but Alma as an enemy or at the very least an obstacle.

Soledad whispered, "Love sucks, and I'm sick of hearing about it. Oh, what the hell, at least Claire had a fiancé who loved her."

Jackpot. Jealousy of Claire was the way to Soledad's loyalty.

"What about you and me?" continued Soledad. "Have we ever had anybody love us? Don't answer that, I know you're going to lie to me. What we want now is to buy a hunk, a hunk of burning love, am I right? Aren't I? And mine's going to be mighty fine."

What a simpleton, thought Alma. Instead she said, "You're absolutely right. Let me get to the point of how we're going to finally get what we want. I told Claire that the old farts are reliving their ancestors' memories. Each one is recalling an incident from the past that couldn't possibly have happened to them personally, yet they feel it with the same intensity as a firsthand experience. Each senior who came into contact with the oil described a memory in detail to Claire and to their companions."

"We are only caregivers, not companions, believe me," said Soledad. Then she started yelling again, "Show me the money, Alma! Get to the point. You're boring me to pieces."

A cranky old voice interrupted from inside the house. "Is that you out there, Soledad? Come in here now. I want to read this to you," snapped Dr. Nunez.

Great, thought Alma. The idiot's yelling finally got the attention of the old man. She would have to think about ways to make Soledad be quiet when she needed it. Alma would not go to all this trouble just to have a big mouth ruin it at the end.

Soledad fumed at the constant attention Dr. Nunez required. She said in her most patient and docile voice, "I'm picking a nice head of lettuce for you, big boss; I'll be right there in a couple of minutes." She whispered in Alma's ear, "He's blind as a bat, but his hearing is remarkable. Now you have to finish telling me the plan quickly."

"Okay, here's what I propose. We find out all the specifics about each memory the senior is having. We already have a good idea: Judge Carrera wants to breastfeed a baby."

"Dumb cow," said Soledad.

Alma was losing her patience with a different dumb cow. She summarized quickly. "Let's start with Mrs. Dougherty. She'll be first. You all seem to think she is easygoing and generous. I know you sometimes keep her company while Yolanda goes to visit her sister downtown, so be sure to contact Yolanda today and offer to watch over Mrs. D while she goes to visit her sister and her baby niece. Got that?"

"Don't piss me off, Alma. Don't talk to me like I'm a moron," Soledad snapped back.

Alma felt like setting Soledad's long hair and equally long phony lashes on fire. Instead she demurely answered, "I apologize, Soledad. It's just that our plan is a good one, but we have to move quickly. Let me continue, ok? Dr. Nunez has known Mrs. Dougherty forever so he'll let you out of the house if you say you're going to go help her. I will explain to Mrs. Dougherty how we can help her relive her memory."

"And you think she's just going to believe you? You think everyone but you is stupid."

"I'll tell her that it involves genealogical research and a DNA cheek swab test to confirm that indeed her memory is accurate. The more medical and scientific we make it, the better our chances. We'll approach each senior with the same respect since we don't want them to think we're deliberately confusing them or they're getting senile or that we are taking advantage of them."

Soledad laughed. "No, we wouldn't want the old farts to think we are taking advantage!"

Alma continued. "We want them to believe they can re-experience their blissful memory. As soon as we see a glimmer of hope in their eyes, we tell them the price of their ancestral memory. Got it?"

"So we give them memories, so what? And how are we going to get them to dish out the dough, genius?" asked Soledad.

"As I said, let's start with Mrs. Dougherty. Her little romantic escapade near her fireplace should be easy to reenact. We won't mention money at all to her; we'll do the first reenactment for free. Once she falls in love again, she'll gladly pay for another love session."

Soledad snorted and said, "Love session? You sound like an idiot. Why don't you call it what it is, Alma? Mrs. Dougherty wants hot sex because she never had any, duh! As if she's alone in that. So who do you think is willing to do an old lady?" Soledad made a face like she smelled something bad.

"You're not the only one who knows people in the porn business. This is L.A., you can buy an actor for nothing. Can you advance me a few hundred dollars to jumpstart this project?" asked Alma.

"Hell no! You're the supposed Ph.D., you figure it out," said Soledad.

Dr. Nunez called out, "Soledad, come back inside, I can't see where I left my notebook," only this time his voice wasn't dictatorial. It quivered with a sadness that Alma picked up on immediately. She was like a predator at a water hole pricking up her ears, sensing weakness.

Alma said, "Soledad, why don't you and I go inside and let me talk to Dr. Nunez while you try to figure out where he hides the key to the safe closet? Leave it to me; I know how to declaw an old cat like him."

Soledad smirked and said, "Tell you what, Alma. If you get the old cat to buy your story, I'll advance you the $500."

After Soledad introduced Alma to Dr. Nunez, she left the library. Alma approached Dr. Nunez very softly and meekly. "Dr. Nunez, may I be of some assistance to you, sir? Is this the notebook that you were looking for?"

Dr. Nunez yanked it from her hand, turned too quickly and lost his balance. Alma was instantly by his side propping him up. She said, "I often lose my equilibrium because I am still suffering from the effects of Bell's palsy. It sure is difficult adjusting to changes in life, but at least you have your notebook of poetry."

"How do you know it's a poetry notebook?" demanded Dr. Nunez.

"It seemed like I saw some stanzas, but I'm probably wrong and just projecting my own desire to be a better poet. I've never told anyone this before, but you seem like such a learned doctor. You don't look like the type to judge. I've started writing poetry again. It has helped me remember so much. In fact, through my poetry I've managed to recover some memories from my past. I'm sorry, this must all seem like gibberish to you. I, I didn't mean to bother you. It's been a pleasure—"

Doctor Nunez clutched his notebook to his chest as Alma helped him sit in his leather executive chair. He rubbed his eyes a few times. He said, "You don't have to go. I haven't talked to anyone about poetry. I tried to with Soledad, but she's not very patient. What kind of poetry do you like?"

Alma's face paled. She was dazed at her lack of memory about poetry. She had more or less liked it in college, but now that she needed to recall any fact about poetry her mind went blank. She was relieved that Dr. Nunez couldn't see her dumbfounded expression. She said, "I enjoyed a wide range of poetry, from the Sufi poets to contemporary poets, but frankly, I would love to hear which poems you like. I think that with your professional background and with the wisdom you obviously have, I could learn so much from you."

Dr. Nunez was not usually susceptible to flattery, but something about Alma's sweet and melodic voice disarmed him. Plus, when he had almost fallen and leaned on her he noticed that she was a trim and petite woman, too. He always had an eye for slightly framed women. He said, "Well, what do I know? I worked my tail off in my medical practice trying to help fat-ass people lose weight for decades, and you know what? There's even more fatties today than ever. It's hopeless! But I feel a bit optimistic when I write poetry. I almost feel that deep inside I was meant to be a poet, not a doctor, does that make sense?"

Alma's mind was racing. She had to extract a great deal of information from this not so tough old cat, after all. She couldn't just jump in and say: tell me about your dreamy mermaid. She had to win him over. "I would think that your poetry is about the ocean and adventure?" she said. "And please excuse me for being a bit forward, since you are such a handsome man perhaps you write poetry about a lost love in your life? I'm just taking a wild guess."

Dr. Nunez laughed like the old flirt he used to be. Before all the sexual harassment lawsuits derailed his prowling, he had been accustomed to getting his way with the female employees in his clinic. These flings never meant anything to him other than recreational sex. He lost both wives due to his philandering, and he didn't miss them at all. In time he lost interest in his bariatric practice, his sex life, and any future romance.

Once Soledad came to keep him company, she had tried to seduce him but the fire inside him had died. By then he found that he preferred the therapeutic massages he got from Claire. Instead of sexual longings, he craved a nostalgic love he felt he had lost somewhere in time.

Dr. Nunez answered Alma with a question of his own. "When you write your poetry do you ever feel that you're writing it for someone from long ago?"

"That's amazing," said Alma. "I've never met anyone who felt as I do." She was ready to reel him in. "Please don't think of me as a silly fool, but when I write my poetry I sometimes feel that I am sending a message to a...oh, you're going to think I'm crazy, but I feel that my poetry is being heard or felt by a centaur. There, I said it. Please don't laugh, Dr. Nunez."

"It's definitely a ludicrous idea, but I've heard weirder ones," said Dr. Nunez.

Alma had misjudged his vulnerability to poetry and to his mermaid. She backtracked and said, "Well, of course I didn't really mean a *literal* centaur. I was referring to the qualities of masculinity and power and passion. Don't you find that your poetry addresses the quintessential qualities of a woman?"

"Now you're making sense. Would you care to read my poetry and give me your frank opinion?"

"I would love to read your poetry," Alma said. "May I ask you a couple of questions?"

Dr. Nunez handed her his notebook and said, "Sure, why not."

Since Dr. Nunez had let his guard down, Alma pressed the advantage. She asked, "Do you find that you write with acute sensibility immediately after Claire's massage?"

Dr. Nunez nodded and said, "Yes, you could say that."

Alma pressed further. She said, "Do you think it's possible that in your relaxed state, after Claire's massage, you can harness memories that have been locked away?"

"Are you going to read my poetry or not?" demanded Dr. Nunez.

"Oh, well yes, Dr. Nunez, of course."

Since he couldn't see far enough to detect what page she was reading, Alma scanned the notebook looking for the word "mermaid," but to no avail. She made pleasant comments such as: "this is marvelous," "you're so perceptive," and "this is so touching that it breaks my heart." On her second go-round with the notebook she found the word *amante,* and remembered this meant lover. Then she saw the six-letter word *sirena*, and recalled its English translation. She read and re-read that heartfelt poem about the *sirena* and smiled confidently at the big blind fish caught in her net.

Soledad walked back into the library with a lunch tray for Dr. Nunez. She announced, "I know how much you like Mrs. Dougherty, and she needs Alma and I to help Yolanda bring down some big boxes from her attic. It will only take around one hour. I know you're the big boss, but you don't mind helping little Mrs. Dougherty, do you? I'll be taking your car, okay?"

Dr. Nunez scowled and said, "Can't Alma stay? She reads better than you."

Alma quickly jumped into the conversation. "I'll be back later and would love to keep reading this lyrical poetry. I promise."

🔲 🔲 🔲

On the way to Mrs. Dougherty's house, Alma asked Soledad about the whereabouts of the key to the safe closet. Soledad said,

"Do I look like I fell off the turnip truck or what? Why would I tell you where the key is? So you can knock me off and go after the gold bars yourself?"

"How do you know they're gold bars if you haven't ever opened his safe?" asked Alma.

"I know everything about that old grouch, but I'm still waiting for you to show me the money first. Then, I might help out," said Soledad.

"If you happen to take a look at the gold bars, make sure that you read the hallmarks and the certification, and obviously count the number of bars in the safe," Alma said. "Did the certification have the .99–"

"You mean were the bars composed of four nines, the purest gold bullion available?" Soledad cut in. "You're not dealing with a country bumpkin, Alma. I know my shit. Anyway, we're almost at Mrs. Dougherty's house. What do you want me to say?"

"I've met Mrs. Dougherty before. All you need to do is keep Yolanda out of the way. I'll take care of the rest."

Yolanda and Mrs. Dougherty were in the rose garden when the women arrived. Soledad claimed that Dr. Nunez needed to borrow the encyclopedia volumes for the letters I, B, and S and offered to help Yolanda look for them.

Alma concentrated on Mrs. Dougherty. "Did you recently have a massage from Claire?"

"Oh, yes, Dr. Ruiz. I'm in seventh heaven."

Alma said, "As a holistic doctor, that's music to my ears. My last patient, whose name I would never, ever divulge, was on cloud nine after her massage from Claire. She revealed to me that she was having the most intense recollections. They were of a very private nature, so I'm afraid I cannot give you details.

Suffice it to say that after she confided in me, I was able to facilitate the resurgence of her memories at will."

Mrs. Dougherty flushed face turned even redder. "Are you saying that your patient was actually able to relive her memories?"

"Why of course, Mrs. Dougherty. You mean you didn't know that memory retrieval is my *forté* in the holistic health field? You may have heard of my research into ancestral memory theory. Well, I was recruited from my research lab deep in the Amazon jungle to come back to Los Angeles to apply my methods on healthy adults such as you. The memory retrieval method is very simple, actually."

"That's so interesting," said Mrs. Dougherty. Alma noted that she was clearly trying not to look too interested. "How does it work?"

"Well, since you ask, I design a personalized memory reawakening program for each of my clients. It begins with the consumption of a tasty 100% natural drink, and then I create the specific environment for the memory. Yes, all my patients have been, let us say, *ecstatic* once their memories have come to life."

Mrs. Dougherty seemed elated; her breathing turned to panting and it seemed she wanted to say something, but simply couldn't. Alma knew that she had passed Mrs. Dougherty's sniff test so she went for the jugular. She asked, "May I please hold your hands? I believe that I can apply my holistic methods to your memory, as well. Let me see."

Alma caused their joined hands to vibrate slightly. She proceeded to whistle in the manner of the shaman in Cusco. She didn't pucker her lips; she protruded her lower jaw and blew air through the gap between her upper and lower teeth. It created an eerie and unfamiliar sound, like a plaintive song from bygone times. When she saw Mrs. Dougherty close her eyes and her lips quiver, she whispered to her, "Let me present you with a gift from ancient times; times when we all felt safe surrounded by the sturdy walls of our warm caves. Inside the cave we felt the intense warmth with our loved ones, aren't I right, Mrs. Dougherty? May I come by tonight and help you as I have helped others? There is no fee whatsoever, but we cannot share this with anyone else because I can only help the enlightened few, such as yourself; those who are receptive to the passions of life. Your elation is my reward."

Soledad threw the three leather-bound volumes of the encyclopedia in the back seat of the car. She asked, "Did you get anything out of the old lady?"

"No, that wasn't the objective," said Alma. "I just had to entice her with the possibility of bliss. Tonight I will satisfy her desires—"

"Whoa!" Soledad said. "That's totally in bad taste. You're going to do the old hag?"

Alma hissed right back. "Don't be so blind. I'm going to get a guy I know from the porn business, but you have to advance me $500 so I can pay him. Mrs. Dougherty will be begging us for more and that is when we ask for the big bucks. How much money do you have on you?"

"I'll let you know after you convince Judge Carrera into believing your ancestral bull. Let's make a bet: If she buys your story, then I'll lend you the cash. If she throws you out, then you have to give me a couple of bags of your mushrooms. Better yet, get the real lively ones that Octavio grows in either Mrs. Dougherty's yard or behind La Linda's fancy guesthouse. We're almost at the Judge's house now. What now, Sherlock?"

⊠ ⊠ ⊠

Upon arriving at Judge Carrera's house Alma found out that Claire was not scheduled to arrive until 4 P.M. Instead of being in a daydreaming state, the Judge looked alert and snappy. Alma immediately decided on another approach. "I really appreciate you seeing me without an appointment, Judge Carrera," she said. "I've been conducting research on the positive effects of the hormone oxytocin that is critical for milk ejection. I'm sure that in your long and illustrious career on the bench you decided on the future of foster children who were abandoned by their mothers. Research by my colleagues has statistically shown that abandoned children were rarely breastfed babies."

The Judge looked irate. "I am neither a scientist, medical doctor, nor social worker. I'm afraid that I will be wasting your time, Dr. Ruiz."

Alma had hoped for a more patient Judge, one who would allow her to paint a picture of gushing mother's milk, but Judge Carrera sat frozen and sour, ready to hammer down her gavel. Alma said, "Time is very valuable, so allow me to arrive at my question, and I do believe only a jurist of your stature could answer it."

Judge Carrera was not susceptible to bootlicking. She cleared her throat in such a way that said: move on now.

"In a nutshell," Alma continued, "oxytocin is produced in the hypothalamus. But the process that makes it fascinating is the release of this hormone from the mother's nerve endings during breast-feeding as a response to the infant's suckling. The skin-to-skin contact also increases the mother's oxytocin levels and increases the flow of milk."

Judge Carrera cleared her throat and said, "Again, I'm not sure what this has to do with me. I'm not an expert on these matters."

"Here's the question that is in your domain: I am now ready to conduct clinical trials on a compounded oxytocin cream that a woman can apply on the skin. This cream is compounded from naturally occurring neuropeptides so it qualifies as a homeo-pathic formula; and therefore, would not require the strict clinical trials of a synthetic hormone. Our pilot group of women in South America was delirious when they applied the compound; they called it the love hormone because the women experienced an excess of feelings of trust, love, and affection. You would not believe the volume of milk that poured from the women's breasts."

"Dr. Ruiz, you are wasting my time," uttered the Judge. "Get to the point."

"My apologies, Judge Carrera. What most surprised us about our research were the results from the group of older women who had never had any children and who were given the compounded cream. By applying just a small quantity of the cream right on the nipple and by the women holding a suckling infant to their breast these women became euphoric and wept for more. Here's my dilemma: I have the homeopathic compound with me, and I also have willing volunteer mothers who want to share their infants for a few minutes to make an older woman happy. Certainly in older times there were nurse-maids who performed this service for women unable to breast-feed; and in fact, there is no law against this charitable act. My question to you is this: could you see yourself participating in such an experiment?"

Judge Carrera sat immobile with a poker face but there were milky drops of drool dripping from her open mouth. Alma didn't wait for an answer; she didn't need to. "I think Claire just arrived for your massage," she said. "I'll check back with you." She left to collect the $500 bet from Soledad.

Los Feliz
April 28, 2011

"So, let me get this straight," said the gaunt, but still handsome twenty-six-year-old porn actor. "What you want me to do is pretend I'm gonna give some old lady the business, but all I have to do is make out with her?"

Alma was losing patience. You'd think a failed actor currently working the oldest profession on a sleazy alleyway in Hollywood would jump at the chance for an acting gig, or at least some fast cash. "Let me repeat it for the third time," she said. "This is a client of mine who wishes to remember a passionate affair with a lover from ages ago. All you have to do is pretend that you're a young sailor named Pablo. My client remembers him as a smaller-framed young man with a sailor's upper body muscles, so you resemble him. You have to be ready at 5 P.M. sharp and shower and shampoo that mop of yours at my house first. Then I'll drive you over to her house. You'll be blindfolded until you reach the foyer of her house. Then all you have to do is say three words."

"Hey, yo, I never had to say no lines before. I just do my thing and that's *all* I need to do, you know what I'm saying?" said the actor with a bawdy swagger.

"Pay attention. From this moment forward your name is Pablo. To the client you are the new Pablo, and you will call her Catalina. You will say these two lines: *Kaixo*, which means hello, when you first walk in. And then you can say I love you, which is pronounced as *maite zaitut*. Repeat those words three times for me," demanded Alma.

The new Pablo looked defiant. He said, "I'm bilingual, but I never heard none of them words before. You said I'd get $300 to bump nasties with a hag. Now you telling me she's more than a hag, she's a grandma, and I gotta say lines. Dude, my fee just went up to $400. But you can scrub my back for free."

Alma's patience was ready to burst. "I'll pick you up right here at 5 P.M. sharp, you'll shower, and then I'll take you to my client's house. You'll be back at your usual corner before 8 P.M. Don't forget that you're going to be lying on a rug near the fireplace, so don't roll around like a fool."

"Say what?" shouted the new Pablo. "You got some crazy bitchnitude. That's hazard pay; you owe me $500. I hate fireplaces, man. That's where the trolls live, man. I'll take the $250 now."

Alma held her ground with this superstitious wimp with bulging biceps. "I'll give you $100 now and the $400 when you leave my client's house. That's the deal."

She handed over the $100 and drove away from the seedy alley in Hollywood and back up Vermont Avenue to the comfort of Los Feliz.

❖ ❖ ❖

Soledad was waiting for Alma under the pepper trees in Dr. Nunez's property. "Do you feel lucky today, well *do* you?" Soledad said, breathless.

Alma laughed at Soledad's agitation. She answered, "Yes, I do feel lucky today. Our new Pablo will be ready at 5 P.M. and as soon as Claire leaves Mrs. Dougherty's house you and I will stop by. How are you going to distract Yolanda for at least 45 minutes? I have to give Mrs. Dougherty a little something and then I'll bring the new Pablo to tempt her for tomorrow's real deal, if you know what I mean."

Soledad laughed. "Yeah, I know what you mean; I could use some real deal myself. But you told me that the porn actor was just going to kiss Mrs. Dougherty. I don't want her to get any gross disease at her old age. Plus, Yolanda told me that Mrs. Dougherty doesn't take any medication whatsoever. She's the picture of health, so don't be giving her anything that's going to make her sick because you know that Yolanda will snitch to Mrs. D's lawyer daughter."

Alma didn't want to put any negative suggestions into Soledad's mind. This was a plan that had to operate with precision, something she had never quite mastered. She was the jack of all trades and now suddenly she had become the master of this mega plan. "Remember, Yolanda is not going to know anything at all," Alma said. "You take her outside by Mrs. Dougherty's rose garden and chew her ear off like only you can do. Tell her some of your long-winded nonsensical stories and make her laugh. You're the best at making a joke out of anything." Or nothing, thought Alma.

"Thank you. I'll take that as a backhanded compliment worthy of a pseudo-doctor, if you get my drift."

Alma had to shake her head at Soledad's quick and biting wit. "Okay, how about a truce? Let's go over the details of our game plan. Tonight before Pablo leaves Mrs. Dougherty's house

I'll make sure that she wants him to come back. Tomorrow she'll be eating out of my hand and I'll get her to write me checks for three very expensive memory retrieval sessions. You need to tell Dr. Nunez that Mrs. Dougherty needs your help off and on for a couple of days since Yolanda's infant niece is not well. He won't like it, but he'll believe it. Also, tell him that I'll stop by to read him some poetry."

Soledad frowned. "I don't like you taking charge of this plan. You're too slow for my taste. I feel like grabbing all of the doctor's gold bars and just leaving town—"

"So you do know where he hides the key to the safe closet." Alma said. "Let's just take that loot tonight and run."

"Naw, I still don't know where he hides the key to the closet. I've only seen the gold bars when he opens the safe and he doesn't see that I'm just a few feet behind him. I would have made a great cat burglar like what's her name in that movie—"

"Never mind your movie trivia questions. You must find the key tonight. I don't care if you stay up all night. And don't forget that you need me to turn gold into its liquid state. You talk tough and say you know people who can help you rip off Dr. Nunez and steal La Linda's car, but you don't know anybody anymore, if you ever did. You've been cooped up with old codgers for years now and all you can do is parrot tough lines from the movies you watch all day long."

"Whatever. You're such a downer. Where's Octavio when I need a little pick-me-up? I just don't think I can wait around more than a couple of days. My luck is getting worse. I just stomped on a bunch of *nuno* mounds when I went to pick some lettuce, and I know those sinister buggers are going to make my life miserable," whined Soledad.

"There is no such thing as a *nuno* or a troll or a gnome or a goblin; it's just your religious upbringing making you feel guilty for wanting to have fun. Concentrate on the money you're going to take back with you to the Philippines. Okay?"

"Easy for you to say, you're not walking around with welts on your legs for the thrashing the *nuno* gave me earlier. Look at my legs, if you don't believe me," demanded Soledad.

Since Alma ignored her, Soledad continued speaking. "By the way, I should tell you that I'm driving Yolanda to her sister's roach-infested apartment to pick up her baby niece tonight. I told her that the baby would cheer up Judge Carrera, and you know what a sucker Yolanda is about helping old people. Have you seen the altar she keeps in Mrs. Dougherty's guest house? She has more saints and rosaries and candles and whatnot; it's a firetrap. Anyway, be ready to act out the Judge's sicko breast-feeding memory tonight, too."

"Are you insane? I can't do two memory retrieval sessions in one evening. I have to prepare and we have less than two hours before new Pablo does his thing with Mrs. Dougherty. You'll have to postpone picking up the baby," said Alma.

"No can do, Maggoo. If we don't close the deal with the Judge tonight I don't know where we can get another baby because Yolanda doesn't want to leave Mrs. Dougherty alone. She says she promised Catlin never to leave her *mamacita* alone and she keeps her promises. She's making tonight an exception since Claire will be giving Mrs. Dougherty a massage while we go to pick up the baby. So that's that," concluded Soledad.

◈ ◈ ◈

While Soledad drove to pick-up the baby, Alma dashed back to her soon-to-be foreclosed house to gather all the items needed to recreate two memories this very night. On her way back to her house Alma spotted Octavio and parked her car behind his van. She marched right up to him as he was loading his gardening equipment into his van. She said, "Octavio, I know you were a shaman back in the jungle, I mean in the Amazon or Cusco or wherever, and I need your help. I'm having a real difficult time right now and I need to calm down. What natural medicine should I take that would relax me but not make me fall asleep? Can you please help me?"

Octavio acknowledged that everything about Alma's body language and the rapid manner of speaking and jittery movements attested to her high-strung nature. He should help her; that is what his destiny had always been since his childhood among the Shuar: to be a healer. He went inside the panel van and was looking for the appropriate herb to give her when he heard Alma's next question. "Can you suggest something that would calm me down but that would not be detected in a urine test?" She must be asking not for herself but for someone else, thought Octavio.

Octavio came out of the panel van empty-handed and said, "Alma, I can't help you. Why don't you go to the health food store and buy some valerian root extract. But you, as a holistic doctor, know that it works best when taken over several weeks. I would recommend that you combine it with lemon balm leaf extract, but again you would know better than I. Good night." He drove off without waiting for Alma's response.

Alma arrived at Mrs. Dougherty's house and sat with her drinking a spiked hot tea and enticing her with talk about loves lost and found. Once Mrs. Dougherty looked deliciously and mildly sedated, Alma went to get the new Pablo. She had sprayed him with verbena eau de parfum earlier but she sprayed his hair and neck one more time. When he started to protest, she covered his mouth with her hand and said, "If you play your role like a real romantic lover tonight, you'll be making $700 tomorrow. Now put this chamois pouch around your neck."

"I'm not putting that on my skin; it stinks. What the heck is in it?"

"Shhh, keep your voice down. Mrs. Dou—that is, Catalina —remembers that her Pablo used to wear a suede pouch around his neck. All I had were an old pair of suede slippers that belonged to my Granny so I did the best I could with it."

New Pablo pretended to vomit, but allowed her to put it around his neck. "Let's get this grandma gig over with," he said. "I want to hit a club tonight."

※ ※ ※

The tiles of the Batchelder fireplace glowed in different hues of natural earth; some as brown as hardened soil and others the light beige of the limestone walls of a prehistoric cave. The usual wrought-iron fireplace screen was not in its place. Its absence made the logs and the flame seem smaller and deeper set in the fireplace cave. The flicker of the low flame highlighted the outline of bas-relief horse tiles and reflected the outlines of the galloping beasts as if they had been painted by cavemen.

The flame periodically illuminated Mrs. Dougherty's pinky cheeks and button nose. She was lying down on her antique Turkish Oushak rug. In all her years she had never lain down on this surface. Tonight its terra-cotta color with sections woven in grass green geometric patterns helped to create a secret pastoral setting in her big home. She smiled in a daze at Dr. Ruiz's kind gestures; why she'd even provided puffy down pillows for her comfort.

Before sending him in to perform, Alma handed Pablo the bottle of verbena eau de parfum. Without her cue, Pablo dutifully hid his left arm behind his back as he sprayed the room. He took soft and measured steps as if he were a stage-trained actor making his grand entrance to fawning fans.

The trail of verbena vapors arrived to Mrs. Dougherty's nose and she inhaled deeply. She tried to look up, but without her glasses, the surrounding dark wood furniture seemed like giant boulders blocking her view. She still tingled from Claire's recent massage so she allowed the spell of tonight to come over her. When she opened her eyes she heard a gentle and manly voice say, "*Kaixo*, Catalina."

The young man smiled at her so sweetly from behind one of the boulders and he knelt down so he would not alarm her. Again he repeated, "*Kaixo*, Catalina." This time he reached out to her with a muscular arm and waved his graceful hand at her as a sailor might wave to his lover when she goes to greet him at the port. The young man smiled and showed her his flawless white teeth set against his full lips. She wanted to touch his lips. Ever so slowly the young man approached her on his knees. She saw the chamois pouch dangling from his neck and she moaned.

New Pablo knew this was his cue to kiss her, but he felt sorry for the wrinkled hag lying in front of him. She was older than his grandmother, but she was small and had a soft face. The brief pity he felt for her vanished and in its place Pablo felt anger rising. This hag has never worked a day in her life, he thought. Not like my grandmother or me. He had always worked hard, even at school. Back in junior high acting class, the teacher had told him to feel the role, to get in touch with the sentiment required for it. He loved that acting class and the ones in high school, too. He had even landed two main roles in high school. He aced the lines from *Romeo and Juliet* and with his chiseled Latin looks he fit the role of Romeo perfectly.

There were some Hollywood agents at one of the performances and they wanted to talk to him about his future in acting.

The hag tried to touch his face and turn him towards the fireplace. Instinctively he knew that she was trying to compare his looks to the original Pablo. He dug deep into the acting methods his junior high teacher taught him. He became Pablo, some dude the hag really missed. He grabbed her hands and let her fondle the stinking pouch. This kept her hands busy and away from his face. He turned so that his face was completely away from the fireplace light. His teacher had said: dig deep into your emotions. He looked beyond the old hag's sparkling prune eyes and fixed his eyes on the memory of Tanya, his main squeeze back in high school. He leaned over and whispered, "*Maite zaitut, maite zaitut.*"

The hag wrapped her arms around his neck and sniffed him like a dog in heat. She breathlessly said, "It is you, Pablo. I can detect your fragrance across the miles and the ages."

His teacher always said to follow the director's directions. A lot of good that did, he thought. He had gone to the agents' interviews without his parents because they couldn't take time off from work and they didn't want him to waste his time with an unachievable acting goal. By his junior year in high school, the agents didn't ask him to come for interviews anymore. After he dropped out of school he tried to go on auditions, but he couldn't even afford to pay for head shots. Since he lived in squalid hollywood and not in capital-H Hollywood, there were other types of movies being shot. When his dad got deported and his mom couldn't work more than two jobs to support a family of seven, including his sick grandparents, he went for an audition from hell, and that's where he had been for several years.

His junior high teacher would have been proud of how well he delved into his inner self on the fancy rug. He showed the hag how much he *maited zaituted* her or whatever he was saying to her over and over in that nonsense language. He did exactly what the crooked-faced director had told him to do. He performed everything except bump the nasties and he left the grandma sighing for more.

❖ ❖ ❖

Mrs. Dougherty followed Alma up the stairs of her home like a brand new puppy. She lay down in her bed curled up in a fetal position and with a whimsical smile on her face. By the time Yolanda returned with her infant niece and Soledad, Mrs. Dougherty was sound asleep. Soledad mooned over the baby, "Coochie, coochie, Sandrita. You're eyelashes are almost as long as your auntie Soledad's."

All three women laughed at Soledad's antics. Soledad offered to change the baby's diaper. "Yes, please change her," Yolanda said. "Do you want to feed Sandrita before you take her to cheer up the Judge?"

"No, Yoli, if you don't mind, may I feed her at the Judge's house? It will give us time to sit and chat with the Judge," cooed Soledad.

❖ ❖ ❖

In a matter of minutes Alma, Soledad, and Sandrita arrived at the Judge's house. Margarita was mildly amused at holding the baby, but passed her right back to Soledad. She told her, "I thought you said you were bringing me a sunny surprise, as in Acapulco gold, and not a baby."

"All in good time," Soledad said. "Let Alma go in and chat up the Judge who is in a happy mood since Claire just left. Alma will feed the baby while we light up."

Alma laid Sandrita on her pink baby blanket on top of the rug in the Judge's living room, and she cleared the area in case the baby tossed or turned. She felt a pang of shame at using an innocent baby to fleece the Judge. She convinced herself that this was a one-time event and in no way would the baby be hurt.

Alma then walked into the library holding a warm baby bottle of milk and a cup of spiked hot tea. She looked at the Judge's dilated eyes and relaxed body posture as she sat on her leather recliner wearing a terry cloth robe. Alma continued yesterday's conversation as if it were perfectly normal. "As I was saying, Judge Carrera, the massage you just had with Claire has released large amounts of endorphins into your bloodstream. As you are aware, endorphins enhance the immune system, they relieve pain, and they release wondrous memories, such as the one we were discussing about women who want to relive their memories of breastfeeding an infant. That is why I've set the warm bottle of mother's milk on the end table next to you."

Judge Carrera glanced at the baby bottle and at the steaming cup of tea. Her lips moved as if she wanted to utter a dozen illogical sentences, but she had dedicated her life to the precise selection of words, so she merely said, "I presume you're going to get to the point of all of this," as she nodded towards the baby bottle.

"Of course, Your Honor. As a holistic doctor I was trained to see beyond the words of my patients. In many ways I'm sure that with your honorable record on the bench you became very wise to the exaggerations you heard. In other words, you instinctively knew the truth. On a smaller scale, I believe—and if I am wrong, please forgive me—I believe that you yearn to hold an infant and nurse her. I detect within you a deep maternal instinct that has never found expression." Alma paused and waited for some sign from the Judge, but the steely Judge did not budge.

Alma continued. "The level of endorphins and the beneficial chemical reactions they release in your body only have a
small window of opportunity to maximize your feelings of
euphoria. In fact, the delta brain waves that prolong the ecstatic
feeling only last a matter of minutes. I don't think that you
should waste any time. From my experience helping many older
women, as I explained yesterday, if you choose to drink the tea,
you should do so now, and in a few minutes you will feel
unimaginable sensations. A tingle will pulsate from the marrow
of your bones and send a quiver to your entire body as you
release a torrent of maternal nutrients to the suckling baby that
awaits your nourishment. You may want to rub some of the milk
from the bottle onto your breasts while I go and get my infant
niece. No one will ever know."

Alma recognized that she only had a few minutes before the
Judge came to her senses and called the cops. She put a pacifier
in Sandrita's mouth as the good-natured baby smiled angelically.
Alma peeked into the Judge's library. The cup of tea was empty
and the judge was practically pouring the mother's milk onto her
sagging breasts.

Alma pulled out the digital camera and the laptop that she
had stuffed into the baby's diaper bag. The laptop was already on
and she busied herself by plugging in the USB cable. She found
the online site where she would upload the video of the Judge.
She checked that the digital camera was ready for videotaping.
She peeked into the library and the Judge was caressing her
breasts. By now the love drug was racing through the Judge's
veins. Alma picked up Sandrita and a comfy pillow. She put the
pillow on top of the Judge's thighs and set Sandrita on the pillow. She heard the Judge weeping with joy at holding the baby,
and she quickly videotaped the Judge attempting to breastfeed
the baby. Fortunately, Sandrita clamped on to her pacifier and
would not touch the decayed breasts, but it didn't matter, the
delirious Judge was over the moon.

Alma quickly uploaded the video and went in to the library to remove Sandrita from the Judge who sat in a soaking terry cloth robe since she had poured all contents of the baby's bottle onto herself. The Judge was in a drugged daze. She muttered, "Bring me the baby. I must feed the baby."

Alma went outside to the heated patio and handed Sandrita to Soledad. She said, "You and Margarita better feed the baby. Here's a new bottle; I dropped the other one. You'd better stay out here, Margarita, since the Judge wants to consult with me on a private matter."

Margarita had the giggles by then, and she just kept on laughing while Soledad, for once, took her babysitting duties seriously.

Alma returned to the library determined to extract $30,000. from Judge Carrera. She knew from dealing with the foreclosing bank flunkies that any check over the amount over $9,999 would require all sorts of paperwork. She walked like a cocky prosecutor into the Judge's library and said, "You can stop rubbing yourself, drink lots of water, and put this pacifier in your mouth because otherwise you're going to hurt your jaws. Here's exhibit number one. This videotape shows the respectable Judge Carrera trying to nurse an infant, and oops, are those Judge Carrera's flopping breasts that she cannot stop caressing? I need three checks written from three different banks. Make each one for the amount of $9,900 or I can take cash; otherwise, this videotape gets uploaded to the Internet and the world will see a very naughty and guilty judge."

The Judge didn't bat an eyelash at the demands; she knew she was now part of a conspiracy. She ambled to her desk and wrote two checks for the amount demanded. She then opened a small safe and took out all the cash she had in there. She didn't even bother to count the money or shut the safe. She didn't say a word. She just chomped on the pacifier and waited to be struck by lightning. She figured the probability of her behavior tonight was about the same chance she had to be struck by lightning or by getting crushed by the big earthquake all Californians know will come. She welcomed a wrathful judgment; she deserved a miserable and painful sentence.

▨ ▨ ▨

Claire drove up to the Judge's house and found Octavio parked across the street. "Hi," she said. "I guess you also forgot something at Judge Carrera's? I left my verbena oil bottle. I need my grandma to blend some more oil exactly like the last batch. I'm not sure what ingredients you two put in that blend, but all my seniors love it. What did you forget in the Judge's yard?"

The moonlight illuminated Claire's face with a piercing glow. Octavio decided that he was looking at truth in the face and he felt compelled to alert Claire about his animal suspicions concerning Alma. He said, "I didn't forget anything, Claire. I'm just hunting demons. I want to ferret out evil."

Claire stepped away from his van. "You're scaring me," she said. "Are you saying that something evil is going on?"

"I'm not sure, Claire. But your innocent eyes just shot a dart into my heart and I had to tell you."

"I know you mean well, Octavio, but when you speak in those metaphorical terms it creeps me out. My grandma talks like that and inevitably what she suggests becomes a reality. I wasn't sending any evil thoughts your way, honest."

"Of course not, you are an angel among these—"

Claire frowned and said, "Stop with the angel compliment; it ticks me off. Please tell me in everyday terms what evil you're talking about."

"It is difficult for me to put into words the vibrations I feel when Alma is around," Octavio said. "She emits the dangerous purring sound of a queen wasp about to sting. Alma has been going from house to house right after you massage your clients. I asked Ofelia if she or La Linda were having a problem with Alma, and she said they were not. I also asked Fatima, but she waved me off and walked back into the house. How about you, Claire? Do you feel that Alma is up to something?"

"Well, she's trying to help some of my elderly clients to understand the memories they've been recalling recently. All my clients seem to look forward to talking to her, especially Dr. Nunez. He told me that she's been reading poetry for him. I think that Alma is very generous with her time. Maybe you're just put-off by her poor disfigured face. I don't think you have anything to worry…oh, there she is now. Hi Alma, hi Soledad."

Both women waved back, got into Dr. Nunez's car, and exited on the circular driveway farther up the street from where Claire and Octavio were parked.

"Just be careful," Octavio said.

"Sure," said Claire. "Sure thing."

Claire crossed the street and rang the doorbell. Margarita opened the door with a stoned smile. She had set the oil bottle on the foyer table so she grabbed it and handed it to Claire. She waved to Octavio and said, "You have no idea how great I feel! Soledad brought me a great surprise—"

"Was it the baby Soledad was holding?" asked Claire, relieved to see that all was well with Margarita and the baby.

"Oh, yeah. The big fat baby was so, so sweet," said Margarita as she burst in stoned out laughter.

Los Feliz
April 29, 2011

Yolanda was surprised at Mrs. Dougherty's insistence. "Please, dear Yolanda," she said, "you must not take no for an answer. I must consult with Dr. Ruiz immediately. She's was so generous with her uh, consultation, last night. Tell her that I am indebted to her and would love to pay for a series of consultations."

Yolanda made the call, and within minutes Alma was in Mrs. Dougherty's living room. She was dressed in clinical white from head to toe. She adjusted the Dr. Ruiz name tag on her white lab coat. She wore horn-rimmed glasses, which Yolanda noted were becoming since they partially concealed the paralyzed right side of the face.

"Yolanda!" Mrs. Dougherty said. "Please cut fresh roses for three vases. And do take your time with your selection—I will need some privacy with Dr. Ruiz."

Mrs. Dougherty couldn't contain herself. She said, "Dr. Ruiz, I feel like a naughty teenager! Do tell me, did I dream of seeing Pablo again or did I participate in an actual memory retrieval session last night?"

Alma tried to respond in what she presumed was a healer's cryptic message. "What you experienced last night is precisely what you felt and what your inner core must be craving still, am I not correct?"

Mrs. Dougherty's pert little face lit up even more. "Why yes, indeed I experienced something beyond my memory or dreams. And I would like to know if it is possible for me to continue reliving my memories of long ago."

"Yes, but in order for us to create the correct environment in which this retrieval session can flourish, it will take—"

"Whatever it takes, I am prepared to offer you compensation commensurate with the service, oh, dear me, please excuse me, I didn't mean to sound like this is a commercial transaction. Please forgive me. I'm just an elderly lady now and well, my daughters seem a tad too eager to manage my affairs, and every day they encroach more and more into my finances, but, well, my heart wants what it wants. And I want more memory retrieval sessions before my daughters swoop down and get their talons into what is mine. Do you think that I am making any sense or am I just rambling on and on?"

Alma approached Mrs. Dougherty at a long and slow pace. She held her hands again, and this time she did not need to shake them. Mrs. Dougherty's dilated pupils and sweaty palms told her all she needed to know. Alma closed her eyes and said, "I am honored that you have trust in my expertise. Last night's session went very well, but I think that you are on the verge of even more intensity. I am only a facilitator and this process can be a bit expensive——"

Mrs. Dougherty clamped onto Alma's hands and groaned. "But, my dear Dr. Ruiz, it's not a matter of how much; it's a matter of how soon. I have spent a lifetime in an icy cave and now I must have my fire. How much do you need to facilitate many more sessions? I am prepared to pay you, but I'm afraid that the checks will have to be written from several bank accounts."

While Alma added up the amount she could ask, Mrs. Dougherty pulled out a leather traveling case with compartments full of precious stone necklaces and diamond bracelets. She said, "I was going to bequeath this jewelry to my daughters, but they would turn right around and sell it for a fraction of the cost, I'm sure. They're more interested in the titles to my properties and so on. I'm sorry to be so crass about these money matters."

Alma tried to look repulsed at the talk of money. She simply said, "My recompense is in seeing you self-actualize, even if it is in the sunset of your life. It is never too late to feel the fury, is it? And after all, how can one put a price tag on what you've missed for a lifetime? We could always wait until you think it over—"

"No, no, absolutely not. I'm afraid that my daughter, who is an attorney, might be coming to visit soon and she's impossible to deal with. Please can you arrange for a daily retrieval session for the next ten days? Can I pay you with these jewels and in cash? Please allow me to write you five checks each for $10,000. Is that okay with you?"

"Your fortuitous number is $9,900. Ten thousand is not your lucky number. Please make the checks in the first amount and I will get to work so that you can feel that same ardor tonight."

In Alma's rush to get to the banks to cash the checks, she didn't notice that three of the checks were from the same bank. She was elated at how easily she extracted money from both Judge Carrera and Mrs. Dougherty. She wanted to close on Dr. Nunez and arrange to steal La Linda's Hispano-Suiza Torpedo and perhaps also arrange for the thieves to steal the Moroccan Matisse. The potential dollar signs from these five elderly victims hovered over her like Amazonian fireflies.

When Alma went to cash Mrs. Dougherty's two checks from two local banks she did not encounter any glitches other than the usual requests for proper identification. She decided to deposit the remaining three checks from Mrs. Dougherty into her own checking account. Then, she cashed one of Judge Carrera's checks at another bank where she had an account, and deposited the second check from Judge Carrera into her checking account. Alma had been opening accounts and chang-ing banks in an effort to thwart the slimy bank that was going to foreclose on Granny's house. She put that worry aside. If she played her cards right, soon she'd be basking in the steamy warmth of the Amazon.

According to Alma's record keeping, she had deposited a total of $39,600 from Mrs. Dougherty and Judge Carrera into her checking account, and she had cashed $29,700 at the different banks. None of the tellers or bank managers had batted an eyelash at the transactions with the clearly handicapped mid-dle-aged Dr. Ruiz. All in all, Alma felt proud of her earnings of over $89,000 in checks and cash, plus the yet-to-be-determined street value of Mrs. Dougherty's jewels. She congratulated herself on the coup she had carried out in a matter of one arduous day.

▦ ▦ ▦

Nothing breeds success like success, and Alma even had the audacity to scheme on how she would snatch La Linda's antique car. But she hesitated at sending in an art thief to steal the

Matisse from Mrs. Hamieh's house. There was something ominous about the diminutive Mrs. Hamieh and her bronze bodyguard-cum-sous-chef, Fatima. Rather than ponder these more complicated possibilities at making money, Alma resolved to cast her net on the big fish: Dr. Nunez.

⬛ ⬛ ⬛

When Alma arrived at Dr. Nunez's home he was shouting at Soledad. "Damn it, girl! Can't you stop flitting around the house looking for your lost earring and read this poem out loud? That's why I hired you."

"Yes, big boss. I'll do as you say. Just sit tight one more minute until I find the gold at the end of my rainbow."

Dr. Nunez screamed, "What are you talking about now? Leprechauns?"

"No, sir, big boss, I was just saying that I'm looking for my gold earring, that's all. But look here, your favorite girl is here. Alma, please come in and read for Dr. Nunez while I keep looking for the gold...earring, okay?"

Alma had removed her white lab coat with its fake name tag, and had put on a plain navy sweater. She smiled her crooked smile, but Dr. Nunez was staring into space. Alma said, "It would be a joy to read Dr. Nunez poetry."

Soledad screeched, "Awesome, I'm outta here."

Alma smiled sweetly and said, "What would you like me to read, sir?"

"Shhh, I told you not to say anything about the poetry I write in front of Soledad. Just read this for me, would you? I wrote it after one of Claire's massages and it sounded like a poem from long ago, but I never had any time to write poetry when I had my medical practice. So where did I get this crazy idea? I need to hear it read by a woman with a heart, not by that babbling Soledad. Go on, read."

"It would be my pleasure," said Alma as she cleared her throat before reading the poem. "*La Sirena Mía*" by Ezequiel Salomón Nuñez, M.D:

Once I sat upon a promontory,
And heard a *sirena* on a dolphin's back,
Uttering such dulcet and harmonious breath,
That the rude sea grew civil at her song;
And certain stars shot madly from their spheres,
To hear the sea-maid's music.

Alma was never a great student of poetry, but she would have gambled all her new-found money on the obvious plagiarizing on the part of old Dr. Nunez. This partial quote was from Shakespeare's "A Midnight Summer's Dream."

"Why are you stalling, Alma? You have to maintain a certain pace when you recite my poems. Keep it up, girl," snapped Dr. Nunez.

Alma continued reading his plagiarized poem:

All my desire and hope is with you

I long just for your company.

My stomach churns and I moan for you,

Who drives sleep away from me.

If only my heart-in-its-chest were glass—

You'd see my love within it.

This stanza was not from Shakespeare, but its inclusion by Dr. Nunez baffled Alma. He obviously grafted it for a purpose. She kept on reading Dr. Nunez's bouillabaisse of a poem; anything to give Soledad enough time to find the key to his treasure chest closet.

Dr. Nunez shouted, "You stall too long between stanzas! Keep up the pace. You're starting to confuse me. The stanza you just read is the most important one, can't you tell? It literally drives sleep away from me because I feel that when I originally wrote it, it must have been in Hebrew, but I only learned enough Hebrew to more or less do my Bar Mitzvah. So how could I have written it in Hebrew? Other times I feel that I wrote it in Latin. Then to confuse me even more, when I have the memory of the lithe *sirena* and me, we are speaking in a kind of old Spanish or Latin. I had some great aunts who had lived in Morocco and they spoke Sephardic Ladino. In fact, many people throughout the world still speak Ladino. I'm not one of them and I don't care about some dying language, but in my dreams or memories or whatever it is that is happening to my memory, I recite my poem in this old Ladino. Go figure."

Alma jumped at the chance to help the old man interpret his underwater riddle and make some more money. She said, "As you may be aware, I can conduct a memory retriev—"

"The only thing you can do is either finish reading my poem or get out of my house!" Dr. Nunez shouted. "You're not any more helpful than Soledad, and at least she makes me laugh every once in a while. Read."

"Of course," said Alma as she proceeded to read with proper poetic inflection:

> I would kiss my *sirena* often under the sea,
> And kiss her again till she kiss'd me
> Laughingly, laughingly.
> O, what a happy life were mine
> Under the hollow-hung ocean green!
> Soft are the moss-beds under the sea;
> We would live merrily, merrily.

"That was better," acknowledged Dr. Nunez. "What do you think of my poem?"

I think that I just read a tampered Tennyson poem, Alma wanted to say. Instead she said, "Dr. Nunez, I believe that you've expressed a deep-seated desire we have to understand the conundrum and the folklore associated with mermaids. You obviously have a sensitivity and appreciation for the poetry of, uh, of the great poets, so your style is very similar to Shakespeare and Tennyson and other geniuses. "

"Well, yes, you're right. I do have an intuitive knowledge of poetry, don't I? If my eyes were still any good, I wouldn't ask you this favor, but do you think that you could help me research the Ladino language I feel I must have known in the past, and the poetry from long ago?"

Alma restrained herself from propositioning Dr. Nunez with a high-fee memory retrieval session on the spot. She was exhausted after what she had achieved with Mrs. Dougherty and Judge Carrera, and she did not want to conduct any research on poetry or Ladino or *sirenas*. Alma just wanted to take his old gold bars and fly back to the Amazon. She had a feeling that the banks might call her up to ask her for more documentation of one kind or another on her recent large deposits. She wished she had paid attention to something about a Currency Transaction Report that the young teller had said. All that mattered now was that she had to keep loose-lipped Soledad from inadvertently revealing their plan to one of the other caregivers. Alma decided that the quicker she could get cash for La Linda's car and spirit away Dr. Nunez's gold ingots, the better. She decided to forego ripping the Matisse canvas off Mrs. Hamieh's Venetian plastered walls; Fatima alarmed her for some unknown reason.

Alma made a subtle suggestion to Dr. Nunez. She said, "Dr. Nunez, your poetry is valuable and you should not just leave it lying about. Surely you've heard about all the theft of intellectual property that is taking place. Your erudite poems are a treasure and ought to be kept in a locked closet or safe. You do have a safe, don't you?"

"None of your damn business what I have. But as a matter of fact, I do keep everything in a safe, don't you worry about me. That's all I'm going to say."

"I'm only thinking about safekeeping your valuable poetry. I would be glad to open the door to your closet or room or wherever you keep your safe. I'll step out of the room since you can still see well enough to open your safe on your own. Let's go lock up your gem of a poetry notebook, shall we? I have to leave for a few hours, but I'll be back with information on the Ladino language and on the poetry memories you're having. It just so happens that I speak a bit of Ladino—"

"Prove it," demanded Dr. Nunez.

"Certainly. *En boka serratha no entra moshka.* This means: If you don't talk about your problems, you cannot find a solution."

"Tell me more," commanded the old man.

"This is one of my great-grandmother's favorites: *Tiempo pedrido nunka se topa.* Lost time is never recovered. Isn't that the truth, Dr. Nunez?"

"I suppose, but I'm a man of science and I deal with the facts I see in front of me."

Alma took a chance to entice him to participate, and pay dearly, for a memory retrieval session. She said, "But now that you are not seeing very well with your eyes, your inner sight is expanding exponentially. Listen to your poetic observations about love and loss, about your cherished *sirena*. You would have to agree that *tiempo pedrido nunka se topa.* We can't lose any more time, can we?"

"I guess not. But we can't go back in time either," concluded Dr. Nunez.

Alma lowered her voice and delicately asked, "What if you could relive your most euphoric memory? At this stage of your life, wouldn't that be worth everything?"

"But I keep telling you it's not my own memory; it's as if I were remembering a memory from an ancestor, which is not scientifically possible," yelled Dr. Nunez as he rubbed his eyes violently. He continued screaming, "I can't see how I could be writing poetry in Ladino. That's not logical, either."

Hearing Dr. Nunez's screams, Soledad came running into the room, but Alma signaled for her to leave. In typical Soledad fashion, she remained hidden outside the room to eavesdrop.

Alma told Dr. Nunez, "It would be my pleasure to help you out with your memories."

She wanted to continue with her proposed mermaid reenactment, but she was exhausted from yesterday's running around and executing the first phase of her plan. The paralyzed right side of her face started to twitch with fatigue and her right eye watered uncontrollably.

Dr. Nunez peered at what he thought was a weeping Alma and said, "Take it easy, Alma. No need to cry and get all nostalgic about the past or about my poetry. Let's be logical. Lead me to my upstairs office, would you?"

Soledad ran up the stairs ahead of Alma and Dr. Nunez and skulked in the upstairs hallway waiting to see if Dr. Nunez would show Alma where he kept his key to the closet where Ft. Knox was stashed away. She didn't trust Alma to share that bit of critical information, just as she might not share the safe's combination with Alma, either.

Once at the entrance to Dr. Nunez's office, he told Alma, "You can leave me here now. What time will you be back to tell me more about the Ladino poetry and such?"

"At exactly five in the afternoon, *mio sîdî,* Ezekiel," answered Alma.

"Whoa, whoa, whoa, what did you just say to me?" asked Dr. Nunez.

"I simply called you *mio sîdî*, Ezekiel, which means 'my lord, Ezekiel' in the old Spanish language of the *Mozárabes* during the Arab rule of Medieval Spain. The Arabs called others the *al-jamiya*, the foreigners, and the indigenous Christians called their Latin root language Latino. The Jewish people of Al-Andalus called virtually the same language Ladino, although they included Hebrew and Aramaic words. Once they were expelled from Spain in 1492, they carried their Ladino language wherever they settled in many parts of the world and added words from their adoptive countries. That's all!"

"What do you mean that's all? That's a whale of a tale. That's what the *sirena* always says in my dream-memory. She says something like: '*Fente mib de nohte, mio sîdî*, Salomón.' And you just said *mio sîdî*, and my middle name is Solomon. You have some explaining to do."

This wily old man was trying to get Alma to do all his memory recollection for free. She remembered how crass and crafty the new Pablo had been about hiking up the prices for his services. She wasn't too proud to learn a lesson from the porn actor pirate. She would pillage the old man's treasure chest and all his booty when she was good and ready. She would do it very, very soon, but she would be the one to call the shots.

Alma simply told Dr. Nunez, "Unfortunately, sir, my client from Bel Air just texted me and I must go help him retrieve his passionate memories since he has been a most generous man with me, a genuine mensch." And she walked out of his office knowing full well that sneaky Soledad would discover where he hid the key.

Octavio pretended to be checking something under the hood of his van. He had done the same thing while he kept a lookout by

Mrs. Dougherty's house early this morning. But now, he had been waiting for too long outside Dr. Nunez's residence and didn't want the neighbors to become suspicious. Ever since last night's conversation with Claire his inner jaguar had purred and growled in anticipation of a bloody hunt. In the past it had purred when he was around Soledad, and periodically when he spoke with Fatima and Margarita, but it always growled around Alma. Now he sensed that she was tracking Claire, and Octavio felt compelled to protect her. Not only because her grandmother, Doña Verito, had generously helped him get on his feet when he first arrived from the Amazon a dozen years ago, but because he had never witnessed a pure glow of goodness such as the light that emanated from Claire.

As soon as Alma left Dr. Nunez's house, Octavio followed her at a distance. When he determined that she was heading down towards Hollywood, he turned his van around and drove back up to Los Feliz to check on Claire who was at Judge Carrera's house.

⊠ ⊠ ⊠

Margarita stepped out to the backyard once she spotted Octavio mowing the lawn. She said, "Octavio, are you going *loco*, you just mowed the lawn yesterday."

"Did I? I guess I forgot a patch here and there."

"You're acting about as strange as the Judge. She even cancelled her appointment with Claire," said Margarita.

"You mean Claire is not here right now?" asked Octavio.

"No, she just stopped by to see how Judge Carrera was doing. But the Judge didn't want to see her. She says she has to rewrite her living trust before it's too late. I took her temperature and her blood pressure, and she's doing fine. Claire told me that seniors get bouts of depression. So I told her, I must be a senior then because living with the Judge has me so depressed, too," said Margarita as she laughed at her tasteless joke.

Octavio asked her, "So, did Claire go to another appointment?"

"She said she was heading to La Linda's appointment. I wish I could get out of this house once in a while. I almost prefer it when the Judge is bossing me around instead of seeing her locked up in her library."

CHAPTER TWELVE

Granada, Spain

1043

Jewish singers and scholars at the Moorish court of Córdoba.
Woodcut after drawing from B. Moerlius, 1881

Granada, Spain
1043

Indignation and resentment burned slowly from the loins of twenty-two-year-old Solomon Ben Yehuda Ibn Gabirol. Throughout his life he learned to swallow his sorrows; to bury deep in his bones the indignation fate had bestowed upon him. Instead of allowing the anger to rise to the surface he preferred to lose himself in memories of his childhood.

When the taunting brought a surge of bile to his throat, he remembered gathering seashells in Málaga, the city of his birth, and this provided temporary peace. He would gawk at the Argonauta shells and wish his bony body structure were inside out, totally external like the nautilus shell. He wished his skin glowed a pearlescent tone instead of being dotted with skin ulcers, the despicable boils that distanced him away from everyone, even the homeliest of girls. Above all, he wished he could live underwater where his nautilus tentacles could reach out for the comfort of a luminescent *sirena*, a mermaid with whom he could explore the sea. He kept all these desires buried deep inside so as not to damage his scholarly character among the Jewish intellectuals of Al-Andalus.

Solomon and his mother loved to reminisce about the seaside town of Málaga in ways that far exceeded the reality of their difficult time there. She encouraged his unrealistic ruminations about the mermaid of his dream as if she knew that he could never win the love of a real woman. She would shower him with blessings to make up for his lack of friends. At night to calm his irascible spirit she would say, "*Bivas, kreskas komo il pishkado en la mar,*" may you live and grow like the fish in the sea. In the morning she would find that he had been unable to sleep and had written another painful poem: "I toss on my bed the whole night through, as on thorns and piercing reeds."

His mother, like all Sephardic Jewish mothers, was adept in ritual medical lore. She was convinced that someone had cursed him with *mal ojo* or had cursed him by *espanto,* fright. Without fail, every night she stepped out into the courtyard and set out a clay pot with sliced radishes and sugar water. With this curative water, *al sereno* or night dew, she treated the boils throughout his body. She recited the cure in Judezmo or Judeo Spanish, also known as Ladino. She said, "*Esto te da la refua, la sheshina, la melezina.*" But the prayer she invoked did not give him health or divine presence or medicine. His boils spread with a vengeance throughout his body.

With the fall of the Umayyad Caliphate, his family moved to Zaragoza, where Solomon's intellectual prowess brought him to the attention of Jewish leaders at court. In Moslem Iberia, the Jews functioned as a state within a state and shared in the prosperity of the region. But for Solomon's tragic fate, just when his intellect was noticed by the right people, his father died.

Despite his emotional and physical suffering, by the age of sixteen Solomon's secular poems were the rage at court.

Wherever he went he heard bits and pieces of his creativity. At sunset he heard one man recite: "See the sun gone red toward evening as though it were wearing a crimson dress, stripping the edges of north and south."

Another lovelorn young man whispered through a window and repeated Solomon's words to his beloved, "All my desire and hope is with you: I long just for your company. My stomach turns and I moan for you."

Solomon's life was beginning to look up when the hotheads at court escalated trifling matters to an outright battle, and his sponsor was killed. Not long thereafter, tragedy struck again when his mother died. Orphaned and without a sponsor, Solomon went to the emirate of Granada. There among the fragrant citrus orchards and trickling fountains, his bitterness turned cantankerous.

In the ambience of shared scholarship among the Arab rulers and the Jewish intellectuals, Solomon's brilliant mind did not escape the attention of the renowned Jewish politician and leader, Samuel ibn Naghrela, also known as Samuel ha-Nagid, the chief. In short order, Solomon was back in the poetic circles of the Nagid, where the scholars no longer spoke in Aramaic or Latin, but in Arabic. Solomon took to languages like a duck to water. In due time, his intellectual arrogance rose to the surface and Solomon began admonishing his co-religionists for disregarding Hebrew.

Despite Solomon's churlishness, Samuel ha-Nagid had a soft spot for Solomon. In court he would say, "Just look at the poor boy, if it weren't for his ill-tempered backbone, the furunculosis on his face would scare everyone away. His anger and his genius are his only saving graces."

All the scholars looked up to the vizier ha-Nagid, but they couldn't bear having a bitter misanthrope such as Solomon in their midst. They could not dissuade the Nagid, and so Solomon pranced around barking at his fellow scholars and complaining about his ills. In return, they taunted him by reciting aloud the same stanza of his poetry over and over again: "My condition worsened and worsened my grief, and in its wake my strength waned." Instead of ignoring his jeerers, he became more belligerent toward them.

The Nagid kept Solomon around because together they reminisced about their earlier years in Málaga, where the Nagid had operated a spice shop. In the chief's memory the spices in his shop were awakened by the breezes of the Mediterranean, and smelled immortal. By listening to Solomon's stories about the *sirena* in the waters of Málaga, the Nagid could taste the salt and hear the waves crashing on the sand. Even at the height of his wealth and power, after all the battles he had won for the greatness of the Taifa of Granada, Samuel ibn Naghrela craved for just one day spent selling the fragrant spices in his Málaga shop.

He appreciated Solomon's lyrical poetry and was impressed by Solomon's initial expression of a philosophical system. Ultimately, the chief had not fought his way to the top to hear his poet crow about his own pain. He demanded that the young poet create majestic poems praising the Nagid; he demanded that he sing his praises.

But Solomon preferred his poetry melancholic and sour. His imagery of shattered glass made his own heart bleed. He wrote: "If only my heart-in-its-chest were glass—you'd see my love within it." Others at court reminded him that court life was about appreciation of the greatness of the dynasty, about elegance, about carnal love, but somber Solomon persevered probing deeper and deeper into the mysteries of life and destiny and faith.

His many enemies saw to it that the Nagid heard about Solomon's disloyalty. They circulated many false rumors or twisted the facts, and soon Solomon was out on the street again.

He roamed from this patron to that sponsor, never happy and never complying with the donor's requests. Acknowledging that he was treated unfairly by Samuel ibn Naghrela, Solomon unwisely wrote unfavorable poems about his former patron.

Eventually, Solomon's thoughts became obsessed with matters greater than one man, no matter how powerful. He overlooked the festering terrestrial injustices suffered by his fellow coreligionists. As he studied, wrote, and meditated, his thoughts elevated to a mystical plane. He no longer thought of the *sirena* or his pus-filled boils or his enemies; he had moved on to the sacred and sublime.

In all his learning Solomon forgot that the Mediterranean climate not only produces immense greatness, but it also begets vengeful people; people who never let the past go unpunished; people who live by the oath of revenge; people who bide by an eye for an eye.

This ancient code of revenge claimed one more victim. They say that Solomon was murdered and buried near a fig tree whose abundant fruit sweetened many lives. The poetic justice of this act evaded some. The evildoers who got rid of this brilliant misanthrope were satisfied that their mediocre talents were no longer eclipsed by his genius. In the charm of the Ladino language, Solomon's mother would have said that her son's virtue triumphed over vice: *A la undura di la mar ki si vaiga todu il mal*, may all the evil go to the depths of the sea.

Los Feliz
May 2, 2011

uke Narvitz sat perplexed in his large cubicle at the bank on Hillhurst Avenue. He reviewed some curious transactions from two of his private wealth management clients. They were both elderly ladies whom he had met on several occasions at their elegant homes near the Greek Theatre in Los Feliz. Judge Carrera was an in-between level High Net Worth Individual with under $4 million of investable assets, but Mrs. Elena Dougherty was on the top end of the HNWI with over $50 million of investable assets. He remembered both women because one was extremely demanding and blunt, and the other was a charming petite lady with a lioness attorney for a daughter.

Luke had been out of the branch for a couple of days the previous week spelunking up in Northern California's Gold Country with his former college buddies. When he returned to his bank job he noticed sizeable checks that both women had written to an Alma Ruiz. The new clerk at the branch had not filled out the Currency Transaction document properly, and she had started her vacation that day, so he couldn't ask her any questions. He told Sam, his co-worker in the cubicle next to his, "There's something odd about all these checks written to Alma Ruiz. I'm going to telephone my clients and pay them a visit. Neither one drives that much anymore."

"Don't get yourself entangled in another mess like in 2009 when you suspected everyone of mortgage modification fraud, or have you forgotten?" Sam asked.

"I don't regret my actions then. Granted none of my VIP clients fell victim to that mortgage mess, but other seniors did get singed badly, or have *you* forgotten?"

"You have a soft spot for your senior clients," Sam said. "I get it. This time look into it with prudence or better yet, why don't you forward your concern to the chief risk officer at the regional office and let him worry about it."

"That's not me and he's a procrastinator who will take forever to investigate anything," Luke said. "I'm going to call these ladies and look into it. Hell, I'll even drive up and visit them on my own time. I feel the walls closing in on me at the branch today."

"Such drama for a guy whose idea of fun is to spend days exploring dark and damp caves!" said Sam.

❖ ❖ ❖

When Luke arrived to visit Mrs. Dougherty she was practically chirping like a cheerful canary. Luke said, "I'm glad that you agreed to see me on such short notice, Mrs. Dougherty. I was up north exploring the caves for a few days and when I came back to the office I wanted to be sure that you had written the checks to Alma Ruiz."

"Oh, please call me Elena Catalina. And yes, it was my pleasure to write those checks. Dr. Ruiz is an authentic healer and is helping me out immensely."

"I didn't realize that these were payments for elective medical matters. I apologize for intruding on your personal life, Mrs. Dougherty."

Mrs. Dougherty's scrunched eyes shimmered with anticipation of a memory retrieval session Alma must have set up with Luke. She hadn't taken an accurate look at Pablo last night, so this might be how he looked in the daytime. She didn't know exactly what was about to take place, but this young man had just given her a clue by mentioning the caves he dwelled in. She smiled flirtatiously with him, and he smiled like an innocent man. She assumed that in today's memory retrieval session she was supposed to be more forward with him and take him to the warm fireplace-cave in her vast living room. Mrs. Dougherty held his hand and rubbed it gently.

Luke, who was used to his grandmother's caresses, thought that Mrs. Dougherty must miss her grandson and was an affectionate lady, so he held both her hands and grinned warmly.

Mrs. Dougherty started to lean forward towards him in an inappropriate way when Yolanda came into the family room and said, "Claire is waiting for you near the fireplace like you requested, Mrs. Dougherty."

Luke tried to let go of Mrs. Dougherty's hand, but she tightened her grip and said, "I would like for Luke to see my cave. It's very large and hot. Come, please."

Luke shrugged his shoulders in bewilderment. Yolanda explained, "Mrs. Dougherty's husband had a huge fireplace built in the living room and Mrs. Dougherty calls it her cave."

When the three of them walked in they startled Claire. She jumped up and said, "You three sounded like a stampede of wild bison. May I know who you are, please?"

Luke loved women with clear healthy skin and with compassionate brown eyes like Claire's. In a city overflowing with artificially enhanced young actresses, Claire's natural beauty glistened like the golden rays of the California sun. Luke wanted to stay and get to know Claire but he was obviously intruding. Mrs. Dougherty broke the unique silent moment exchanged between Claire and Luke. She said, "Claire, I'd like for you to meet Pablo. He's come back to make sure that I am all right."

Luke quickly corrected her. He said, "Hi, I'm Luke Narvitz, and I came to visit Mrs. Dougherty on a banking matter. Excuse me for interrupting your session."

Mrs. Dougherty asked Luke, "Will you be coming back later on this evening?"

"No, Mrs. Dougherty. You've verified your transaction with Alma Ruiz. I don't need to come back."

Mrs. Dougherty looked very confused. She pouted and tears gathered in her eyes. She said, "But you must come back to me. That's why I paid Dr. Ruiz. She said you'd be back."

Claire and Yolanda exchanged looks of concern. "Yolanda, please help Mrs. Dougherty onto the massage table," Claire said. "May I escort you out, Mr. Narvitz?"

▦ ▦ ▦

Once outside the front door, Claire wanted an explanation. She said, "May I please have one of your business cards?" She pulled out her cell phone and called his branch office. Sam picked up the private wealth management line and he verified that Luke worked in his department. Claire apologized for her brusque approach.

Luke smiled and said, "I'm so glad that you care for Mrs. Dougherty's safety. I was very concerned about certain checks that she had written and I wanted to verify with her in person. As a matter of fact, just by being here and speaking with you about Mrs. Dougherty's matters could get me fired, but heck, I can't stand the thought of someone potentially taking advantage of my senior clients. I treat them as I wish people would treat my grandparents, don't you?"

"You can say that again. I live with my grandmother and she's my best friend. Sounds old-fashioned and positively pathetic, but I benefit from her love and wisdom."

"Sounds awesome to me! I guess we're both fortunate to have our grandparents nearby," said Luke.

Claire's blood rippled slightly at Luke's comment, but she tried to ignore it. It had been so long since she felt excitement over meeting a man. She remained puzzled with Mrs. Dougherty's behavior, so she said, "Why did she ask you if you were going to come back this evening? Is she in any trouble?"

"No, she's not in any trouble, although I was taken aback when she called me Pablo. I may be meddling here, but I assume that you interact with her doctor, Dr. Ruiz."

Claire thought carefully about her answer. Finally she said, "You and I are both constrained by our professional codes as to what we can say about our clients. I will say that the mention of a Pablo perplexed me, too. As far as Alma Ruiz, she's a holistic doctor with whom many of my clients here in Los Feliz consult. That's really all I can say."

Luke nodded in agreement. "It's a litigious world, isn't it? Well, I have to pay a visit to Judge Carrera."

"What a coincidence, she's also my client."

Luke liked the way the sunset made Claire's golden skin gleam. He said, "I hope to see you again. Please call me and we can have a glass of wine and make a list of all the taboo subjects we can't talk about."

"It's a deal," said Claire as she went back into Mrs. Dougherty's house feeling unusually uplifted by her brief conversation with Luke.

⊞ ⊞ ⊞

Margarita answered the door and told Luke that Judge Carrera could not meet him after all. "Sorry, Mr. Narvitz, but I thought that she would be feeling better by now. She likes to talk to important bank people and big lawyers like when she was a sitting judge. Today she just sits very depressed. I'm sorry that you drove up for nothing."

"Has she been sick for some time?"

"No, she was happy yesterday after her massage with Claire. Then she saw Alma Ruiz and the baby. After they left, she started crying and writing her will again, I think she called it by another name, but she's not talking to anyone today."

Luke knew he was overstepping his boundaries, but he liked going out on a limb. He asked, "I'll wait out here, but can you please give Judge Carrera my card and tell her I would like to ask her a couple of questions concerning the checks she wrote yesterday."

After a few minutes Margarita returned to the front door. She said, "I'm sorry Mr. Narvitz, but the Judge is very upset. She's saying she's so ashamed. She doesn't even want me to call Claire to ask her to come and give her a calming massage. The Judge never cries. I must go to her."

All Luke had time to say before Margarita shut the door was, "Sure, I understand, but please call Claire and tell her to call my cell number as soon as possible. Please."

Luke drove up to the observatory at Griffith Park to wait for a call from Claire. He figured that if Margarita relayed his message, Claire might call him back within the hour and he could be back down the hill in minutes. He was perturbed by the fact that Judge Carrera, who had written two large checks to Alma Ruiz, was now rewriting her living trust and crying uncontrollably. This was not the behavior of the imperturbable Judge he had met on many occasions in the past.

⬚ ⬚ ⬚

Soledad traipsed to the farthest corner of Dr. Nunez's back yard. She dialed a number and spoke quickly. She said, "I don't care if I sound like a white woman, I'm *pinay* from Manila, moron. If you want to make major-major bucks you'll hightail you're scrawny *pinoy* butts to the two houses I told you about and figure out how you're gonna move the car and the yellow painting later on tonight, but no later than tomorrow. Don't screw up!" She hung up and ran to the front of the house to wait for Alma. She had no intention of sharing the proceeds from La Linda's car and Mrs. Hamieh's painting with Alma.

Within minutes Alma drove by and hailed Soledad to her old car. Sitting low on the shabby back seat was the new Pablo, blindfolded. Alma said, "You don't need to come tonight to Mrs. D's house. Pablo knows what he has to do and I'll keep Yolanda busy in the greenhouse. She's such a farm hick who likes to tell me about all the curative plants Octavio has growing in there."

Pablo pulled his blindfold down and said, "Why can't I bump nasties with this fine looking *mami* instead of the grandma?"

"Pull the blindfold up or I'll throw you out of the car," hissed Alma.

Soledad was flattered by his proposition. She told him, "All in good time, cutie. You wanna go back to the Philippines with me?"

Alma drove off in a tizzy.

✦ ✦ ✦

Octavio determined that Claire was safe in Mrs. Dougherty's house. At a distance he waited and watched as she briefly spoke with a young man in a shirt and tie. The young man left and headed up Vermont Canyon Road toward the observatory. Suddenly Octavio had a distinct urge to stop and check on La Linda and Ofelia. Their round-the-clock dancing had become a wildfire with sparks of obsession that seared not only La Linda, but scorched Ofelia, as well.

Earlier that day Octavio tried to speak with a withering Ofelia but she waved him away. He left oranges and pomegranates on a basket outside the back door, but only the squirrels nibbled at the fruit. Tonight he walked in the darkness of the side yard and whistled by the open window of the practice room. The ornamental wrought iron on the window and the block-out curtains did not allow him to peek in. La Linda shouted, "Go away, Octavio, we must continue practicing."

"I came by to fix a broken sprinkler. I'll just be a minute."

La Linda laughed coarsely and said, "You're a nocturnal being like Ofelia and me."

Octavio seized the opportunity and said, "Yes, perhaps I am. May I speak with Ofelia for just one minute?"

"Okay, but she can only take a short break. We have much to accomplish."

Ofelia stepped outside and sat on a bench near the cork tree. Her skin glistened with perspiration. Her long black hair was pulled back into a chignon whose tendrils hung soaking wet onto her neck. "Ay, Octavio, La Linda wants to achieve the impossible. I'm bone tired."

"You must tell her that you cannot help her as much as she demands. You are getting too thin. May I make you a revitalizing tea and leave it at the back door with some fortifying fruits and nuts?"

Ofelia said, "No, thanks. I've heard that your herbs and mushrooms make people hallucinate. I have to be clearheaded at all times. I never know when my daughter might call me and want me to go help her escape from whoever is holding her captive. Ay! Do you think I will ever find her? She's so young and beautiful."

Octavio tried to live according to the Shuar code of truth, but he couldn't tell Ofelia that her daughter was long gone. Months ago when he first heard about Ofelia's missing daughter he had lurked in the seediest dens of Los Angeles hoping to find her daughter. At the time he had been confident of his tracking and hunting skills. After all, he had managed to paddle in the oily muck of what was once his pristine Amazon paradise for years on his own. He was certain he could find an innocent maiden. But in Los Angeles the more he probed about Ofelia's daughter the more threats he received. He came to understand that she had disappeared as easily as the turquoise Glaucous Macaw had flown into extinction. Octavio hung his head in shame knowing that he would have to deceive Ofelia. "I think she is fine," he said.

Ofelia started to cry. She had never seen Octavio look down to the ground as he spoke to her. He was spitting dark lies to her and they both knew it.

The rustling leaves of the cork tree whimpered along with Ofelia. She sighed and said, "Ay! *Me duele hasta la médula.*"

Octavio's own bones rattled with the pain she oozed from deep in her bone marrow. He would never know that kind of love or mourning for another person. That was not his fate. His destiny was to manifest the spirit of a *kakáram*, and thus far he had squandered away his shaman gifts. He had to make amends.

La Linda yelled out from behind the curtains. "Octavio, fix the damn sprinkler and get out. This isn't a flamenco show for tourists. We're not twirling around in our polka-dotted dresses stomping like fools. This is flamenco *puro*; it's pure and raw and painful. Ofelia needs to get back here and put her heart and soul into the music."

◈ ◈ ◈

As Octavio walked around La Linda's guesthouse he spotted three slight men gaping through the garage windows at La Linda's Hispano-Suiza Torpedo. The second they saw him they ran towards the front of the house. He chased them fearlessly and caught the slowest runner by the neck. He opened his mouth wide as if ready to bite him and at the same time he pulled out his blade from the leather protector hanging at his belt. The gasping runner said, "We were just looking at the car, man. You don't need to be so aggro. My homies there are calling the cops right now. You're attacking a minor and I'm on a public sidewalk."

His confederates laughed and started to videotape the assault. One of the men said, "We know you're the 'shroom man, and we're going to let the cops know about it. Soledad said you're Tarzan and you shrink heads. Guess what, Tarzan? We're coming back to decapitate you."

Octavio cut the runner on the shoulder and tasted his blood. The runner escaped and dashed into the waiting car of his friend. He yelled, "Kiss your head goodbye, jungle man!"

◈ ◈ ◈

The cover of dusk did not cloud Fatima's vigil around Mrs. Hamieh's house. The previous night she had dreamt that wolves roamed her property. At first she thought that in her sleep she was simply hearing the howls of the feasting coyotes near the Griffith Observatory, but as the dream progressed the wolves' fangs protruded ominously as they tried to break into Mrs. Hamieh's house. All day long Fatima had kept her machete near her, but out of sight of her fairy godmother. That's how she regarded Mrs. Hamieh, and she cherished her like a celestial being. As evening approached Fatima left Mrs. Hamieh sitting comfortably and laughing at a silly television show. Fatima said, "I'm going to walk around your property for a while, is that okay with you, Mrs. Hamieh?"

"Of course, my girl, of course. It's beneficial to walk after dinner."

On her fifth walk around the property she saw the wolves at a distance. Fatima pulled her red bandanna up to the bridge of her nose and swung her machete as if she were ready to lasso a fat calf. The glint of the metal caught the attention of two of the three wolves. They had been trying to open a side window on the first floor. One of the wolves had some kind of weapon in his right hand, but this did not deter Fatima. She shouted at them in her native Tzeltal dialect, "Don't ever let me catch you coming into my village! You are trespassing on the land that has belonged to the Maya since the beginning of time. *Viva la Revolución!*"

The wolves looked at each other in amusement at the small female trying to scare them with her toy sword and yelling in some strange language. Fatima thought that these wolves even laughed liked humans. Fatima swung the machete swiftly at a low lying branch of the large coral tree whose branches towered above the wolves. The branch and its higher thorny branches dropped on top of the wolves, snaring them to the ground.

These city wolves could not react in the darkness with the agility of a Maya woman accustomed to black nights and the evildoers who crept behind the shadows of trees. Fatima swung the machete once again with surgical precision that removed the pinkie finger of the bigger wolf. His visceral howl initiated an accompanying chorus of all the canines in the hills of Los Feliz. As the wolves ran to their waiting car, Fatima picked up their dropped gun and the warm pinkie with great care. Just as her words and screams revealed that a Chiapas rebel still inhabited the marrow of the docile sous-chef, the bloody pinkie pulsated with the spirit of the Maya *huay chivo*; the legendary Maya evil sorcerer capable of transforming from beast to man.

▣ ▣ ▣

Later that evening Alma and Soledad lounged under Dr. Nunez's pepper trees. Their exaggerated chameleon poses broadcasted that each one held a secret from the other. One second they behaved as best friends and the next they argued about the execution of their plan. Alma did not tell Soledad that Judge Carrera had handed over $28,000 in cash, and Soledad withheld the location of the key to the safe closet.

Alma said, "Since we can't determine where he hides the key, I think I'll have to tempt Dr. Nunez with a fine reading of the rest of his love poems. I'll even interject Ladino sentences to take him back in time. As I read his poems I'll coax him into consuming one of my concoctions, and soon he'll reveal all we need to know."

"You go ahead and try; he only drinks his favorite scotch. You'll never get a penny out of the old tightwad. Let's concentrate on getting more money out of Mrs. Dougherty and the Judge. They already paid once, and they'll do it again. Speaking of which, I'll take my share of their payments tomorrow morning. Don't try to cheat me, either. I'm leaving in two days come hell or high water."

Alma didn't suspect that Soledad was keeping the key's exact whereabouts locked in her brain since Alma's own thoughts were fixated on the respect she could demand once she got a hold of Dr. Nunez's gold ingots. Alma came up with another idea: "What if you get dressed like a mermaid and jump in the pool. I'll pick up a costume in Hollywood tomorrow morning. We'll wait till tomorrow night and then I'll tell Dr. Nunez that you're waiting for him in costume to recite his love poems. Once he steps out toward his pool, you disappear and leave him begging to see the *sirena* again. His desire for his *sirena* is overflowing with pheromones. Don't tell me you haven't caught a whiff of his lusty and musky scent?"

"Gross," shouted Soledad. "Makes me want to puke! Why do you bring up the most disgusting ideas, Alma?"

"Because I've done research on pheromones in humans, and it's fascinating. Let me tell you—"

"I'll pass on knowing anything about hairymoans or whatever you called stinky body odor," objected Soledad.

Alma persisted with her explanation. "Here's why pheromones are important to our conversation. People think that their sense of smell is their least important sensory system, when in fact, it is critical to sexuality. Did you know that women are very sensitive to the odor of the anal glands of a cat-like mammal called a civet? Perfumers use civetone to make long-lasting fragrances."

Soledad pounded the grass with her fists as she laughed out of control. "Cat's ass perfume? Only in America. I'm going to miss this crazy country when I leave in a couple of days. But what is the connection to our money scheme?"

"You yourself said that Dr. Nunez's sense of hearing escalat-ed since his eyesight declined. I think that the properties in

Claire's massage oil are heightening the sensory faculties of the oldsters. You know that her grandmother is a natural healer and Octavio has been giving her all sorts of organic, yet possibly psychotropic ingredients, to put into that oil, don't you?"

"Who cares about the oil, Alma? I'm way beyond that now. Let's just get all the money we can from Mrs. Dougherty and Judge Carrera. You just told me that Mrs. Dougherty's session tonight with Pablo was steamy. Let's hit her for more sessions, get her money, and run."

"You're two steps behind me, Soledad. First, I'm counting on olfaction to trigger an insatiable desire in Judge Carrera; one she will gladly pay an additional amount to satisfy. I've instructed Margarita to keep the soiled mother's milk robe on or near the Judge. When I conducted experiments with breast-fed babies, I discovered that infants could detect their own mother's milk by sniffing milk-drenched pads from a range of other women's milk. The infants instantly displayed a sucking response once they smelled their mother's milk. I am confident that Judge Carrera will sniff the soiled robe and pay me, I mean us, to let her try to breastfeed Sandrita again."

"You are one sick puppy, Alma, but I'll buy your story. How do Dr. Nunez's hairymoans fit into our plan?"

Alma gladly responded. "They are called pheromones. Since you're not willing to act the part of the mermaid, I've already selected your understudy who will fill the mermaid's scaly costume in ways you never could. Pablo introduced me to her and she's eager to act out the part. She's even going to read lines of poetry to Dr. Nunez in Ladino. You should hear her luscious purring voice. Believe me, she exudes sex pheromones. Why she's hanging around the likes of Pablo puzzles me. She has a university degree from Ecuador and she is an art conservator trained in Spain. Her name is Monty and she can imitate any woman's voice. Since Dr. Nunez's hearing is elevated, she will belt out her eerie siren's song. Dr. Nunez will gladly hand over the key to his safe closet for a full memory retrieval session with Monty, the *sirena* of his dreams. While she's driving him wild with passion, she'll throw the key our way and we exit L.A. forever."

"Get real, Alma. The man is going blind but he's a clever shark. He'll never believe that there is a real mermaid in his pool. You've been drinking too much of your wacky concoctions," said Soledad.

"Once I almost convinced my old stubborn boss, Dr. Yepez, about my theory on how ancestral memories are transferred through the DNA," Alma countered. "I was recommending that he do clinical trials using the divination plants that the people in the Amazon have been using for ages. I told him to make a tincture of *salvia divinorum* since it is low on toxicity and low on addictive potential. He seemed interested on what I was explaining. He even took notes."

Soledad interrupted her. She said, "Get to the point, Alma. You probably bored him to pieces, too."

"How did you know? Did I already tell you the story? I'll have you know that he pissed me off so much by ignoring my theory that I got even with him. I torched his precious data and most of his lab."

Soledad sat up instantly and said, "Awesome, I've never met a pyromaniac. Did you get arrested?"

"Are you kidding? Nobody cares about an insignificant fire as long as people don't get hurt. I always get even with those who do me wrong, Soledad. Don't ever forget that!"

Los Feliz
May 3, 2011

At exactly one in the morning Ofelia crept out of La Linda's house. The tidal wave of longing for her daughter crashed any logical faculties she had left after her exhausting day of flamenco with La Linda. She didn't think about her actions, she simply followed her lunacy, and this was the black hour in which she would unleash her rage and find out the whereabouts of her child. She drove down the foggy hill inattentively and nearly ran over a mother raccoon and her kits. Even animals take better care of their offspring, Ofelia thought, as she scratched her face in despair.

By the time she arrived at the first strip joint, with a crazed and scratched face, she got shoved out by the usual doorman. He slapped her around and said, "This is the last time I'm going to throw you out of here. I've told you already all the girls who work here want to work here. We don't force no girls to dance or do nothing, if they don't want to. Face it, you're such a *loca* that your daughter ran away from you!"

By three in the morning she had made her way towards the Valley. Adrenaline rushed through her body so she didn't feel her face swelling. The tidal wave of anguish and rage had completely taken over her body and short-circuited her nerve endings. She looked in the visor mirror and saw a one-eyed purple octopus ready to strangle the men responsible for violating her innocent daughter. She was underwater now and prepared to drown. She stormed the revolting strip joint and managed to grab a glass. As she broke it against a table top she attempted to slice a man who dared to smile lecherously at her. She lunged at him but another man ripped her blouse off. The two men tossed her to and fro, and fondled her with abandon. With only one eye somewhat open, Ofelia misjudged her distance from the men and she kept on slashing at the revolting stench in the air. Ofelia screamed, "Give me my daughter back and I'll let you live."

In her deranged state, Ofelia attempted to yank a petite dancer off the stage. The touch of the dancer's skin was dry and scaly, not like the coconut-oiled skin of her daughter. The dancer wobbled in her six-inch stiletto heels and hissed at Ofelia, "I ain't your daughter, bitch!"

Somewhere in that putrid grotto, with its stench of three-day-old fish, Ofelia detected the smell of her daughter's sweet breath of hot chocolate and warm *churros*. She saw a strand of her daughter's obsidian hair glistening on the stripper pole as a platinum-blond dancer twirled drunkenly around it. Somewhere behind the stage Ofelia heard the faint and muffled cries of her daughter calling out to her, "*Mami, mami.*" She ran towards the shadow behind the stacked crates of empty beer bottles. Instead of seeing her daughter, Ofelia saw an old cleaning woman. The woman pointed toward a service door and said, "*Mami*, you'd better leave right now or they're going to cut you up."

Ofelia's internal riptide forced her right back to her daughter's abusers. She charged them fearlessly. The men at the bar cheered her on and threw soiled napkins and cigarettes at her. The dancers on stage barely noticed the ruckus with the glazed and unfocused fish eyes of girls who had already drowned, but didn't know it. One of the men ridiculed the small size of Ofelia's breasts so she slashed her own chest and hollered, "You can cut me to pieces in exchange for my daughter, bloody swine."

Ofelia's enraged sideshow titillated the men in the audience and they ordered tequila shots by the double fist. Finally after filling all the orders for shots, two brawny guys punched her and carried her to her car. The guy with the work gloves drove her car as she lay passed out and bleeding in the back seat. After a couple of blocks he parked the car, left Ofelia in the back seat, jumped into the other man's car, and they drove away.

▧ ▧ ▧

At exactly five in the morning, Octavio woke himself up by coughing and growling. He drank water and crawled back into his soft bed. Again he coughed, but this time he realized that it wasn't a simple cough, he was roaring like a jaguar again. He'd overslept in his cave of an apartment and did not pay attention to his cell phone ringing. His inner beast heard the ring and woke him up with a growl. When Octavio heard his voicemail, his uncontrollable primal roar woke up his neighbors in Echo Park. They knew better than to ask him to shut up; they both respected and feared him. When they saw him hightail out of the apartment, they heaved sighs of relief.

Octavio drove around unfamiliar neighborhoods trying to locate La Linda's red sedan. Ofelia's cryptic phone message about blood and dancing and her lost daughter made no sense to him. The one thing he did understand was that she was hurt and hiding in the back seat of La Linda's swanky sedan near the giant donut sign by the bus stop. When he finally located the red car, Ofelia lay motionless and unable to unlock the car doors. He had no choice but to break the front passenger window, unlock the doors, and lift Ofelia into his van. The handful of bystanders at the bus stop was glad for the drama that helped them wake up for their ride to work. One slumped-shoulder man whispered, "I bet she had it coming. She went out with some hotshot in his expensive red car and wouldn't put out for him. Now her poor husband has to pick her up and take her home to take care of his kids. Our women are no longer faithful like they were back in our countries."

The younger bus riders turned the volume up on their headsets and directed their bobbing heads up towards the chocolaty donut in the sky, oblivious to the world around them. A woman in an orderly's uniform said, "Let's mind our business. Can't you see the poor lady is bleeding her heart out? Have some compassion."

■ ■ ■

Instead of treating her instantly in this unfamiliar street, Octavio felt Ofelia's pulse, and listened to her breathing. The surface cuts on her face and chest had stopped bleeding. He touched her tongue and gums. They were moist and pink, so he drove back towards Los Feliz. He didn't dare take her back to tempestuous La Linda. The best place to let Ofelia recuperate would be Mrs. Dougherty's guesthouse adjacent to his greenhouse, but lately Mrs. Dougherty had been acting too jittery and talkative. She would interfere with too many questions. She might also tell her daughter about the incident and her daughter would make sure to report it to the authorities. Dr. Nunez's guesthouse was nestled by lush trees, but meddlesome Soledad would broadcast the incident to the neighborhood. Judge Carrera was out of question since she did everything by the book. Mrs. Hamieh and Fatima were his only resort, so he stopped his van in their driveway.

❖ ❖ ❖

Both women were waiting for him at the massive front door as if he had called to warn them of his arrival. Mrs. Hamieh spoke first. "Mercy me, I didn't think it would be this bad."

Fatima nodded and said, "She's alive; that's a relief! In my dream I saw her touching a baby camel, so we knew what to expect, didn't we?"

"Indeed we did. In my dream I saw a fish moving from seawater to freshwater, so we may never know all the details of what happened to Ofelia. Please Octavio, lay her down in the guest bedroom down the hall to your right. We will clean her up while you bring us her medicine, won't you, dear?"

Both women busied themselves with cleaning the wounds and applying an ice compress to Ofelia's ballooned face. Mrs. Hamieh told Fatima, "Ofelia's physical wounds will heal quickly, dear. You must rush over to La Linda's house. Her bladder must be ready to explode, and you know what a demanding diva she is. Be patient and help her out the best you can. I'll check with you later on today."

❖ ❖ ❖

At eight in the morning Claire met Luke for a cup of coffee on Hillhurst Avenue before they headed to their respective jobs.

Each one tried to hide the excitement about seeing each other again. Luke greeted her formally and said, "I'm so glad you're able to meet me this morning. As we agreed yesterday, we're both undoubtedly meddling into our clients' personal business, but I'm willing to take a risk for their well-being. I stopped at Judge Carrera's house yesterday as per my appointment with her and she would not see me. Her assistant told me that she was distraught and I did hear her sobbing, and as you know, the woman is made of steel, so the weeping was way out of the ordinary. Now, here comes my unprofessional behavior and grounds for dismissal. Judge Carrera also wrote one large check to Alma Ruiz two days ago. I've never met Dr. Ruiz but a co-worker remembers her because she apparently has a noticeable facial disfigurement. He said that she may have first tried to cash two checks from Judge Carrera." Luke took a deep breath and said, "Heck, I think I'm going to fire myself for my loose lips. I have to tell you Claire, something about these two special clients and their recent check-writing is not passing my sniff test."

Claire smiled at his candor and his genuine concern. She said, "Funny you should mention sniff test, because several of my clients started behaving differently ever since I changed their massage oil. I know that sounds hocus-pocus, but I noticed how deeply satisfied they all seemed when I used my grandmother's own blend of aromatherapy oils."

Luke said, "Let me get this right: your very elderly clients seemed happy and wanted more massages after you used a unique hand-blended oil made with love by your grandmother. And what is wrong with this picture, please tell me?"

They both laughed at his humorous summary. The other customers at the coffee shop turned and saw two gorgeous people flirting and enjoying each other on a glorious sunny day in Southern California. Claire said, "There is a quirky side effect from my massages. It appears that the scent in the oil brings back memories of long, long ago for some of my senior clients. Lately, I've been hearing some rather unusual recollections about their youth, some of which are totally implausible. But none of my clients ever mentioned writing checks or losing money or anything to do with finances. In fact one of the clients calls the oil "utter bliss." Now I guess I have to fire myself from my job, too, right?"

"In that case, I guess I'll have to sacrifice my body and be your only client," answered Luke.

▩ ▩ ▩

Octavio's van zipped from one house to another. At Dr. Nunez's house he gathered leaves of the *puca panga* dye plant. He would use the leaves to make an infusion as an eye bath for Ofelia. He would also make an extract in water to help treat her anemia and start her on this liquid in a few days. He snuck into Mrs. Dougherty's greenhouse and left quickly with the leaves, stems, and flowers of the *sapo huasca* toad vine. He had to hurry and crush them into a thick mash that he would apply to Ofelia's body to reduce the inflammation and relieve pain. Octavio grabbed some *chami or mimosa pudica* leaves in case Ofelia wanted to sleep, and rushed to his van.

As he put all his plants into his van a surge of yellow-green bile exploded from his liver and convulsed his thoughts into anger and revenge. With a jaguar's acute vision he glanced at all the tools he could use to inflict pain and destroy the men who attacked Ofelia. Hanging in his van were all the serrated edges and steel blades he could wield to puncture and saw his enemies, but the only weapon he missed was a large phallic-shaped branch of the *capinuri* tree. He could pulverize them with that.

It would not be difficult for Octavio to find the den of iniquity near the giant donut sign where the cowards and criminals lie low. He recalled that he had been there months ago asking about Ofelia's daughter as he showed her photo to the depraved animals who frequented such places. At that time, two younger men had told him that they may have seen her three years ago at an ESL class in Hollywood. They spoke to him in fluent English to prove that they had been quick studies. They also heard that Ofelia's daughter was a housekeeper in the Hollywood Hills. Before they showed him their guns, they warned him not to ever return or parts of his body would be leaving in the trash truck.

That memory turned his bile deadly mustard brown. Octavio's retractile forepaw claws were ready to hold their prey. His tongue's rough edge tingled at the taste of peeling the skin away from the criminals who dared to paw at Ofelia's breasts. He was prepared to peel the criminals' flesh to the bones and then gnaw and grind them to their malignant marrow.

❖ ❖ ❖

That day Claire approached each client with a renewed optimism that her massages were therapeutic for her senior clients. Luke had made her realize that she offered a healing service. At Mrs. Dougherty's house she was surprised when Soledad opened the door instead of Yolanda. Soledad was nonchalant. "Come on in," she said. "Yolanda had to run an errand with Margarita. Mrs. D will be with you once her consultation with Dr. Ruiz ends."

Suddenly the mention of Alma Ruiz sent a chill up Claire's back.

While Claire was setting up her massage table, Mrs. Dougherty dragged into the living room with a gloomy expression, and said, "I'm afraid I don't need a massage and I don't want to be near the fireplace. Dr. Ruiz just left. She said I should take a break today since I'll need my full energy for tomorrow. Besides, Pablo can't come today."

Claire had to ask, "Who's Pablo, Mrs. Dougherty?"

Mrs. Dougherty looked downtrodden when she answered, "Oh, he's, he's a special friend of Dr. Ruiz. I'm going up to my room now."

▨ ▨ ▨

Thinking that everyone has an off day, Claire packed up her table. The cancelled appointment left her some free time, so she stopped at Judge Carrera's house to check on her. She rang the doorbell and knocked several times. Then she remembered that Margarita had taken Yolanda on an errand. As she walked away she thought she heard Alma Ruiz shouting at the Judge. She walked around the house and called out to the Judge, but no one came to the door. Perplexed by knowing that Mrs. Dougherty, Judge Carrera, and Dr. Nunez were without their own caregivers, she made a note to telephone all three later in the afternoon. She did not like the feeling in the pit of her stomach, yet she couldn't identify why she was concerned.

When she reached Mrs. Hamieh's she spotted Octavio entering the house just before her. This was very unusual, as Octavio always remained alone and working outdoors. Mrs. Hamieh took her by the hand and sat her down. She said, "Brace yourself, Claire. I have Ofelia in the guest room, and Octavio and I have been mending her bruised and beaten body."

"Oh, no, was she in a car accident? How is La Linda?"

"We don't know for certain what happened to Ofelia, but La Linda did not go with her. Fatima is with La Linda now. It appears that Ofelia snuck out of the house in the wee hours of the morning and took it upon herself to look for her daughter in some very nasty places. In the process she was beaten and cut. Thankfully, she contacted Octavio and he brought her here.

We didn't think she should return to La Linda's house; you're familiar with La Linda's cantankerous demeanor."

"If it's okay with you, I would like to go in and visit Ofelia," said Claire.

※ ※ ※

Ofelia sat on a plush mohair divan in the large guest room. Octavio finished applying a glossy lotion on Ofelia's face and walked out. The swelling on most of her face had subsided but her eyes were still closed shut. The women had bandaged the cuts on her chest, and dressed her in a thin linen caftan.

Ofelia spoke up when she heard Claire's voice. She said, "I don't know what came over me. Earlier in the evening I heard the coyotes howling, and their wailing echoes reverberated in my bones until they escaped through all my pores at exactly one in the morning. I reacted so irrationally, so instinctively, that I scared myself. I had an awareness of death; not just my own or La Linda's, but of a bottomless water well of death. It doesn't make sense does it?" Ofelia tried to get up.

Claire told her, "You've had a shock, Ofelia. Why don't you stay here and I'll go and check on La Linda and Fatima."

Ofelia stood up again and said, "Please take me with you, La Linda needs me."

Both Mrs. Hamieh and Claire attempted to get Ofelia to sit down, but she started to walk out of the room, bumping into the dresser. Mrs. Hamieh said, "Ofelia, daughter, please sit down and let Claire go and straighten things out with La Linda. You'll call us and let us know what La Linda says, right Claire?"

Ofelia screeched, "No, I must be with La Linda, she knows all about pain."

Mrs. Hamieh said, "If you insist, I'll go with you, too."

⊞ ⊞ ⊞

On the short ride to La Linda's house Claire talked Ofelia and Mrs. Hamieh into waiting in the car while she went in to prepare La Linda for Ofelia's bruised body.

La Linda sat sullen in her practice room. Fatima tried to accompany her with the rhythm La Linda desired. La Linda yelled, "Listen, this is the *compás,* this is the basic rhythm unit: there are 12 beats. The strong beats are on the 3, 6, 8, 10, and 12. Come on, Fatima, use your strong hands, clap with intensity, and use your *palmas.* Can't you feel the rhythm in the palm of your hands?"

"Can I just use the tambourine?" asked Fatima.

La Linda replied, "What's the point? This is a *siguiriya* I'm performing and it is uncommon to accompany *siguiriyas* with hand clapping anyway. Forget it. When is Ofelia coming back?"

Claire explained the few facts about Ofelia's irrational behavior and the beating she received at dawn. La Linda said, "Well, of course. The *duende* overcame her, as we all knew it would, didn't we? For God's sake, her daughter has been missing for three long years and she inherently senses the truth. The *duende* drove her to that hellish joint so she could go *mano a mano* with evil, with death, with destiny. You say Ofelia's tragedy took place at dawn and she admits her irrationality and her awareness of death, correct?"

Claire and Fatima nodded in agreement.

"Of course! It's always at dawn! This is Ofelia's *cante jondo,* her innately deepest lament of death and pain and suffering. This is *duende* and she must let *duende* bury its roots in her."

Claire said, "Don't you think tranquility would be better for Ofelia?"

La Linda threw four sets of castanets on the wooden floor one right after the other. They created their own brief flamenco performance. La Linda said, "Did you hear that? That's flamenco without *duende*." She yelled, "Tranquility will never be a possibility for Ofelia. Let me tell you what the great Federico García Lorca said about his search for *duende*. He said that it was not an angel who guides you or gives light nor is it a muse who dictates and prompts. No, absolutely not! García Lorca said that *duende* burns your blood like a poultice of broken glass. Those were his exact words. And didn't you tell me that Ofelia had bits of broken glass and blood oozing from her heart? How much more do you need to see before you believe? García Lorca and others have said that *duende* is a mysterious power which everyone senses and no philosopher can explain. It was true in 1930, it was true one thousand years ago, and it is true today." She added, "Fatima, please bring me some *aguardiente;* I need fortification."

Fatima sat immobile for a few seconds. In her mind, she saw the broken glass from the bus and the blood of the people drowning in the river near San Cristobal de las Casas. As she ran down the road, she felt an overwhelming heat run up from the soles of her feet. It had been *duende*. Her heart was in pieces then and it had cauterized into an abnormal, yet content shape, under the generous warmth of Mrs. Hamieh. She'd had dreams of changing her world up in the hills of San Cristobal de las Casas, now her mended heart smiled at the scent of warm honey and almonds.

La Linda drank her strong *aguardiente* and continued. "García Lorca knew what he wrote about. He was a poet, author, and musician…and he died a violent death. He used to say that an old guitar maestro told him that *duende* is not in the throat. *Duende* climbs up inside you, from the soles of your feet. It brings out your deep-seated emotions. A rejected lover I once had sang in anguish that his intestines burned yellow hot as in

a forge when he remembered me and cried. La Linda whispered,
"Listen," and she belted out her ex-lover's words:

¡*Aaayyy!*

Así como está la fragua,

(Just as the forge)

hecha candela de oro,

(Throws a fire of gold,)

se me ponen las entrañas

(So do my insides)

cuando te recuerdo, y lloro.

(When I remember you, and weep.)

The women didn't need to understand each word that La
Linda sang. La Linda held on to her gut while she sang, as if
indeed, her intestines were on fire. La Linda concluded by saying,
"This is flamenco: the pain of grieving, the loss of a loved one, the
treacherous actions of a friend, the decay of our bodies." She
slapped her legs with ferocity, and then sunk very low on her
chair. She said, "Make no bones about it; we are all *flamencas*.
Our instincts dominate our lives and we've been dealt fatal blows,
but we continue to survive and to say to hell with all of you."

The women heard Mrs. Hamieh's chirpy voice leading
Ofelia to the front door of La Linda's house. Fatima ran to open
the door and guide Ofelia to the studio. The flutter of the privacy sheers in the studio opened slightly and La Linda caught sight
of Octavio listening to her discourse on flamenco and *duende*.
He thought that she was referring to the Shuar understanding of
the instinctual *arutam* of a shaman. La Linda yelled at him,
"You've done enough, Octavio. Please leave."

Mrs. Hamieh walked right up to La Linda and said, "Enough already, La Linda. We have not spoken in decades. Let bygones be bygones. Let sleeping dogs lie."

"You mean dead dogs, don't you? You know how much he loved me and you took him away from me," hissed La Linda.

Claire and Fatima each held one of Ofelia's hands as they scrambled to find a chair for her. They couldn't believe the animosity between Mrs. Hamieh and La Linda.

Mrs. Hamieh said, "You still can't accept fate, can you? He was my husband and it was you who tempted him away temporarily and that is why you came to live in Los Angeles. You are an Andalusian Gypsy and should have stayed with your people. But look at us now. We are old and decrepit. Don't you think we should spend our last days doing good deeds?"

"I think that I should slice you into tiny pieces. You and your sinewy belly dancing were never a match to a dynamic dancer like me. I commanded attention," cried La Linda as she struggled to find her dagger.

Fatima stood in front of La Linda and stared at her coldly, daring her to raise a finger against her godmother. Claire tried to intervene, but had to balance Ofelia, who took off on her own and stepped up to the elevated dance floor in the practice studio.

The emotional drum skin in the studio was taut to the point of tearing. Claire attempted to calm La Linda, who started to clap and snap her fingers. She shouted to Ofelia, "*Alé*, Ofelia. This is our *pena negra*, our darkest pain. It's more than despair and resignation; it's more than wounds and crimes. It's the anguish of nothingness. *Alé!*" Claire tried to get up on the stage to bring Ofelia back down, but without thinking Fatima understood La

Linda's otherworldly motives and prevented Claire from walking up to the dance floor.

Fatima clapped the same rhythm that La Linda started. Mrs. Hamieh sat next to La Linda and heaved and sighed as she tried to keep up with La Linda's rhythm. All three shouted words of encouragement to Ofelia. La Linda shouted, "Your *pena negra* is as old as humanity. You are trying to catch black birds with nets of wind, as García Lorca would say. You are a *bailaora*, you must dance."

The clapping and cheering escalated. Mrs. Hamieh screeched, "*Baila, Mora*. Dance for Beatriz de Robles and all the Moriscas who withstood the torture in the caves of Alpujarra, dance!"

Ofelia's eyes remained sealed shut, but she knew every square inch of the dance floor. She raised her arms in graceful arabesques. La Linda shouted, "Yes, that's it. Your arms are as exquisite as La Argentinita, the famous South American *bailaora*. You are dancing with the timeless arabesques of blood and bone that García Lorca so admired. Dance, *alé!*"

Mrs. Hamieh shrieked, "You are like Telethusa in the Phoenician days of Cádiz. She danced forcefully and artistically. Two thousand years later we still remember her hypnotic dances."

Ofelia lifted the lower half of the thin caftan with both hands and scraped the sole of her shoes on the wood floor like a brush drum. She progressed in intensity by using her heel, the sole and the point of the toe. She stomped and tapped all the time keeping her head downward.

Ofelia twirled and whirled ecstatically. She seemed in a trance. The bandages on her chest were soaked through with blood and ointment. Claire and Fatima finally walked up to the stage and brought Ofelia down as Mrs. Hamieh wrapped her arms tightly around La Linda's quivering shoulders.

Los Feliz
May 4, 2011

At five in the afternoon, at the conclusion of her last massage therapy appointment for the day, Claire vigorously rubbed the last of the oil on the nape of her sore neck. Suddenly she felt an electrical current run through her body. What her mind's eye saw alarmed and excited her. In that split-second bolt, she understood why her clients became both dreamy and agitated as their respective hibernating memories woke up with a roar.

When Luke picked up his cell phone, Claire didn't waste any time. "Okay, this will be the oddest question I have ever posed and you will ever hear, but here goes: Did we ever meet outside a cave that you were exploring some time back?"

He paused and answered, "The question is definitely intriguing—"

"Please don't play games with me. Can you answer my question?"

Luke said, "Yes, but I want to talk to you in person. Are you anywhere near Hillhurst Avenue?"

Within minutes they met at a wine bar, but by then their ethereal connection had faded and they were both composed, serious professionals who couldn't recapture their fleeting epiphanies. The notion of discussing a subject as extremely paranormal as having a memory of each other in their ancestral pasts embarrassed both of them, so they reverted to talking about their mutual clients. Claire was the first to break the last thread of their momentary connection. "I stopped to check on Judge Carrera a while ago, but neither Margarita nor the Judge would open the door. When I walked around her house, I heard Alma Ruiz's loud voice. She was haranguing the Judge about something that I couldn't exactly make out. I tapped on the window, but they ignored me."

Luke's disappointment at not recapturing their special connection showed itself through his bitter comment. He said, "So you left while Alma was screaming at Judge Carrera?" He caught himself and added, "You don't have to answer that. I'm a bit on edge today. I was reprimanded pretty severely at the bank today for not following investigative protocol. And guess what I did instead of sticking to my principles?" Again Luke did not wait for Claire's response. He continued, "That's right; I apologized to my supervisor. I suppose we both *do* have something in common, after all. Seems to me we both get a charge out of being aware of the unsaid and intangible communications with others, yet when it comes right down to it, we're both conventional. We toe the line."

Instead of justifying her behavior at the Judge's house, Claire looked down at her wine glass and said, "I also stopped by to check on Mrs. Dougherty and she asked me to come by tonight for a 7 P.M. massage. I usually don't work past six in the evening. Mrs. Dougherty told me Alma arranged for Pablo to return at 8 P.M. I'm determined to meet this Pablo in person and see what is going on with Mrs. Dougherty."

Luke smiled at Claire and said, "Mind if I join you in meeting Pablo? I'll be outside Mrs. Dougherty's house at eight, even if I get fired tomorrow."

And they clinked their glasses in agreement to break the rules.

◫ ◫ ◫

Alma stopped at a shabby Craftsman style bungalow in Hollywood in one of the grimiest streets no tourist would ever visit. She carried an iridescent mermaid costume as if it were a case of valuable caviar. She entered directly into the miniscule living room which had cots and large boxes strewn on the once pristine wood floors. The slim woman who answered the door had cropped brown hair and dressed in androgynous tight jeans and a black t-shirt. Alma said, "You sure look different from yesterday, Monty. Are you sure you can fit into this curvy mermaid costume? I thought you told me you had your long hair tucked into your hat."

Monty yanked the costume and said, "Wait here. In a couple of minutes you will be mesmerized by a mermaid with flowing tresses. Just wait."

Amidst the empty fast food wrappers, oily plates, beer bottles, and plain filth, an innocent mermaid appeared at the roughhewn doorway. She tossed her long auburn hair behind her shoulders and sang a hypnotic siren song in a plaintive voice. The mermaid kicked the fish tail up and down with her dainty toes as she sang:

Yo me enamoré de una sirena;

De una sirena; de una mujer

Una mujer muy hermosa

Although entranced by the fishtail sounds of the song, Alma had to keep this mermaid under control. She said, "Monty, you cannot pronounce the word *mujer* as you would in Spanish. Also, you must elongate the first two sentences in this manner: I once fell in love with a mermaiiid; of a mermaiiid; of a woman. In Ladino you must pronounce the letter j like the English consonant cluster *sh*. So the word *mujer* becomes *moosher*, do you understand my direction?"

Monty's amber eyes enlarged like a cat ready to eat a rat. She said, "Oh, yes, Alma. I was told you are quite the task master, no?"

Alma sensed a recalcitrant mermaid who needed a firm hand. She said, "This is your opportunity to make an easy $500 if you follow my direction."

Monty advanced towards Alma taking minute steps due to the tightness of her scaly tail. She was nearly nose to nose with Alma when she purred and said, "I have much to learn from a doctor in so many fields. I hear that you are a holistic doctor, a botanist, a genealogist, and now a linguistic professor. Please tell me about your education and about the tragedy to your face."

Alma wanted to step back, but was cornered by the protruding slats of the sofa. Like a deep water eel, Monty simply reached out and put her arms around Alma's neck and held on tightly. She repeated, "I want to hear all about your exciting life. I think that if you are willing to pay me $500 for a few minutes of singing and swimming, and you've already paid Carlos, I mean Pablo, $1,200, then you must have very deep pockets, no?" Monty tried to reach her hands into Alma's jean pockets.

Alma swatted Monty's hand away and said, "This is a one-time gig for you and it is Pablo's last performance. I have to return to my research abroad in a couple of days, so listen to the details of your performance. I'll pick you and Pablo up in one hour. For now rehearse your lines while I stop by the car repair shop and see what they can do about my car."

"I know the lines by heart. Besides didn't you tell me that these lines are a hodgepodge of lines from the poetry of Avicebrón, an eleventh century poet? Get real! How is an old man who has the hots for a mermaid going to know what I am singing in Ladino?"

Alma held to her guns. "You must sing and recite the lines I selected from various poems because I can't be sure which poem is the one he remembers as having written for some girl he loved, a girl he calls *sirena*. We must entice him with the trigger words."

Monty laughed and said, "I think this whole gig is a fiasco and it's not going to work. Starting with your car. We'd better take a cab to our gigs tonight since your junker will never make it."

"Never mind my car, it only has to last one more day. On the way back up to Los Feliz, you'll practice your lines with Pablo. He's a darn good actor, by the way."

"Yes, I've seen all his movies—twice," said Monty.

Alma was too rushed to worry about Monty's sarcasm. "Once we drop Pablo for his acting job at my other client's home, then you will wait in the car until Soledad comes to escort you to the backyard swimming pool. I'll leave the window to the client's first floor den open and you'll approach the window and sing your lines very dramatically and loudly. The only line that I know for sure he must hear is: *Fente mib de nohte, mio sîdî*, Solomon. Say that line clearly, it simply means: Come to me at night, my lord, Solomon. Then, walk back to the pool. Once I pull back the drapes you will dive into the pool and make that tail splash repeatedly. This is a client who must believe that he is seeing a mermaid. As his psychologist, I have been working to overcome his—"

Monty slipped out of her tight and scaly tail and sat legs wide open on the edge of the raggedy sofa in her threadbare thong. She said, "I'm wondering, in your expert opinion, how does a pathological liar compare with a sociopath, dear Dr. Ruiz?"

"I don't have time to waste. You either want to earn the $500 or I'll hire any skanky actress to play your part," snapped Alma.

"Not in less than two hours you won't! And certainly not one who can speak Ladino convincingly, and one who understands your animal desires and who can travel with you. I can be the face of your foreign research. We can research all sorts of vibrant subjects together, no? Surely you're not so delusional to believe that people will trust you with your hideous grimace, do you?" asked Monty.

Her blunt force truth knocked the wind out of Alma and left her momentarily speechless.

Monty said, "That's why I'm asking you if you understand the difference between a pathological liar and a sociopath. Let's me refresh your memory, Dr. Ruiz. A pathological liar has excessive anxiety of being caught in a lie whereas a sociopath has total disregard for social norms and rules and is incapable of experiencing guilt. A habitual liar creates a myth or imaginary fantasies to reinforce her low self-esteem whereas a sociopath acts any way she chooses and has a very low tolerance for frustration and will lash out." Monty let Alma gasp for air, and then she continued. "I'll let you in on a little secret, just to show you that I am a good business partner. My name is Montserrat Joa and the police have been looking for me for a couple of years in connection with the trafficking of young Ecuadorian women. I can leave this country any time I want but I won't do it until I have enough money to live abroad in style. You can provide that style with the loot you and Soledad are hiding. You can make up any lie you want about us. I can be your research assistant, your lover, your daughter from a very handsome ex-lover, or whatever you wish. I can protect you and your money since pathological liars also have other impulse control disorders such as compulsive shopping and pathological gambling. Am I right? Sounds enticing, no?"

Alma was fuming instead of breathing. She threw $100 on the stained sofa and said, "Be ready in one hour. You talk too much. Incidentally, the last person who tried to analyze me was old Dr. Yepez. He went on and on about factitious disorder and confabulation and complex narratives. All I needed to do to shut him up for good was to set a torch to his lab. So what was that you were saying about creative thinkers not being able to discharge aggression? Cat got your tongue? I'll let you know what we can do together after your swimming and singing performance." She stormed out of the decrepit bungalow.

An hour later, Pablo and Monty heard a puttering car creep into the bungalow's driveway. Alma honked the car horn and they both ran across the dry grass to the car, laughing like two garden gnomes on a mischievous spree. Monty almost tripped a couple of times, and Pablo helped to balance her. Monty said, "I see they fixed your car. If I had taken it to the garage, they would have lent me a sports car, right Pablo?"

"You do have your ways to get what you want. Hey, Alma, don't we have to wear a blindfold?"

Alma was feeling giddy herself. She said, "No, tonight is our last performance. But I don't like the way Monty almost fell down twice. You'd better not be stoned, Monty. You have to be sober to pull off acting like mermaid that dives into the pool, got it?"

Monty answered, "Don't worry about my acting. Just worry about your car making it up the hill."

⊞ ⊞ ⊞

Soledad proceeded with her end of the plot for tonight's three final memory reenactments at the homes of Mrs. Dougherty, the Judge, and Dr. Nunez. First, she drove Yolanda to her sister's apartment downtown and left her there while she purportedly ran an errand. Soledad drove back up to Los Feliz and was waiting at the door of Mrs. Dougherty's house when Claire arrived at 7 P.M. After the massage was under way, she brought Pablo back into the house and told him to wait until Claire left and then to go ahead and charm Mrs. Dougherty in his usual fashion.

⊞ ⊞ ⊞

Meanwhile, Alma sat in Dr. Nunez's den reading his pitiful poetry and serving him his nightly scotch. She brought him a special bottle of single malt. As was his grouchy fashion, Dr. Nunez complained. "This scotch tastes awful," he said. "Serve me my usual."

Alma put on her most charming persona and said, "Now you're hurting my feelings. I bought you the most expensive twenty-five-year-old bottle of scotch to show you how much I appreciate you letting me read your lyrical poetry."

The curmudgeon reluctantly said, "Fine, fine, fine, I'll drink it but it's making me sleepy. Thanks anyway. Keep reading the poems and use your Ladino words. They sound like the *sirena* I once loved. I think that was her name: *sirena*."

⊞ ⊞ ⊞

Soledad sneaked out of Mrs. Dougherty's house and rushed back
to Dr. Nunez's house. She did not want to miss a minute of the
mermaid's reenactment. She left the car running on the street
and went inside. As if on cue, she escorted the mermaid from the
back seat of Alma's car to the backyard patio and left her right by
the opened den window while she dimmed the patio lights.
Anyone looking from the inside would only see the darkness of
the patio and the turquoise blue water of the pool and its cas-
cading waterfall.

Soledad took off her shoes so she would not make noise as
she ran up the stairs to crack open Fort Knox. She would only
have a couple of minutes to get the gold bars from the safe into
the duffel bag, and get back into Dr. Nunez car. She heard the
mermaid start to sing:

Fente mib de nohte, mio sîdî, Solomon.

(Come to me at night, my lord, Solomon.)

Yo me enamoré de una sirena,

(I fell in love with a mermaid)

de una sirena, de una **moosher,**

(With a mermaid, with a woman)

me ha enviado una frasca llena de fragancias,

(She has sent me a bottle full of scents)

Cada una como de verde y oro,

(Each one like emerald and gold—)

Dr. Nunez struggled to stand up as he said, "Shut up, Alma.
Can't you hear that beautiful song? How can that be? I'm

hearing my *sirena* sing her haunting song. Damn it, girl, help me stand up, will you?"

Alma took her sweet time steadying Dr. Nunez. She had to allow Monty to take her tiny steps closer to the pool before pulling back the drapes to give Dr. Nunez his reenactment. She assumed that Soledad was completing her task of filling up the duffel bag with the gold bars.

Dr. Nunez yanked the drape off its track and cried out to the mermaid:

All my desire and hope is with you, my *sirena*;

I long just for your company.

My, my eyes cry out for you,

Who drives my sleep away.

Monty stood at the edge of the pool. She teetered tottered at the edge. Although clearly off balance due to her usual cock-tail of drugs, she somehow managed to turn around to wave to Dr. Nunez before diving into the pool. Her opalescent tail reflected like diamonds on the surface of the water. The tail slapped the water repeatedly and then slowed down. The long hair wig floated away dragging a stream of blood.

Alma prepared for stage two of their plan, which was to sit Dr. Nunez down on his reclining chair and tell him that she would go outside and ask the mermaid to wait while she escorted him out. But Dr. Nunez's passion for his *sirena* energized him and he ran out to the pool. He had lived in this house for decades and he knew every step by heart. The more Monty flapped her tail and arms in the panic of drowning the more the diamond waters reflected light. Dr. Nunez followed this beacon with open arms. He shouted for the *sirena* to wait for him in what he hoped was Spanish or Ladino, "*Espérale, mía sirena! Yo era, yo soy Latino!*" If Monty had heard him, she would have ridiculed his syntax. Dr. Nunez had said: "Wait for him, mine mermaid. I was, I am Hispanic."

Alma struggled with a split-second decision. Should she turn off the lights to the pool to give Monty time to get out of the water on her own two legs or should she go up to check on what was delaying Soledad?

At the same time of Alma's confusion as to what to do next, Pablo made the instinctive decision to leave Mrs. Dougherty's house before the end of her massage with Claire. Pablo had walked around the house and picked up a couple of silver picture frames, a German knife set from the kitchen, and a few loose dollars stuffed in a kitchen drawer. Pablo had an inkling that the old grandma would demand him to do the nasty tonight, and he just wasn't feeling it. It wasn't that he felt sorry for the grandma or that he suddenly had a pang of remorse about his actions. He simply found her neediness repulsive and he thought he might have to hurt her. Severely. Instead, he walked out of her house like a thief in the night with his meager loot and headed down the hill towards Hollywood.

Proving that there is no honor among thieves, Soledad did not follow Alma's plan. She threw the heavy duffel bag into the backseat and dashed into Dr. Nunez's car. She drove frantically and giddily down the hill. She kept shouting inside her car, "Yeah, baby. Can buy me loooove; money can buy me love!" She nearly missed hitting two joggers as they carelessly crossed in front of her. She swerved to the right and hit a trash can. Instead of slowing down she accelerated with vigor and didn't see Pablo waving her down. Through her dangling false eyelashes she saw knives flying in the air and felt the car run over Pablo. She lost total control of the vehicle as it skidded into a tall cement wall.

⊠ ⊠ ⊠

Alma ran up the stairs and gaped at the opened and empty safe. She rushed to the second-story window and looked out. Instead of finding Soledad trying to bring Dr. Nunez back into the house, she saw Dr. Nunez dive into the pool and grab his *sirena's* tail. She heard him cry out, "My beloved!" as he attempted to hold on to a drugged out and injured mermaid. Whatever, thought Alma. Let them engage in their bizarre sext acts. She had to find Soledad and the duffel bag full of gold.

Even in his previous lecherous days, Dr. Nunez loved to wrestle his medical assistants into submission as they slapped away his probing thick digits. The mermaid bit Dr. Nunez's left hand, and he instinctively put his right hand into her crotch. The lustrous tail slid down and wrapped itself tightly around his legs and the mermaid's kicking left leg. This was a professional mermaid costume and its sturdy curved wire sprung around both their legs and snapped shut. Dr. Nunez experienced a surge of adrenaline unlike anything he had felt before. He took a deep breath and went down on the sinking mermaid. The second surge of severe pain to his chest turned off his dim light forever.

The mermaid's costume did not include the vital gills required for rough underwater recreation. Despite her stupor, Monty realized that even her treasure chest of sociopathic attributes could not help her struggle against the rusty old anchor holding her down at the bottom of the pool.

Alma's search had turned up nothing. No Soledad and no gold. She ran to the front of the house and looked for Dr. Nunez's car, which Soledad used as if it were her own. It was nowhere in sight.

Alma returned dejectedly to the swimming pool area to get the old man out of the water. He had to have cash hidden somewhere in the house. Perhaps she could sweet-talk him into paying her, after the fact, for being the madam in his mermaid escapade.

At a distance Alma could see two floating bodies obscuring the glimmer of the water. Alma's twisted face twitched uncontrollably and her watery right eye blinded her with rage. The only plan she had managed to execute flawlessly was the accidental execution of two blundering idiots. Even the two-faced, snake-in-the-grass Soledad had outwitted her and would soon be on an airplane bound for her home and her family back in the Philippines with a fortune. But Alma had no family, she had no home, and she had no friends. For a lifelong charlatan, this moment of truth was impossible to comprehend. She had to leave both this grisly pool scene and this country immediately. She had wanted to accomplish so much in life, but the only traces she left wherever she went were murky smudges people wiped off with disgust.

Alma walked back to the house and turned off all the pool and landscape lights in an attempt to buy time before the bodies would be discovered. She got into Granny's old car, but it refused to start. She trembled at the awareness that her brief and pathetic life had come to an end. She got out of the car, grabbed her backpack, pulled her fedora down tightly, and started her walk to hell.

Since sunset, Octavio made the rounds checking on Claire and her customers. Mrs. Hamieh and Fatima offered him dinner and sent him off with pistachio *macarons* as he went back to his van. Margarita answered the door sullenly and told him to mind his business. He eavesdropped on La Linda and Ofelia, and was relieved to discover that they were taking a break from dancing and were singing woebegone songs.

Earlier in the evening he had seen Soledad driving recklessly, but he ignored her since he was headed to Mrs. Dougherty's house expecting to see Alma's old car in the driveway alongside Claire's. He parked across the street and spied on Claire and the young man who had been there the other day. They both stayed outside the entrance door looking around as if waiting for someone. Eventually, Mrs. Dougherty came out in a disheveled and flimsy robe and looking very confused. Claire said goodbye to the young man and took Mrs. Dougherty by the hand back inside.

Perplexed by not finding Alma anywhere, Octavio drove past Dr. Nunez's house to see if she was there. Although the old man was frugal, Octavio had never seen his property in such darkness. He grabbed a flashlight and went to check the property. His sixth sense rang its warning before he aimed the flashlight at the pool. Octavio ran to the pool and jumped in to rescue Dr. Nunez. Immediately he knew that any attempt to rescue him and the thin woman was futile.

Octavio had seen many floating bodies of man and beast in the still tributaries of the Amazon. Particularly after the oil company intentionally disposed of the toxic waste into the hidden rivers and streams back in the 1990's. Octavio witnessed his revered wildlife float by indistinguishably with a thick coat of black slime. Their carcasses stunk to high heaven, but tonight he smelled a singular rat the size of Alma Ruiz.

⧆ ⧆ ⧆

Alma avoided going back to Granny's house. There was nothing of value waiting for her there. She carried her passport and all the cash and jewels she had fleeced from the old suckers in the backpack on her shoulder. Alma pulled down her fedora on her face and walked by the crowd of emergency vehicles surrounding Dr. Nunez's car. Whoever had been trapped under the car was carried off on a completely covered gurney. For once she was relieved knowing that throughout her life she had gone unnoticed by everyone just as she did tonight.

⧆ ⧆ ⧆

As Alma approached the intersection of Catalina Street and Los Feliz Boulevard, Octavio's van pulled up beside her. He rolled down the passenger window and said, "They're out to get you, Alma. Get in the back of the van and cover yourself with my garden tarp. Quickly."

Alma saw more and more police cars with their sirens blaring heading towards the car crash. She jumped in the back of the van. "Why should I cover myself with this abomination? I didn't do anything. I'm sick and tired of L.A. Besides Granny's house doesn't belong to me anymore, but my research awaits me in Cusco. Why are you heading back towards the accident?"

Octavio recognized Alma's confused state and rambling illogical monologue. She was behaving no more differently than a trapped tapir who will try to charge or bite knowing full well that it is no match for a stealth jaguar. Octavio answered her truthfully. He said, "I'm heading back on Los Feliz Boulevard to Commonwealth Avenue and then we'll head up Vista del Valle into the heart of Griffith Park. Once there you can calm down, we can talk, and I can help you reach your final destination, okay?"

Alma didn't like not being in control, but his option did make sense, and she covered herself with the malodorous tarp. She asked him, "Can you take me to the airport?"

"I will help you reach your desired destination, certainly. Do you mind if I spray a deodorizer onto the tarp?" Octavio didn't wait for her response. He strayed directly onto the green tarp at about the area covering her head.

Alma lifted the tarp off her face, and Octavio sprayed her face. Alma sat up, but she saw the flashing red lights of the police cars and decided to lie down again. She yelled at Octavio, "Don't spray me again or I'll get out of this car."

Octavio pulled his van over to a parking lot on Los Feliz Boulevard. He said, "Please feel free to do as you wish. This is a good place for you to wait for the bus. It's fairly busy and people won't notice you at all. You're used to being neglected, right?"

Alma felt oddly calm despite her chaotic evening. Octavio's comment about her being neglected was accurate and she felt glad that he had phrased his observation without any rancor. "I didn't say I wanted to get out of the van," she said. "Just don't spray me with a flowery deodorizer. I've had enough with exotic fragrances and hallucinogenic massage oils. Were you and Claire trying to euthanize the old people with some topical crushed mushrooms or whatever?"

Octavio said, "We can sit here and talk about the euphoric qualities of the blissful oil I prepared for the elderly, but I'm fairly certain that a police car will be pulling up to observe the bus stop. Are you interested in talking under the canopy of Griffith Park or not?"

"Yeah, let's get out of here. But can you please go in to the convenience store there and buy me a bottle of water, I'm parched."

Octavio pointed to a small cooler in his van and said, "I have a couple bottles of water in there. I always fill them myself with specially filtered water, is that okay with you?"

Alma grabbed a bottle gulped down the entire thing. She asked Octavio, "It still stinks in here under the tarp. Do you think—"

"Shhh, don't say a word, there's a police car pulling into the lot. Get under the tarp, while I go out and pretend to tighten my gardening equipment." As he walked out of the van, he once again sprayed the tarp.

When Alma next sat up, she was outdoors on a hillside under a dense canopy of trees surrounded by thick shrubs. She asked Octavio, "What the hell just happened? Weren't we just in the parking lot?"

Octavio sat very relaxed next to her on the ground and said, "You are obviously exhausted, so I let you sleep and carried you to this quiet spot until things cool down in Los Feliz. What do you think your final destination should be?"

Alma liked the way he asked her about her future. Perhaps he was trying to include himself as a part of the plan. She answered, "I want to live in a peaceful place where people pay attention to what I have to say. I want to be able to just be myself, plain old Alma Ruiz. I would love to roam around the new town and its nearby surroundings and see beautiful flowers and unique birds in the sky. Would you like to come with me to such a place? Is there such a place?"

Octavio offered her a drink from his thermos after taking the first swig. She followed suit despite its bitter taste. Octavio said, "There is definitely such a paradise and I like the way you can already picture it. It's a place where your namesake, that is your soul, your *alma*, will find repose. Here, let's finish this drink. It will relax both of us as we talk about finding peace in this utterly confused world."

Alma protested. "I don't like to get high. I like to be in control at all times. What's in this drink?"

"It's all natural. You've seen me growing all my plants in Mrs. Dougherty's greenhouse and in the other properties. I share my knowledge of nature with people once they are ready to travel on," said Octavio.

Alma didn't quite understand his oblique references to travel. She asked him point blank, "Are you or are you not going to drive me to the airport so I can fly to South America?"

"Of course, if that is what you wish. I just want to be sure that you are traveling to the appropriate paradise. That is why I am asking you about how you envision it. Let's take Mrs. Dougherty's idea of paradise. She yearns for the protection of a warm secret cave, am I not correct?"

Alma's eyes started to close and her speech began to slur. She said, "I don't want to live in a cave…thash not paradishe."

Octavio asked her very respectfully. "Do you mind if I rub your neck with this massage oil?"

"Go for ith. Tell me about my paradishe…."

Octavio rubbed the intoxicating oil onto Alma's neck. He then rubbed it on her wrists. Alma inhaled the aroma and said, "Utter blish." Soon Alma felt her neck and wrists alluringly numb. She managed to say, "My paradishe is…"

Octavio pricked her finger with a rose thorn. Alma didn't respond. He treated her with the respect that a Shuar warrior must always give a strong adversary. He must contain his opponent's *arutam* tightly inside a shrunken head or the life force might attack again and again.

Octavio poured psychotropic *datura* drops into Alma's droopy mouth. He had to decide if he would follow the ancient Shuar ways and carry Alma's head around his neck or if he would follow the way of the priests who once rescued him and convinced him that he should continue helping cure the ill. He waited for a sign and it appeared in the shape of a scrawny coyote.

Once Octavio made his decision with conviction, he slit both of Alma's wrists in the way that she would have eventually taken her own life. He picked up all his paraphernalia and covered her with the coat from her backpack. He took all the money and jewels out of her backpack and planted them in a bag of manure in the back of his van. He'd been in California long enough to know that you need money to make money. Lastly, he blew a poisonous dart at the lingering coyote.

Octavio covered his tracks and took off in his van. He drove all around Griffith Park until he saw the tiny creek with enough water to perform his last shamanic rite. He decapitated the coyote and gently placed its head in the water in tribute to the shattered and destructive *alma* of his adversary, Alma Ruiz.

16

Los Feliz
Summer 2011

ike coyote bones left out to blanch in the sun, the traces of bliss experienced by Claire's clients also faded away. Claire continued to massage her remaining elderly clients, but the oil no longer ushered them into their previous reveries. It was as if the hardiest bass notes in the verbena fragrance had evaporated into the balmy Santa Ana winds. The magic and ecstasy that had briefly uplifted her clients blew west into the depths of the Pacific Ocean.

Over summer, the elderly residents of Los Feliz saw less and less of Octavio's verdant van. His barbarous mushrooms no longer ruminated in the mossy corners of their yards. Little by little he dismantled Mrs. Dougherty's greenhouse. The pungent earthy tang of the Amazonian plants waned. In their place now grew lemon trees whose blossoms scented the air with Southern California aromas. Mrs. Dougherty looked out from her living room window and shrugged her shoulders enigmatically at Octavio as he trimmed back her verbena shrubs. She stood at the window momentarily and then returned to sit next to the Batchelder fireplace, her eyes fixed on the disappearing Pegasus bas-relief. She started to make a comment to Yolanda, but instead leaned over and scratched the uneven surface of the tiles as if they contained a braille-like secret message. Yolanda began to worry about this gesture. "Mrs. Dougherty," she said, "you are going to ruin your pretty nails if you keep scratching the tiles."

"Yes, you're right, dear, but I want to disintegrate the tile. I want to scratch away at the body of the Pegasus and turn him into dust. I want to see this whole fireplace turn into its original prehistoric cave, does it make sense?"

Yolanda recognized that Mrs. Dougherty's mind was becoming more fragile than the fading horse. Yolanda selected her words carefully. She said, "I think that many of us want to be somewhere else. I would love to be taking care of my children. So I think that maybe you must want to see your daughters, too. Did they play near the fireplace on cold nights when they were young?"

"They were both serious girls who did not waste time sitting by the fireplace. No, I am thinking that I must have lived in a cave a long time ago. In fact, the more I think about it, the more I will have this fireplace dismantled and turned into a proper cave. Do you think that Pablo will ever come back?"

"I never met Pablo, but I heard that he has returned to his home far, far away and will not ever come back," said Yolanda. She saw tears welling up in Mrs. Dougherty's eyes, so she asked her, "Would you like me to ask Lawyer Catlin to come and visit you, or better yet, why don't I fly with you to visit her?"

"Catlin does not like surprises of that nature. Besides she's very busy and can't see me. We would be better off flying to Mexico and visiting your children," answered Mrs. Dougherty as tear drops streamed down her rosy cheeks.

Yolanda jumped up and hugged Mrs. Dougherty. She said, "You would love my children and they would love you. They miss their grandmother; you would become their American *abuelita*. My aunt takes care of them, but she has her own grandchildren and she's very tired. You are very kind to ask me, but if I go back to Mexico, I may not be able to come back."

Mrs. Dougherty stayed silent for a while. She stopped scratching the tiles. She went to her desk and opened old files. She found the contact information for a trusted travel agent and she made an appointment with her estate attorney. She reminded the attorney that her appointment was confidential and her daughters would not be privy to the information. Once Mrs. Dougherty's plan was set in motion, she called her daughters. Catlin's cold-hearted response did not take her by surprise. Catlin said, "Mother, get to the point. I'm walking into the conference room."

Mrs. Dougherty said, "I am going to spend a year or longer with Yolanda's family in Oaxaca, Mexico."

Catlin said, "Fine, whatever. Do you want me to put the Los Feliz house up for sale and roll the proceeds into our trusts or what?"

Mrs. Dougherty knew in her bones that she would never return to her sylvan retreat in Los Feliz. She said, "Sure, sweetheart, do as you wish."

Catlin said, "Don't get me started, mother. You always say that and then when I act to put your welfare first, you refuse to move into a perfectly upstanding senior home. Are you certain that you want to go live in Oaxaca? You know that I won't be able to fly down there quarterly, like I do now."

Mrs. Dougherty had to get one last jab in. "Well, you haven't been down to see me since last year, what's the difference?"

"The difference is that I am swamped with work and worrying about you day and night. Just because I can't fly down to L.A. doesn't mean that I don't care, for pity's sake," snapped Catlin. "My meeting is about to start. Do you need me to do any arrangements?"

Mrs. Dougherty could detect a sigh of relief in Catlin's voice. She understood the unsaid things her daughter had just revealed to her. Mrs. Dougherty had outlived her value to her daughter. Her advice would never be heeded and she had proved her love to her daughter with a worthy inheritance. Her daughter's keen intellect had propelled her to great heights, but she had left her heart on the ground.

Mrs. Dougherty replied, "No, thank you, Catlin. I believe I've taken care of all my arrangements. Would you like me to give you Yolanda's address in Oaxaca? Do you think that you could fly down for their festivities for the Day of the Dead in November?"

Catlin replied, "When are you going to learn how to text me information? I'll hand you over to my assistant so you can give her your address. As for the November event, I can't see myself walking around looking at a bunch of marigold altars to dead people. I'll call you, mother. Make sure that your cell phone works and take a battery charger, for pity's sake. I'm late to my meeting."

Within a matter of weeks Mrs. Dougherty reveled in the charm of the cobblestone streets and Spanish Colonial architecture of Oaxaca. Her sweet demeanor and wide-eyed interest in the beauty of the crafts and arts on display throughout the city made her a favorite among the merchants. Soon she was chatting in her rusty Spanish, much to the glee of Yolanda's children. She enjoyed cooking three daily meals; something she had never done in all her privileged life. In the early evenings Mrs. Dougherty would burn *copal* resin incense so that its pine and citrus fragrance would protect her and the children. She took great pleasure in helping Yolanda bathe the little ones. Mrs. Dougherty's duty was to dry them off with soft towels. As she dried their tiny toes, she giggled and told them in her choppy Spanish, "*Deditos limpios, no come duende*," and they all laughed together at her silly refrain, "Clean little toes, the *duende* won't eat."

* * *

For a few weeks after Dr. Nunez's drowning, Octavio left a basket of figs for La Linda and pomegranates for Ofelia by the dance studio door. Sometimes the basket disappeared indoors for a day or two, and other times the fruit rotted in the basket. He whistled for Ofelia through the fluttering curtains in La Linda's studio, but he never received a response other than the tap, tap, tapping of flamenco shoes, and the constant clapping of the women's palms. The energy field coming from their studio was as great as the *arutam* power force that would have emanated from a half-dozen Shuar shamans, if there were that many left in the world. Octavio perceived that the joint destiny of Ofelia and La Linda did not include him, and he left. The only trace of him ever having been at their estate was the tendril of a Cat's Claw liana that was intertwined with the hardy cork tree next to the dance studio.

* * *

At Mrs. Hamieh's property Octavio groomed her herb and vegetable gardens. For a few weeks, Fatima worked side by side with him as he taught her how to properly care for the ripening fruit and vegetables. Mrs. Hamieh stepped out of her kitchen to see their progress. She asked Octavio, "Do you think that we have enough land to plant vegetables and herbs to supply one restaurant?"

"It depends on how many customers the restaurant feeds daily," said Octavio. "I think that if it were your restaurant you would know how to include just the right amount of your organic produce into each dish."

"Well, what it if were a restaurant that Fatima could operate, can you help her figure out what she might need?" panted Mrs. Hamieh. Octavio stopped gardening and stood next to Mrs. Hamieh. He looked into her eyes and they both could see that her flame was extinguishing. Her shallow breathing and weakness said it all. She nodded at him confirming his thoughts. She perkily added, "Please, Octavio, help Fatima and me maintain a delicious garden for our customers." She quickly became very fatigued and returned to the comfort of her kitchen.

❖ ❖ ❖

Mrs. Hamieh had been experiencing variations of the same dream. Every night the sun appeared in her dreams, and every day she analyzed its evolving significance to her past and present. In one dream, the sun fell apart in the sky just as her child had fallen apart and died ages ago in infancy. Her infant's Mediterranean DNA had been too intense and defective. The sea as in Thalassa and the blood as in Haema had created thalassemia major, the blood disease from the same sea of Aristotle, Hannibal, and Telethusa. Throughout the generations, this genetic blood abnormality had avoided hurting her ancestors, but in her baby's body the bone marrow produced an abnormal form of hemoglobin that could not sustain life. When her baby died she could never fill the hole left in her heart. Without any other children to help her mend, Mrs. Hamieh had fallen lower than the sun in her dreams.

In another dream, Mrs. Hamieh was holding the sun, and indeed, her errant husband had returned to her after his fiery affair with La Linda. The next night the sun appeared in a clear blue sky meaning that her husband would spoil her. This dream had become a reality, and now at the end of her life, her wealth had multiplied. But it was the string of dreams in which she spoke with the sun that urged her to settle all legal matters to benefit her late-in-life goddaughter, Fatima. Speaking with the sun meant death. In her conversations with the sun Mrs. Hamieh always managed to coax one more day of existence.

In a matter of a month, Octavio drove Mrs. Hamieh and Fatima to a charming restaurant on Sunset Boulevard near Elysian Park. Octavio carried a debilitated Mrs. Hamieh like a bride over the threshold of the restaurant as she panted in anticipation. Her neighbors and well-wishers applauded the grand opening of Fatima's Bistro. The carved stone doorway was in the shape of a large, seven-foot-high, keyhole. But it was the detail of the door that took everyone's breath away.

The Marrakech red, parquet wood, antique door was inlaid in camel bone whose old marrow had left its mark with yellowed striations. The ancient bones seemed to jump out of the red door. They symbolized the importance of the marrow in the production of blood: the source of life. Mrs. Hamieh knew that Fatima would understand that she and Mrs. Hamieh were in some way related by a blood thicker than hereditary blood. In the heart of the door rested a polished brass, life-size, hand knocker. Its pinkie and thumb were extended outwards as a talisman warding off the evil eye.

Fatima followed Mrs. Hamieh and Octavio as they entered the restaurant. She carried a large clay pot planted with a fragrant verbena shrub. She placed it prominently on the round entry table. She surreptitiously dug her pinkie finger deep into the soil until she felt the chopped-off pinkie bone of the larcenous wolf. She would need the shape-shifting power of the *huay chivo* to help her run this restaurant without fear.

In the previous night's dream, Mrs. Hamieh had seen the sun falling to the ground and a stork had swallowed it whole. She exhaled woefully during the restaurant's successful debut party, and accepted the fact that she would never see another sunset.

⊠ ⊠ ⊠

When Octavio stopped by to check on Judge Carrera, he found the house empty. Neither Margarita nor the Judge were anywhere in sight. He peeked through the windows and a moving van company employee came out to speak with him. He said, "Sorry, man, but I guess they forgot to tell you that the house was sold. Maybe the new owners will need your services."

Octavio asked, "Do you know where the Judge has moved?"

The man looked at his manila folder. He said, "Says here that a Judge Carrera is now a resident in a senior community down in Orange County. It's a facility for seniors with diminishing capacity. Man, it's so sad to see all these old *abuelitos* get locked up. Even if it is a nice place, it's not right to put them way, you know what I mean, man?"

⊠ ⊠ ⊠

Octavio's van was last seen on the steep streets of nearby Echo Park. It was totally empty inside. The remaining exterior graffiti had been entirely erased by time and wear and tear. Octavio had planted an array of healing plants near Doña Verito's cottage, and then he disappeared. Some say that he went back to the Amazon with the riches he acquired in Los Angeles. They say that he casually picked up Soledad's duffel bag full of gold bars from the chaotic accident scene. After all, no one ever notices a gardener bending down near a shrub or tree. Octavio's assimilation to modern California life was exemplary. He spoke English flawlessly and he transferred his skills for creating essential oils for the elderly to essentially awakening the senses of a new demographic. They say that he is now in the San Francisco Bay area, a secretive healer known only to a handful of wealthy techies who believe he gives them their inner strength and marketing advantage. They flaunt their priceless talismans of shrunken animal heads. The techies say he's turned them into fearless warriors for a modern age.

▩ ▩ ▩

With her gnarly hands, Claire's grandmother tended the terraced hillside blooming with the cuttings Octavio left for her. Due to the hilly topography of her tucked away home and its huge and overgrown agaves, it was easy for the healing plants to proliferate without notice. Besides, in this large immigrant neighborhood overlooking Echo Park Lake, Doña Verito was a cherished healer. Even the toughest gangbangers left her plants alone. She continued her private consultations with her regular clients, but she extended her healing touch to whoever made the hike up the narrow stairway leading to her cottage. In such an old neighborhood near downtown Los Angeles, the numerous public stairways that zigzagged up the hilly streets were a welcome anachronism. Some stairways were wide and elegant and others were precipitous and dangerous. Doña Verito's old wooden steps were known to only a few of the long-time residents who lived in tiny cottages, steps away from each of the landings of its time-worn steps.

As more and more clients made the long hike up to seek a consultation, Doña Verito's concern for Claire grew. She did not like the insincerity of the newcomers to the neighborhood. They feigned an interest in Doña Verito's healing methods and concocted ailments simply to hear her explain her findings or to watch her go outdoors to select the well-suited natural cures. Instead of seeking a cure, they were gathering exotic facts for their soulless screenplays. Many of the newcomers were employed in the periphery of the film industry and they started to see her as their ancient muse. They knocked on her door at odd hours of day and night and offered her more and more money to heal their psychosomatic illnesses. They pretended forthright interest in her, but they were just mining her for more details about life in the Amazon. One man even dared to make his own video that went viral showing his purportedly frightening midnight hike up the narrow steps in Echo Park, and his consultation with the "Amazonian witch," as he had tagged the video when he uploaded it to the Internet.

Doña Verito recognized that she had always been an old soul and that her *duende* lived within her for decades. By adhering to its deep-seated rage, she had channeled all her tragedies into healing others. But she intuitively knew that Claire did not belong in this tenuous healing ambiance. To be a healer one must give all, and this was not Claire's destiny. After each genuine patient left Doña Verito's cottage, she felt that her bones were being drained of their marrow. All she had left were the shadows of her patients' despair floating in the empty cavity of her bones. Each tragic patient sapped more and more of Doña Verito's energy, and she did not want this diminishing life for Claire.

She wanted her to be young and carefree. She delighted in hearing Claire laugh on the telephone with her new young man. She encouraged Claire to take La Linda's offer and travel with her and Ofelia to the south of Spain for an extended period of time.

Doña Verito felt that her own time to pass on was nearing and she didn't want Claire to witness death once again. When she found out that Claire's new boyfriend, Luke, was also going to Spain in September, Doña Verito hounded Claire into accompanying La Linda. She said, "Clarita, you know that Ofelia can't handle La Linda all by herself, they need your help. Besides, Luke is going to Spain, too. He told me that he would love to travel with you once you get there."

"Did he tell you that his hobby is exploring caves?" Claire said. "That is what he is going to be doing there. I don't want to have anything to do with caves. Period."

Doña Verito said, "Don't worry about the caves. If I promise you that Luke will never set foot in another cave ever again, will you go to Seville?"

Claire nodded yes.

◈ ◈ ◈

La Linda's house became a hub of activity with the finest auction houses vying for her prized Hispano-Suiza Torpedo and her collections of valuable art and jewelry. She settled this matter as efficiently and rudely as she did all things. She yelled at the prim and proper estate representatives. "Get the hell out of my house, you vultures! Your only job is to get me the highest prices. Did you know that every leading man adored me? They gave me all these gifts. That's right, every single one of them. They competed for my attention, not for my love, mind you. I only have passion for one thing, and that is flamenco. So get out of my house and do your job and let me get back to flamenco."

As they left her property one tall man was heard to say, "Surely, she doesn't believe she can make a flamenco comeback, does she?"

Another not so diplomatic woman said, "She's a total wack job, Jimmy, and I wouldn't pay a cent to see her do anything."

The tall man said, "She's definitely a tyrant and a perfectionist, so imagine how difficult all these years have been for her. But she does have a heart. She's leaving her estate to a range of charities and also to her companion, Ofelia. Ofelia is really a fit and attractive woman, isn't she?"

The crass woman replied, "Jimmy, I'm sure you find her upcoming wealth very alluring."

Seville, Spain
September 17, 2011

In September the festival atmosphere reigned supreme in Seville. Flamenco aficionados from all over the globe swarmed the city to participate in this ancient art of song and dance. Granted, the crowds were not as thick as those at the Bienal de Flamenco on the even number years. La Linda was compelled to make her comeback in 2011 since she felt that by 2012 she would only be a fantastic memory for her fans.

Luke sat anxiously in his seat at the Palacio theatre in Seville waiting for Claire to settle La Linda and Ofelia back stage. The audience buzzed with incredulous remarks about La Linda's comeback. It simply could not be possible for a *bailaora* in her eighties to accomplish such a thing. It would be a feat for the annals of flamenco history, not unlike the tragic deaths of Tomás El Nitri or Curro Pablas. Curro died while singing his final *siguiriya* to his lost love, Dolores the Untamed. Their wild love affair back in 1869 ended with Dolores's husband stabbing

Curro in the stomach while he sang: "¡*Ayyy!* I'm destined for the graveyard, don't let me die alone!"

The only other *bailaora* anyone could recall dancing well into her eighties was the remarkable La Macarrona, who after international acclaim and a posh life in Paris, ended up penniless and dancing in the flamenco taverns of Seville in 1945 at the age of eighty-five. She could still enchant admirers with her traditional style of dancing that emphasized her upper torso and graceful arms and hands. Her genuine Gypsy fatalism came through to the very end. She said, "I've taught a million students to dance, but no one remembers pure flamenco anymore. Time erases everything."

Although it had been decades since anyone had seen La Linda dance, her artistic genius and her tempestuous character were the talk of the preshow crowd. Claire finally joined Luke at their seats. He kissed her gently and snuggled his nose into her long dark hair. He said, "I love the smell of your hair. I think my Basque grandmother must have worn the same perfume because I remember that fragrance from when I was a kid."

"It's verbena, my grandmother's favorite. I'm glad it brings you beautiful memories,"said Claire. "I'm so happy to see you here, but I apologize for cutting your caving trip short."

Luke kissed her hand and said, "It was a farewell trip to spelunking. Didn't your grandmother tell you? I promised her never to explore caves again."

The house lights dimmed as the announcer began his long-winded commentary. Claire whispered to Luke, "La Linda is ready to make her comeback!"

Luke commented. "Don't you mean, she's ready to make her debut as a singer? It is impossible for her to dance from her wheelchair."

▣ ▣ ▣

As the curtain rose, the audience remained silent. The stage was totally black except for a light beaming on a solitary *cantaora*. La Linda sat on a chair whose large metal wheels had been covered with embroidered black shawls known as *mantones de Manila*. These shawls harkened back to the golden age of Spain. An era when its galleons sailed under the expert hands of Basque sailors who searched for riches from the Philippines, to Mexico, to Peru, and North America.

The stage light moved up to illuminate the face of the singer. There was a sudden collective gasp from the audience when they recognized La Linda. The silence was followed by the most perfectly painful lament anyone had ever heard: "*¡Ayyyy! ¡Ayyyy!*"

The wail stunned and electrified everyone. La Linda reached out frantically to her audience as if she wanted to grasp all their faces in her veiny and bony hands, as if she wanted to transmit her anguish by touching them. In the blackness of the theatre people felt a spark enter their bodies through their feet. Luke wrapped his arm around Claire who shook uncontrollably. La Linda's rapture exploded; her bewitching song enchanting and paralyzing the audience. Her *siguiriya*, the deepest of the deep song forms, the *cante jondo*, was one no one had ever heard before, yet it seemed very familiar to them. With a scorched throat she sang of her *penas negras*, her darkest pains:

¡Ayyyy!

My pain is bottomless,

I have fallen in a well

And I can't find the way out!

The frenzy in the audience was contagious. Their own *penas negras* rose to the surface and for a split second they understood what Garcia Lorca wrote: "at this hallowed instant, those who are present feel a communion with God through the five senses."

The audience was intoxicated with their heightened awareness of life and death. La Linda continued singing her heart out. Instead of singing about the death of one's mother, the central theme of *cante jondo*, La Linda called out to Ofelia who was hiding near the stage. She dedicated the next song to her and told the audience that Ofelia was her *protégée* and would be the next great *bailaora*.

The audience applauded and shouted Ofelia's name. La Linda began to sing again and continued wailing her tragic song. Step by slow step Ofelia made her way to center stage. The beam of light remained on La Linda and the audience could only see the silhouette of a lithe and petite woman moving her arms and hands in the arabesque style of long ago. Her head looked down in respect for the greatness of La Linda's performance. La Linda's song progressed to its poignant theme, her reason for dedicating the song to Ofelia. It was a song about the endless sorrow of a daughter's death. La Linda belted out her Gypsy *caló* lament:

¡Ayyyy!

Se murio la hija mía;

(My daughter is dead)

Ya no hay en er

 mundo hijas,

(There are no daughters in the world,)

¡Hija, la que yo tenía!

(Like the daughter I had!)

!Ayyyy! Ayyyy!

La Linda's *duende* generated lament cast a spell over the audience and echoed with their collective agony. No one had ever experienced such an awareness of the suffering of their ancestors.

Entirely overcome by *duende* and Ofelia's pure flamenco performance, the audience did not notice that La Linda had stopped singing. That in fact, she had stopped breathing. Ofelia's dance was improvised, it was intense, it was technically flawless, and she had lost herself entirely in her sorrow and rage. The audience shouted encouragement after encouragement. "*Alé*, Ofelia, Alé," but she didn't hear them. In typical Gypsy tradition, the crowd instantly gave her a new nickname, La Furia. They screamed her name, "La Furia! La Furia!" The fury inside her detonated into her dance. She was dancing for herself and she was dancing for her daughter; for all the lost daughters throughout the ages whose traces vibrated through her body with the steely backbone of *duende*.

Afterword

nlike the intoxicating fragrance of verbena, it was the stuffy and aged odor in the archives of San Sebastian and Seville, Spain that inspired me to write about my ancestors. After showing my credentials at the archives, and slipping on the required white cotton gloves, I was allowed to leisurely inspect countless records dating back hundreds of years. The not so good- natured staff at these archives warmed up to me and my investigations after meeting my then rambunctious pre-teen sons who stopped by daily to drag me out of the intrigue of the archives and back to the reality of being a mom.

My research in genealogy, combined with family lore, led me down numerous dead ends. After several years of piecing together fact and fable, it became clear to me that the many histories of the ancient Mediterranean and the New World were my legacy, and I did not need to prove which specific ancestor did what. Once I came to this realization, individual ancestors remained intact in their oral histories, and I was able to create this novel that is primarily made-up of a kaleidoscope of fictional characters.

The historical characters and events appearing in this novel are as follows: Ojer de Berástegui, whose name appears as Ojer de Velástegui in the records, was a Basque crew member on the famous *Pinta* caravel of 1492. The lack of mention of his name on many of the Columbian records was resolved by the recent scholarly citations of his participation on the first voyage of Columbus and in the Indies trade. In this instance, oral tradition, including my family's inherited nearsightedness, trumped the records by generations. As for the other historical characters and events, there is no direct connection to my ancestors.

The 17th century Basque Witch Trials that took place in Zugarramurdi are well documented, as are the officials of the Spanish Inquisition: Juan de Valle and Alonso de Salazar Frías. Numerous pre-historic caves, replete with ancient art work, dot the foggy Basque landscape. The blood feud battles between the Oñacinos and the Gambinos destroyed many families. Among the participants in this feud were the Lords of Velástegui from my bucolic ancestral village of Velástegui (or Berástegui) in Guipúzcoa, Spain. The linguistic enigma of the Basque language continues to intrigue scholars in the field. It is the last remaining descendant of the pre-Indo-European languages of Western Europe.

I took poetic license with the poetry of the 11th century Sephardic Jewish poet, Solomon ibn Gabirol, also known as Avicebrón, by quoting a hodgepodge of his stanzas. The poems in this novel are from his early career and do not reflect the depth, intellect and religious fervor of his later work.

The tribulations of the 17th century Moriscos, and in particular Beatriz de Robles, are well documented. Telethusa was a 1st century Phoenician dancer from Cádiz.

Colonial life in the convent of Santa Catalina, mentioned herein, is an amalgamation of two convents established in 17th century Cusco: Santa Catalina and Santa Clara. The Monasterio of Santa Catalina was founded in 1605 on the masonry foundations of the Inca *acllahuasi*. It is now a museum of Spanish Colonial art. The recorded financial arrangements managed by the convents during the Spanish Colonial period mirror those discussed in this book. The Lieutenant Nun, Catalina de Erauso, was a Basque, cross-dressing, military, officer who fought for the Spanish crown in Chile.

The Shuar are one of the indigenous people of the Ecuadorian Amazonian region. The dumping of billions of gallons of toxic oil sludge into the rivers and streams in Ecuador in the 1990's is a complicated tragedy, the details of which can be found from reliable sources on the Internet.

All the 19th century flamenco artists mentioned were remarkable performers whose contributions to flamenco are still remembered. The love affair between Tomás El Nitri and La Andonda, including her predilection for knives and his on-stage death, are factual. The great Spanish poet, Federico García Lorca, wrote eloquently about flamenco and *duende*.

※ ※ ※

I am very grateful for the support of my writing endeavors from my friends: Lisa Renee Baker, Melody Burbank, Sarah Faber, Aida Gandinni, Loreal Goodin, Dr. Mae Kinaly, Heather Parks, Sylvia Sacal, Alaina Skidmore, Dr. Mozelle Sukut, Kathy Smolanovich, Carolyn Weik, Rebecca Zapanta, and all the members of my book club. Many thanks to my editor Catherine Knepper for her great insights.

As always and forever, my love and gratitude to my phenomenal husband Peter and to my loving sons, Jay-Paul and Peter, with whom I have shared countless adventures, from listening to Ladino speakers in Istanbul and the Sea of Galilee to enjoying hours of flamenco in Granada and Sevilla.

Monarch Beach, January 1, 2012

Glossary

KEY:

B   – Basque
FI   – Filipino
F   – French
L   – Latin
LA – Ladino
MA – Maghrebi Arabic
MO – Mozarabic
Q   – Quechua
S   – Spanish
SH – Shuar dialect

abuelitos – (S) Grandparents.

acllas – (Q) Brides of the sun.

acllahuasi – (Q) Palace for the brides of the Inca sun.

ad nauseam – (L) To a ridiculous degree.

aguardiente – (S) Moonshine.

alé, guapa, alé – (S) Flamenco cheer equivalent to: go for it—
    good-looking.

alegría – (S) A flamenco song form.

al sereno – (S) Night dew.

aquellarre – (B) witches' coven.

amikri – (SH) blood brother.

Amor Seco – (S) Spanish needles herb.

amuse bouche – (F) Appetizer before a meal.

arutam – (SH) Life force.

auto de fe – (S) A ritual of public penance.

belarberza – (B) Healing herbs

belar osasungarriak – (B) Medicinal herbs.

burualdi – (B) Stubborn one.

bailaora – (S) Gypsy caló meaning: dancer.

café cantante – Singing café.

camu camu – Myrtle tree.

cantaora – (S) Gypsy caló meaning: singer.

cante jondo – (S) Gypsy caló meaning: deep song.

capinuri – Tree of the Amazon Basin.

centros – (S) A settlement in the Amazon Basin.

chicha – (Q) Fermented alcoholic drink.

chorizo – (S) Sausage.

churros – (S) A fried dough pastry.

compás – (S) A measure or bar.

converso – (S) Jews who converted to Catholicism.

curare – (SH) Moonseed plant.

datura – (S) A psychotropic plant.

duende – (S) Spirit.

en masse – (F) In a group.

epa – (B) Hello.

Esto te da la refua, la sheshina, la melezina. – (LA) This will give you refuge, blessings and medicine.

Euskal Herria – (B) Basque country.

Ezo! Toma que te toma – (S) Flamenco cheer.

Fente mib de nohte, mio sîdî – (MO) Come to me at night, my lord.

fueros – (S) Ancient laws.

Gitano caló – Gypsy dialect.

gitanos – (S) Gypsies.

Gora Euskadi – Long live the Basque homeland.

granadilla venenosa – (S) Red passion vine.

Huay chivo – (MD) Maya, shape-shifting, evil, sorcerer.

ingeniero – (S) Engineer.

jaleos – (S) Shouts of encouragement.

jamás – (S) Never.

juergas – (S) A flamenco get-together.

jengibre - (S) Ginger plant.

Kaixo – (B) Hello.

kakáram – (SH) An exceptional warrior.

Kari shina – (Q) Man-like behavior.

lagundu – (B) Help.

La Linda – (S) The pretty one.

lamia – (B) A creature of Basque mythology.

la sirena mía – (S) My mermaid.

leilas – (MA) An early Moorish dance.

loco – (S) Crazy

locutorio – (S) Waiting room in a convent.

mal ojo – (S) Evil eye.

Mi amada – (S) My beloved (feminine).

mujer baronil – (S) Masculine woman.

Maite zaitut – (B) I love you.

Malleus Maleficarum – (L) Witches' Hammer.

mamacita – (S) Mother.

mano a mano – Hand to hand combat.

me duele hasta la médula – (S) It hurts me to the marrow.

medina – (MA) The historic quarter of a city.

médula – (S) Bone marrow.

mestiza – (S) Mixed race (feminine).

mi hijita, toma más leche – (S) My little daughter, drink
    more milk.

mora – (S) Moorish woman.

mujer – (S) Woman.

natem – (SH) Psychotropic plant.

Nuno – (FI) Troll or gnome.

pena negra – (S) Darkest pain.

Piñon Blanco – (S) A nut shrub of the Amazon Basin.

Pinay – (FI) Filipina woman.

pobrecitos – (S) Poor things.

pobrecita – (S) Poor thing (feminine).

puca panga – (SH) Toad vine.

riad – (MA) A traditional Moroccan house.

salvia divinorum – (L) Diviner's Sage plant.

Sangre del Grado – (S) Dragon's Blood tree.

siguiriya – (S) Flamenco tragic song style.

sirena – (S) Mermaid.

soleares – (S) Flamenco song form.

tonás – (S) Flamenco song form.

tristeza – (S) Sadness.

tsantsa – (SH) The shrunken head of an enemy.

tsentsak – (SH) Invisible darts.

txoko – (B) Tavern.

uwishin – (SH) Elder.

verdad – (S) Truth.

yagé – (Q) A hallucinogenic brew.

zambras – (MA) An early Moorish dance.

About This Guide

We hope that these discussion questions will enhance your reading group's exploration of Cecilia Velástegui's novel, **Traces of Bliss.** They are meant to stimulate discussion, offer new viewpoints and enrich your enjoyment of the book.

QUESTIONS FOR DISCUSSION

1. In the novel there are multiple levels of the symbolism of caves. They range from a place of safety to the representation of the female womb. In what ways did the cave represent the mysterious and unexplored parts of the characters? In what ways did caves symbolize the unconscious mind? What aspects of the mind did caves represent?

2. Mrs. Dougherty has always been surrounded by household help. What made her so attached to Yolanda and Octavio?

3. Mrs. Dougherty lived in a palatial estate. Why are the small details of her house, such as the fireplace or her garden, so important to her?

4. Mrs. Dougherty's daughter, Catlin, is depicted harshly. Do you think that her cold demeanor hid good qualities?

5. Foliage, trees, and medicinal plants played pivotal roles in the lives of the characters in the novel. Describe how the canopy of the trees influenced the caregivers via-à-vis the canopy of the trees in the Amazon region where Octavio grew up? What did the oak trees mean to Mrs. Dougherty? What was the meaning of the cork tree to Ofelia, La Linda, and Octavio? What was the symbolism of the canopy of trees at Griffith Park for Octavio and Alma at the moment of her demise?

6. The Spanish Inquisition's draconian measures destroyed lives and villages. In what ways did its injustices affect future generations of the people from the Bertizuan Valley in the Basque country?

7. The Basque Witch Trials seared frightening memories for Pablo and Catalina. Do you think that one generation's pivotal/traumatic memories can be passed down to future generations? Is it possible for the visceral reactions felt by the original generation to be experienced by its descendants?

8. When Octavio was first introduced, his behavior was a product of the values of the Amazon region. What were those values? How did Octavio's values change over the course of the novel?

9. The notion of primordial lands was evident in the Basque homeland of Pablo and Catalina, in the ancient Al-Andalus of Solomon ibn Gabirol, in the Andalucía of Tomás El Nitri and La Andonda, and in the Amazon region of Ecuador for Octavio. In what ways did these ancient places mold their inhabitants? After the Basque diaspora and the deforestation and destruction of the Shuar lands, how did the inhabitants cope with the changes? Based on the reaction that La Linda received at her comeback performance, how has Andalucía managed to retain its character?

10. The destruction of the Shuar territory due to oil excavation angered Octavio. Did he exhibit any outward retaliation towards the oil companies either in the Amazon or in California? Did his reactions indicate that he was more of a healer or more of a jaguar?

11. Given the hierarchal and societal restrictions on women in Cusco in 1623, was the Abbess justified in her aggressive tactics to obtain more funds for the Santa Catalina convent?

12. Using today's idiomatic expression, "playing with the big boys", how would you assess the financial strategies

employed by the Abbess? How do you evaluate her management style of the convent? Was she justified in using these tactics?

13. Why did the Abbess and Judge Carrera's yearning to nurse a newborn make them behave irrationally?

14. How did Alma Ruiz use her permanent disfigurement due to Bell's palsy as a means to connect with the caregivers and the elderly? When she decided to venture outdoors during the daytime, how did her attire show her state of mind?

15. Were the caregivers empathetic to Alma's affliction or were they consumed with their own problems?

16. Both Soledad and Alma exhibited contempt for the elderly, but their reasons stemmed from different sources. Discuss their reasons for their disdain of the elderly.

17. The many interpretations of *duende* are introduced early on in the novel. It was equated to a gnome, a troll, a *nuno,* and a goblin. What are the commonalities of these creatures in folklore and how are they different from the concept of *duende* at the heart of this novel? Why are these folkloric creatures introduced in relation to the caregivers and why are some of the caregivers fearful of them?

18. Soledad had lived in California for two decades. Besides speaking English perfectly, how did she show her acculturation to modern American life?

19. Do you believe that the specially blended verbena oil that Claire used in her massage therapy had the power to trigger emotional memories?

20. Octavio was very specific about which herbal medicine he applied both in the Amazon as a youth and as a healer to Ofelia. What did his meticulous healing character reveal about his state of mind and his self-perception?

21. Tomás el Nitri and La Andonda were historical flamenco singers from 1860 Seville, Spain. In what ways did their passion for each other and their art support the Gypsy ethos?

22. The flamenco world of Seville in 1860 indicated the depth of emotions felt by all who cherished this art form. Do you think that in order for such an art form to survive it must be propelled by a surge of emotions?

23. What do the snippets of flamenco lyrics reveal about the themes in the music?

24. Early on in the novel, why was the fact that La Linda was in a wheelchair and unable to dance not apparent?

25. Has Mrs. Hamieh's reliance on dream divination been a crutch or has it been therapeutic for her state of mind? Will her positive influence on Fatima continue after her death or will Fatima resort to her own Maya perspective and values?

26. The barbaric reach of the Spanish Inquisition is evident in the historical chapters. Do you think that any traces of its cruelty are still felt today?

27. Both Dr. Nunez and Solomon ibn Gabirol are depicted as misanthropes. Dr. Nunez appears to have had many opportunities for love and fulfillment and wasted them. How does Solomon ibn Gabirol find fulfillment in his life?

28. Did any one of the caregivers truly care for her employer? If so, how did she show it?

29. Given that the English translation of the word *alma* is soul, in what ways was this name appropriate for Alma Ruiz?

30. Ofelia was traumatized by not knowing the whereabouts of her missing 19-year old daughter. Will La Linda's channeling of Ofelia's grief into her dance be a permanent release for Ofelia or will Ofelia revert to despair knowing that her daughter was a victim of sex traffickers?

Bibliography

Bennett, Bradley C., Marc A. Baker, and Patricia Gómez Andrade. *Ethnobotany of the Shuar of Eastern Ecuador.* New York: The New York Botanical Garden Press, 2002.

Berntsen, Dorthe. *Involuntary Autobiographical Memories: An Introduction to the Unbidden Past.* Cambridge. Cambridge University Press, 2009.

Bilbao Azkarreta, Jon. Ed. *Amerika eta Euskaldunak: America y los Vascos.* DEIA, Diario De Euskadi, 1992.

Burns, Kathryn. *Colonial Habits: Convents and the Spiritual Economy of Cuzco, Peru* Durham and London: Duke University Press, 1999.

Castner, James L., James A. Duke, and Stephen L. Timme. *A Field Guide to Medicinal and Useful Plants of the Upper Amazon.* Gainesville: Feline Press, 1998.

Cohen, Martin A., and Abraham J. Peck. Ed. *Sephardim in the Americas: Studies in Culture and History.* Tuscaloosa and London: The American Jewish Archives, 1993.

Cole, Peter. Ed. and Trans. *The Dream of the Poem: Hebrew Poetry from Muslim and Christian Spain 950-1492.* Princeton and Oxford: Princeton University Press, 2007.

Cole, Peter. Trans. *Selected Poems of Solomon Ibn Gabirol.* Princeton and Oxford: Princeton University Press, 2001.

Cruces Roldán, Cristina. *El flamenco y la música andalusí: Argumentos para un encuentro.* Barcelona: Ediciones Carena.

Edwards, Gwynne. *Flamenco.* New York: Thames and Hudson, 2000.

Erauso, Catalina. *Memoir of a Basque Lieutenant Nun: Transvestite in the New World.* Trans. Michele Stepto and Gabriel Stepto. Boston: Beacon Press, 1996.

Erauso, Catalina. *Historia de la Monja Alférez, Catalina de Erauso, escrita por ella misma.* Ed. by Ángel Esteban. Madrid: Cátedra, 2002.

Fuchs. Barbara. *Exotic Nation: Maurophilia and the Construction of Early Modern Spain.* Philadelphia: University of Pennsylvania Press, 2009.

García Lorca, Federico. *In Search of Duende.* Ed. And Trans. Christopher Maurer, New York:New Directions Publishing Corporation, 1998.

García Lorca, Federico. *Poema del Cante Jondo Romancero Gitano*. Doral: Stockcero, Inc. 2010

García Lorca, Federico. *Collected Poems*. Ed. Christopher Maurer, New York: Farrar, Straus and Giroux, 1988.

Garmendia Arruebarrena, José, *Cadiz, Los Vascos y la Carrera de Indias*. San Sebastian: Editorial Eusko Ikaskuntza, S.A., 1990

Giles, Mary E. *Women in the Inquisition: Spain and the New World*. Baltimore: The Johns Hopkins University Press, 1999.

Gómez, Agustín. *De Estética Flamenca*. Barcelona: Ediciones Carena.

Gouda, Yehia. *Dreams and their Meanings in the Old Arab Tradition*. New York: Vantage Press, 2006.

Gould, Alicia B. *Nueva Lista Documentada de los Tripulantes de Colon en 1492*. Madrid: Orión Editorial, 1984.

Greene, Molly. *A Shared World: Christian and Muslims in the Early Modern Mediterranean*. Princeton: Princeton University Press, 2000.

Henningsen, Gustav. *The Witches' Advocate: Basque Witchcraft and the Spanish Inquisition (1609-1614)*. Reno: University of Nevada Press, 1980.

——— *Jews of Al-Andalus*. Hephaestus Books.

Kramer, Heinrich, and James Sprenger. *The Malleus Maleficarum*. Trans. Rev. Montague Summers. New York: Dover Publications, Inc., 1971.

Leblon, Bernard. *Gypsies and Flamenco*. Trans. Sinéad ni Shuinéar. Hertfordshire: University of Hertfordshire Press, 2003.

Levack, Brian P. *Witch-Hunt in Early Modern Europe*. Harlow: Pearson Longman, 1987.

Lévy, Isaac Jack, and Rosemary Lévy Zumwalt. *Ritual Medical Lore of Sephardic Women: Sweetening the Spirits, Healing the Sick*. Urbana and Chicago: University of Illinois Press, 2002.

Lieberman, Julia R. *Sephardi Family Life in the Early Modern Diaspora*. Hanover and London: University Press of New England, 2011.

Lowney, Chris. *A Vanished World: Muslims, Christians, and Jews in Medieval Spain*. Oxford: Oxford University Press, 2005.

Netanyahu, B. *The Marranos of Spain: From the Late 14th to the Early 16th Century*. Ithaca and London, Cornell University Press, 1999.

Netanyahu, B. *The Origins of the Inquisition in Fifteenth Century Spain.* New York: Random House, 1995.

Pérez, Joseph. *The Spanish Inquisition.* New Haven: Yale University Press, 2005.

Pérez-Mallaína, Pablo E. *Spain's Men of the Sea: Daily Life on the Indies Fleets in the Sixteenth Century.* Baltimore: The Johns Hopkins University Press, 1998.

Perkins, John, and Shakaim Mariano Shakai Ijisam Chumpi, *Spirit of the Shuar: Wisdom from the Last Unconquered People of the Amazon.* Rochester: Destiny Books, 2001.

Perry, Mary Elizabeth. *Gender and Disorder in Early Modern Seville.* Princeton: Princeton University Press, 1990.

Perry, Mary Elizabeth. *The Handless Maiden: Moriscos and the Politics of Religion in Early Modern Spain.* Princeton: Princeton University Press, 2005.

—— *Poetas de España del Siglo XI.* Memphis: Books LLC.

Pohren, D.E. *Lives and Legends of Flamenco: A Biographical History.* Madrid: Society of Spanish Studies, 1971.

Russo, Ethan, MD. *Handbook of Psychotropic Herbs: A Scientific Analysis of Herbal Remedies For Psychiatric Conditions.* New York: Routledge, 2010.

Sachar, Howard M. *Farewell España: The World of the Sephardim Remembered.* New York:Alfred A. Knopf, 1994.

Silverblatt, Irene. *Modern Inquisitions: Peru and the Colonial Origins of the Civilized World.*Durham and London: Duke University Press, 2004.

Stanton, Edward F. *The Tragic Myth: Lorca and Cante Jondo.* Kentucky: The University Press of Kentucky, 1942.

Toledano, Haim Henry. *The Sephardic Legacy: Unique Features and Achievements.* Scranton and London: University of Scranton Press, 2010.

Totton, Robin. *Song of the Outcasts: An Introduction to Flamenco.* Portland and Cambridge:Amadeus Press, 2003.

Webster, Jason. *Duende: A Journey into the Heart of Flamenco.* New York: Broadway Books,2002.

About the Author

CECILIA VELÁSTEGUI is the author of the acclaimed novel **Gathering the Indigo Maidens.** She was born in Ecuador where she spent her childhood. She was raised in California and France, and has traveled in over 50 countries. She received her graduate degree from the University of Southern California, and speaks four languages. She serves on the board of directors of several cultural and educational institutions. She lives with her family in Monarch Beach, California.

Flamenco Dancer
All flamenco dance images: iStockphoto.com

Flamenco Dancer

Flamenco Dancer

Flamenco Dancer